OF HUMAN BONDAGE

In a Digital Age

By

Dominie Mary Stemp

Table of Contents

Dedication

Dedicated to Almighty God. And to my husband, Matthew, who brought out the writer in me!

About the Author

After studying writing courses, Dominie wrote biographical articles for the Catholic Herald and Catholic Life Magazine until she became disillusioned by the Catholic Church under the so-called Pope Francis. She lives with her husband and her youngest son in East Sussex.

Her blog is www.dominiestemp.blogspot.com

MAIN CHARACTERS

Martin Charmer (Mab) - Beatrice's husband

Beatrice (Bea) Charmer (née Eclectic) - Martin Charmer's wife

Anne & Matthew Charmer - Martin's parents

Therese & Robert Eclectic - Bea's parents

Viscountess Isabelle De Tra-Vail-Dur (née Tentateur) - Étienne De Tra-Vail- Dur's wife

Viscount Étienne De Tra-Vail-Dur (Isabelle's husband)

Paulette & Édouard Tentateur - Isabelle's parents

Benoît - Isabelle's brother

Anne-Marie - Isabelle's friend

Lucy - Bea's oldest sister

Tessa - Bea's youngest sister

Florence Triste - Martin's first girlfriend

Michael Oak - University housemate

Rebecca Prissy - another girlfriend

Freddie Charmer - Eldest son

Cecily Charmer - Daughter

Rufus Charmer - Youngest son

'And God created man to his own image: to the image of God he created him: male and female he created them. And God blessed them, saying: Increase and multiply, and fill the earth, and subdue it....'

Genesis chapter 1, verses 27-28. DOUAY-RHEIMS VERSION.

'And Adam said: This now is bone of my bones and flesh of my flesh; she shall be called woman because she was taken out of man. Wherefore a man shall leave father and mother, and shall cleave to his wife: and they shall be two in one flesh.'

Genesis chapter 2, verses 23-24. DOUAY-RHEIMS VERSION.

'Whosoever shall look on a woman to lust after her hath already committed adultery with her in his heart.'

St Matthew's Gospel, chapter 5, verse 28. DOUAY-RHEIMS VERSION.

Marriage Law in the UK - 1985 states that;

'Marriage is the union of one man and one woman, entered into freely, to the exclusion of all others, for life.'

Catholic Ecclesiastical Laws of Marriage state that;

The two essential qualities of Matrimony are unity and indissolubility. Unity forbids adultery and dangerous friendships with members of the opposite sex.

Indissolubility means that the marriage lasts for the life of the bride and groom.

"Wonders of the Catholic Faith" by Fr F Radecki, page 98.

Part 1 - Broken Heart

Chapter 1 - The Broken Heart

It was the summer of 1980 when life in the Garden of England was much simpler. The pre-digital era was rapidly drawing to a close and hurtling towards the 21st Century - there were no mobile phones, no internet and only 3 channels on British television. The only way to communicate with people was via letters, postcards and landline telephones; if you wanted to see people, you actually had to meet physically in *real* places.[1]

Grammar school leavers - Martin Charmer and Christopher Wright had just finished their 'A' Levels - and were off to the Belgian countryside to stay with a family so that they could improve their French and have a fun time meeting Belgian teenagers. Martin was also due to spend his gap year in Paris and therefore needed to speak acceptable French.

The young men were 18 and wore the typical clothing of the English upper middle classes - cotton shirts under plain woollen jumpers from St Michael (aka M&S) and plain cotton trousers with brown leather loafers. The colours were tastefully quiet and super conservative - and definitely no loud tracksuits and trainers! The simplicity of the pre-internet era meant there wasn't much choice in many aspects of English life, including men's fashion.

Christopher knew the family very well, as his parents knew them through a business connection. He briefed Martin on the Calais ferry while they were on deck, and there was a gentle breeze,

'Oh, and by the way', he said in his clipped English accent - 'they're a *very* conservative family - *very* Catholic - so *don't* make fun of their religion - I know you, so watch it! - and not only that - they happen to be rather chic too - I mean Martin, there is this famous book published every year called "High Life De Belgique" - it has all

---

[1] 1st January 1983 - birthday of the internet.

the aristocratic and upper-class families in it - together with their telephone numbers. And yes - they're in *that* book', raising his blonde eyebrows several times at Martin, 'OK - there are two daughters and a son - around about our age or possibly younger, I think.

'Are they pretty?' Asked Martin, 'Erm… not bad looking.'

Martin was deeply impressed by all this information, and he decided that he was going to make an impression - although an introvert - he was exceptionally good with people and engaged well. He loved meeting new people and was very charming when he wanted to be. He made sure that his appearance was smart and that his poker straight mousey brown hair was combed. He was very proud of his highly polished chestnut penny loafers with leather soles.

The young men arrived at a charming old white house in the quiet Belgian countryside of the Wallonia region, and they noticed the hard tennis court next to fields - and a small pool set in an immaculately mown garden lined with trees. A very well-groomed tall lady of about 40 greeted them in the circular gravel driveway - Martin assumed this was the mother of the family. She clearly looked after herself, he thought - tall, slim and smartly dressed with shoulder-length solid brown hair which didn't seem to move - a hard style which mature women seemed to have then - he thought. She was quite tanned, which showed off her jewel-like smiling blue eyes. And indeed, she was the mother and, holding out her exquisitely manicured hand, introduced herself to Martin as 'Paulette Tentateur.'

And in his best French accent and charming smile, he simply replied, 'Enchantée.'

She looked delighted and said what a good accent he had. He laughed good-humouredly while she hugged Christopher as though he were a long-lost son.

Christopher spoke very good French, and he chatted to Paulette about his family news while out of the corner of his eye, Martin spotted a tall slim young girl doing dance moves with a much shorter girl. They were at the far end of the garden where the sun was dancing in the tree leaves. The tall girl looked quite similar to Paulette he thought as he stared in wonderment at this gazelle- like wonderment with wavy brown hair cascading over her slim shoulders - doing the most graceful moves he had ever seen in his entire life. The shorter girl was not so elegant - and had a very short masculine pudding-bowl hairstyle - with an air of impatience about her.

Paulette beckoned the girls over to meet their young guests for the week.

The taller girl, who had just turned 17, glided up in bare feet - demurely dressed - wearing a yellow fitted jumper and a denim flared skirt which finished just below the knee. Martin was totally mesmerised by the shyness and grace with which this girl moved - and could barely speak when she held her hand coyly out to him to introduce herself as 'Isabelle.' Her voice was as dulcet as her movements, and he thought she did resemble her mother, except her eyes were green and not so jewel-like. She observed Martin's awkwardness and his blushing as he half whispered, half choked,

'Enchantée' - followed by another two attempts in a louder voice. She smiled in amusement at his efforts and laughed prettily while going to embrace Christopher, whom she had known for several years now. The shorter girl was in boyish shorts and an Argyll jumper and was giggling at Martin's attempts to speak French. In a loud voice, she took Martin's hand and, shaking it said, 'I am Anne-Marie, a friend of Isabelle - delighted to make your acquaintance.'

'You speak good English,' said Martin noticing the extraordinary difference in the two girls - one so feminine and one so ungainly - totally the opposite of each other. Anne-Marie's smiling face lit up her plainness, and Martin could see that she had a cheeky sense of fun. He warmed to her immediately.

Paulette beckoned the guests inside, 'Christopher, you know where your room is - you take Martin, and you can take your things - come - you must be tired, no?

While the youths were unpacking in the twin bedroom, Martin wanted to know more about the family.

'Hmm -you didn't tell me about Isabelle Chris.' 'What about her?'

'I can't get her out of my head - she's like an angel, isn't she?'

'Oh do you think so? - well, she is very nice, but oh - do you think she's pretty then?' As he looked Martin straight in the eye - with his curly blonde hair flopping over his eyebrows.

'I have *never* come across femininity like her - she's my idea of utter perfection, Chris - her whole manner - her carriage - *that that* voice.'

'Oh, I see - ah - you *have* fallen for her' - while he fell on his bed laughing, 'Oh Martin - you really have, haven't you? Oh - is it love at first sight, Martin?'

'Well, haven't you?' Martin frowned.

'Well, actually, no - not my type - but she does have some nice friends - who we'll no doubt meet when they host their usual tennis parties. Oh, and I wouldn't get your hopes up, Martin - they are a closed lot that lot - they only marry their sort - you know - Catholics who happen to be in that book. You fail on both counts - as he observed Martin's scowling face.

'Really?' Said Martin while taking in the country views and admiring the tasteful antiques in the house. He checked his appearance in the mirror - he felt confident that his hair was tidy, unlike his companion's unruly long curls. He thanked his genes that he was above average height and well-built with regular features.

Before supper that night, the guests helped their hosts in the kitchen, and Isabelle was quietly laying the table while chatting about the plans for the week. When they all sat down, Paulette brought in a steaming bowl of hot potatoes - which they would all start to peel at the table.

'Is a family custom - we pill potatoes at the table,' laughed Isabelle as she observed Martin's amused expression.

Martin charmed the family with his efforts at speaking French and his good manners. Paulette, Isabelle, and Anne-Marie seemed intrigued by this English man, who Isabelle eventually confided to Anne-Marie,

'This English boy Marteen - he has the most beautiful eyes, and so chouette - he's so kind.'

'I agree - he is not bad looking, but I sense Isabelle that he doesn't have eyes for me' while giving her friend a knowing look.

The following balmy days were taken up with tennis parties, country walks, picnics and an outing to Brussels. Martin loved chocolate, and Isabelle introduced him to the Belgian brand CÔTE D'OR.

'Oh, this is much better than English chocolate Isabelle' while swooning over the sweet smell wafting out of the factory.

'You zink so - yes?'

'Yes, I do think it's much better chocolate than English chocolate. Now I must take some photos of our group. Could you all sit on that bench?

Christopher and Paulette couldn't fail to notice how well Martin and Isabelle were getting on. They seemed inseparable, thought Christopher - but it seemed more than just a friendship. He quizzed Martin when they went to bed.

'You and Isabelle are getting on jolly well, aren't you?' As he winked several times at Martin.

'Yes - it's amazing, Chris, she's the only person I have ever met who I can talk to just about anything - and yes, you're spot on - I *have* fallen in love, and I feel sick - so sick I had to be sick behind the garage - oh please don't tell anyone, especially not her!' Christopher was visibly shocked at this honest admission by his best pal.

'Oh, you'll get over her - it's only a crush, Martin - we're going home in a couple of days, and you'll soon forget her once you start your job in Paris.'

'I'll never ever forget her, Chris - I'm determined she will be my friend as long as I live. You know, she is my first true love, don't you?'

'Gosh, you really mean it don't you - well, you're pretty obvious about your feelings - you can't take your eyes off her, can you - and you will put on that silly er lovey voice' - it's hilarious listening to you.

During supper, Isabelle's father Édouard - who always wore old-fashioned grey suits asked the men about religion in England. It was a topic of great interest to him. He was a kind man who liked to smile a lot, and he loved having English guests - his English was excellent, and he liked practicing his English.

'Oh, we're Church of England as you well know Édouard', said Christopher as his curly fringe swept across his forehead - 'Which means we are really C and E, or Christmas and Easter. We aren't very religious, actually - we are, I suppose, typical English middle-class Anglicans. We go to church at Xmas and Easter, and christenings, weddings and funerals, and that's just about it. There aren't that many Catholics in England, but I tell you what Édouard - they're a vociferous lot! I guess they feel they have to be, as they were persecuted under Queen Elizabeth I. It was illegal to be Catholic at one time, you know. English Catholics have a persecution complex to this day.

'And you, Marteen - are you religious?' asked Isabelle as she cocked her head sideways towards him, her eyes serious.

'Well, I don't know, really - I just find it very hard to believe in what I can't see, that's all. I'm what you call agnostic.' Isabelle gave him a sad look.

Édouard had never considered persecuted Catholics in England before - he was genuinely interested in English history and religion. He was an intelligent, hard-working man, a very devout Catholic who was also an altar server in his parish. His strict Catholicism was part of who he was as a person, as it was with his wife and children.

On the last day of the holiday - Martin was feeling sick with the thought that they would be going home soon, so he wanted to tell Isabelle how he really felt about her. He wanted to be alone with her. He didn't know how she felt about him, but her body language and the way she gazed at him - surely she felt the same? He hoped.

There was to be a mini-tennis tournament with some other teenagers in the area, and Isabelle and Martin sat on the grass watching the tennis. Their minds were not on tennis one iota. Christopher noticed they looked a bit sad as he got up to take his turn on the tennis court.

'You're funny, Martin - never thought I'd see you like this - you love-sick dog.' He knew Isabelle wouldn't understand this saying, as she looked puzzled.

'What does he mean - sick dog Marteen?'

'I need to tell you something important, Isabelle.'

He had a pained expression on his usually happy face. She gazed into the beautiful eyes and suggested they walk towards the field. She knew he loved her - he didn't need to say anything - she could see right into his soul - and she loved him too. But she knew it was futile - a non-starter - as she strode like an angel with the gentle breeze waving her cascading hair. Martin's eyes never left her, and as they got to the hedge - they looked each other in the eye, not saying a word.

It was so quick when he swiftly pecked her on the mouth - she stepped back, startled but not saying a word. He was mortified and went red in the face and wanted the ground to swallow him up. Isabelle, in her sweet innocence, looked serious and serene. And then she smiled, and he stopped blushing.

But deep down, he knew it was a rejection. His heart broke in 2. The hurt was too much to bear. He didn't think he could get over this. I will never get over this girl - *never ever* - she's in my heart forever. If she can just be my friend, then I can be happy. That's all I ask.

Meanwhile, sitting by the pool in her Dior shades, Paulette had been observing her daughter and Martin keenly - she had watched the pair getting on extraordinarily well since they met, and she knew her daughter. She knew she was captivated by this English man - this charming Protestant man with a good French accent. She had watched her daughter at the dinner table giving shy glances towards Martin - and his gauche flirtiness. This friendship was very different, she thought - but it could only ever be just that - just a good friendship and nothing more. She and her husband had high hopes for a suitable match for their eldest daughter.

'May we keep in touch?' Asked Martin as he forced himself to act normally - 'Would you like to come and visit us in England?'

'Of course, we must always keep in touch Marteen, and yes I would like to visit you and meet your family - it would be so so chouette.' He weakened at her voice.

'That's settled then - I will ask my parents if you can come and stay when I've finished my job in Paris - shall we write to each other to confirm arrangements?'

'Ah yes for sure.'

She looked radiantly happy. She now regarded him as her best male friend. No one would take that away, she thought - we have a bond so strong. But she was immensely sad that her state in life meant she couldn't consider him as a future husband - he wasn't Catholic - and her parents were very clear that their children were to marry Catholics, as mixed marriages were considered very dangerous by the Church due to the inevitable conflicts that would arise.

Before the Second Vatican Council of the early 1960s, it was forbidden for Catholics to marry non-Catholics unless there was a very serious reason for them to do so. After the Council, which was very ambiguous in its documents compared to past councils, the rules relaxed a bit - but for Belgian upper classes, it was still considered bad form to marry non-Catholics.[2]

Isabelle and other high-born girls would meet their future spouses at carefully arranged dances known as the 'Cours de Danse.' Only children from the 'High Life de Belgique' would be invited, ensuring suitable matches were made.

When Martin returned back to Hersterlamb in Kent, an intense correspondence started with Isabelle - the letters were very long, detailed and emotional. The letters continued for many years until well into the internet age. As a result, a very strong bond developed between Martin and Isabelle - which would one day prove to be a stumbling block in his later middle age.

A new chapter was about to begin in the life of Martin Charmer - soon he was off to work in Paris for his gap year before setting off to a smart university in the South West of England - a university which had a reputation for well-heeled students from private schools and Oxbridge rejects.

---

[2] See Appendix under Mixed Marriages.

Chapter 2 - Final Year at Truro School.

It was 1980 and the first day of the autumn term at Truro School. Eldest child and daughter, 17-year-old Beatrice Eclectic, Bea for short, and her younger sister Lucy got into the back of their father's big brown Granada while he drove them from Scorrier to Truro - a 20-minute drive. This was the 10th school of their lives, having lived abroad for much of their childhood and moving a lot in England. As a result, Beatrice was rather indifferent to making new friends as she always had to say goodbye after 1 or 2 years.

Bea was not looking forward to her final year in the 6th form as she was dreading seeing her boyfriend of over one year and really needed to finish it, having failed several times so far - she didn't love him and found him quite dull. He was her first boyfriend, and she asked Lucy what to do. The two sisters were only a year apart and very close.

'Just tell him the truth, Bea - that it's run its course and that you're going to be too busy with your exams - ha ha' laughed Lucy knowing full well that Bea swapped all the hard 'A' Level subjects for easier options.

'He proposed to me in his latest letter - I mean really,' said Bea with an arrogance that comes with being one of the first few girls to go to a predominantly male school. Lucy was very much looking forward to going to an all-boys school, having spent the last two years at a convent in Birmingham.

Both girls had inherited their mother's wavy thick hair, and as a result, Beatrice kept hers unflatteringly short. Both girls were extroverts and had discovered the joys of dyeing their hair with henna powder and temporary hair colour sachets - with mixed results. At their ages, it didn't matter what they did to their hair - they had youth on their sides and were blessed with regular features.

'I'm going grey at the sides', said Bea, 'And I'm not confident enough to be grey at 17!'

'Bad luck - you take after mummy', said Lucy as her long dark blonde tresses tumbled over her brand new blazer. The girls were swiftly dropped off at the front entrance and made their way through the old musty corridors of the 1882 purpose-built school towards the new 6th form centre. Their father, Robert, had left the rat race in Birmingham and was the new bursar.

The school was Methodist - which was the main Christian denomination in Cornwall in the 1980s. This worried their mother, Therese, as it was not Catholic. It was considered quite bad for Catholic children to go to non-Catholic schools, even though many Catholic schools had become diluted in their Catholic ethos since the Second Vatican Council of the 1960s. Therese would send her children to catechism camps to make up for it, not realising that many camps had diluted the teachings.

Therese's devout mother, Ursula, also taught the children their faith and used a little red pamphlet popularly called "The Penny Catechism."[3] She would tell her grandchildren all about the apparitions and miracles at Lourdes, Fatima, and other places. Her strong missionary spirit led her to hand out miraculous medals and missionary rosaries to complete strangers. She always wore a patterned headscarf in church, which was still a requirement, but most women and girls had abandoned it during the chaotic time of the conciliar changes.

It was assumed that Beatrice would go to university straight after 'A' Levels - and in the 1980s, university tuition was free, and students were given means-tested grants to pay for their accommodation and other living expenses. That autumn term Bea applied to Exeter University in Devon and was offered a place to read modern languages, subject to getting 3 Cs at 'A' Level and passing maths 'O' Level.

---

[3] The Catechism of Christian Doctrine - 1958 edition. Revised editions not as accurate. See Bibliography.

‘Wow - that’s pretty achievable’, said a delighted Beatrice to her equally delighted parents. Therese said, ‘I think Exeter has to give a certain percentage of places to Cornish students - that’s what I heard anyway.’

‘I still need maths...grrr…maybe 3rd time lucky.’

The romance with her first boyfriend was over, and Bea had a series of short-lived boyfriends - none of them serious - she got bored as soon as they got serious. Being at an all-boys school had made her hard-hearted and spoilt. She was taught from an early age to keep boys at arm’s length with a ‘treat em mean, keep em keen’ attitude. It worked. Her father, although an agnostic, told his daughters that men would not respect them if they were ‘easy.’ He used to add,

‘And they certainly won’t want to marry “used goods.”’

Whenever potential boyfriends walked up the garden path to visit them, he would ask, ‘Who’s this oaf, buck, or yob arriving?’ And swiftly beat a hasty retreat upstairs.

Bea took this aspect of her faith very seriously and vowed to save herself for her future husband - she wanted very much to marry young and have many children.[4] Bea didn’t care if this was out of step with her contemporaries’ ambitions to be career girls - she was strong-willed and didn’t go with the flow. Her grandmother’s mantra of people, places, and things being “God’s will or *not* stayed with her for life.

The Eclectic family was not long in the country house in Scorrier. They moved to Truro itself so that the children could walk to school. Beatrice achieved the grades for university - just.

She got a summer job as a lone cook at a small granary restaurant - and was told by the owner to ‘just get on with it and cook a main

---

[4] See Bibliography “Clean Love in Courtship” by Fr Lovasik

vegetarian meal for any customers.' She was a self-taught cook since the age of 12. She saved up her wages and bought a new autumn wardrobe for Exeter University. Her mother teased her and likened it to a wedding trousseau.

Chapter 3 - Paris and Florence

In September 1980, Martin started his gap year job in a large department store in Paris. He lived in a relation's archive room in an office block. It had no facilities, and there were public showers nearby. His best friend Christopher decided to join him at the last minute, and they adopted a diet of baguettes and Camembert, and red wine every night. They slept on old mattresses.

The young men were going to be shop assistants, and they were the only English speakers in the shop, but they quickly made friends with their co-workers and took up smoking very strong Gauloise cigarettes and other questionable substances in the staff room, which was in the basement.

'It's all part of the experience,' said Martin to the more reserved Christopher, who replied, 'Well, I'm glad you got over Isabelle pretty quickly then?'

'Er….em….I'll never get over her, Chris, and we're very much in touch, and she's coming to stay with us when I finish here.'

'I hear an older man is interested in her - he's finished his conscription now - and he's from an ancient noble family - he'll become a Viscount one day- just the sort her parents want.'

'I'm sure she has many admirers, Christopher,' Martin said quickly, annoyed that his friend brought up the subject.

The weeks went by quickly. The youths improved their French, found the job tiring as they had to move furniture, and always looked forward to their evening of Camembert and red wine. Sometimes they treated themselves at cheap restaurants.

The French staff were a mixture of young and old people - and Martin made sure he was friendly to all. One young woman, in particular, was very helpful to them - and would always deal with any tricky customers on their behalf. She was from the poor quarter of Paris and spoke hardly any English. She was of average height and build and had a mass of thick dark corkscrew hair down to her shoulders and smooth olive skin. Martin found her quite attractive. Her name was Florence Triste. She had a certain maturity and feistiness about her, and her silky long eyelashes fluttered when helping the men. Martin soon started flirting with her, and she reciprocated keenly. He wasn't sure of her age but guessed she was around their age. He knew it wasn't the done thing to ask a woman her age.

One day in the stuffy, smoky basement during their lunch break, Florence beckoned Martin to look in one of the storage shelves behind the rest area - she wanted to show him an item.

'Marteen - I show you thees light.'

Martin innocently went like a lamb to the slaughter, and once he was out of sight from the rest of the staff - a pair of soft hands grabbed his stomach from behind. He turned around, startled, and Florence planted a long, hard kiss on his rosebud lips. 'OH Florence what…'

She shushed him to be quiet while staring into his eyes.

It was the start of an intense romance - Florence was Martin's first girlfriend, and the romance continued until he started university. She was slightly older, and she schooled him in the ways of love. She was a knowledgeable teacher, and he was a very willing pupil.

It was all Christopher could bear, 'Well, you won't want me hanging around with you, will you? - you don't waste any time, do you, Martin' laughed Christopher, 'I could see it coming, though - what is it with you and women?'

‘Actually, she’s the one who made a pass at *me!* - I have to say Chris - she’s the opposite of Isabelle - there’s something very fresh about her - she’s got a lot of get up and go - she’s going to show me parts of Paris tourists don’t see. We’re going to have a lot of fun.

‘Spare me the details.’

Martin had a new confidence about him and enjoyed walking the streets of Paris arm in arm with his new ladylove - he felt very much at home in a French-speaking country. Florence was not a feminine dresser and preferred to wear jeans, t-shirts, and flat shoes. Martin didn’t generally like girls in trousers, but he was too content to let that worry him.

Florence was deeply in love with Martin, but he wasn’t in love with her. He was very fond of her, but that was it. When it was time to return to England, the pair would keep in touch, and Martin invited Florence to meet his family. Florence couldn’t wait, hoping he felt the same way as her.

Chapter 4. Florence & Isabelle

In the late summer of 1981, Martin was looking forward to starting at Exeter University - he had managed to save a lot of his wages from Paris and felt happy with life. He hadn't forgotten that he had invited Isabelle to stay, and now Florence was also coming to stay. He was glad to have passed his driving test and to have the use of a car - the remoteness of his family home made it necessary.

Martin's parents, Matthew and Anne, were looking forward to meeting their son's Parisian girlfriend and Anne got the spare room ready for the first of the arrivals - Florence. They were traditional conservatives and explained the house rules to their son - it was very simple but clear, but before Anne could speak, 'Yes, I know,' said Martin, 'not under our roof' - he had heard this said to his older siblings often.

It was Florence's first time out of France, and when she arrived in the Kent countryside - she couldn't hide her happiness at seeing her beau again and all his plans for their outings. She was completely besotted with her English man, but to her great sadness, she sensed the feeling wasn't mutual.

'Will you still write to me when you go to your university Marteen?', 'Of course I will, Florence,' he smiled affectionately at her.

He didn't dare tell her that it would be difficult for them to continue their romance while living in different countries and going on different paths.

Florence found it hard trying to understand all the family members, and she had little in common with them. She was from a big city, and her career path was working her way up in a department store - albeit a fashionable one. She was from a very different background and culture from Martin.

When it was time to say goodbye, she was very tearful, and Martin promised to keep writing to her.

A few days later, Martin reminded his parents that Isabelle was coming for a flying visit - they raised their eyebrows at each other, and Anne, with her cigarette in one hand, said, 'So is Florence a *serious* girlfriend, Martin - she is a nice girl - very quiet though.'

'I don't think it can last - I didn't tell her, but I can't see this continuing once I start at Exeter.'

Martin's father, Matthew was more interested in Isabelle, 'And why is Isabelle coming?'

'Oh, I invited her last summer, and we've been writing to each other all this time - she's just a very good friend of mine.'

Anne gave a knowing look to her husband. Her son's guarded expression told her he was keener on Isabelle than he was making out.

Martin couldn't believe how changed Isabelle was when she arrived - she was a young woman now, and her girlish shyness had disappeared - her clothes were very chic and grown up - her tall slim figure had filled out, and she had a very feminine shape - a typical hourglass. Her impeccable manners were polished, and her English was much improved since he last saw her. She was quite plain, really, but her carriage gave her a beauty that was hard to define. Martin's parents found her extrovert character delightful, and they thought about how different Isabelle and Florence were. They could see that their son was extremely keen on Isabelle. A bit too fond, perhaps.

Martin had so much to tell her, and on the first night, the pair stayed up all night talking in low voices in Isabelle's room - which had 2 small single beds. His heart sank when Isabelle mentioned a man she had met at one of the smart dances - a slightly older man from a very aristocratic family going back to the 13th century. They had started to go on dates together, and her family thought he was rather a good catch for her, as he would carry the family title one day.

He was clever, he didn't drink or take drugs, and he was an entrepreneur. Martin felt privileged to know *all* about him.

In his turn, he spoke of his time in Paris with Florence and that he felt it wasn't going to last. He looked her straight in the eye, and his voice lowered, 'You know, Isabelle, I still feel the same way about you, and you only have to say it, and Florence will be history', and quietly crawling over to her he took her hand and kissed it. He thought this time there might be hope, but her body language said no, and he bitterly thought, twice turned down.

Isabelle smiled sweetly - how she loved the attentions of her English man with the beautiful eyes and rosebud mouth. She held his heart in the palm of her hand, and she knew it. Oh how she knew it! It gave her sweet power.

A tired Martin appeared in the kitchen after a sleepless night in the same clothes and was greeted by his disgruntled father, 'Well, good morning, young Martin - and we noticed your bed wasn't slept in - what were you up to?!

'Oh no, no - don't get the wrong idea Pa - we were talking all night - she isn't interested in me - she has a serious boyfriend now. You know we're just very good friends, and she confides in me.'

Anne emerged from mucking out the horses and, with a cigarette in her fuchsia pink lipsticked mouth, gave her son a raised eyebrow look and, with her hands on her hips, said - 'Well, I must say Martin - you do look exhausted by the way - are you sure there isn't anything going on between you and Isabelle? -you're very different when you're around her, quite different from the way you are with Florence.'

'Well, yes - Isabelle will *always* be my dearest friend, and Florence won't be my girlfriend for much longer as I don't have much in common with her, and she lives in another country. I doubt I'll ever see her again. She had her use to me in Paris, and I enjoyed her company, but it's over.'

Isabelle eventually joined the Charmers and apologised for being so late in getting up. She wanted to ask the family what they thought of the latest British royal wedding between Prince Charles and Lady Diana Spencer. Anne - who was much more talkative than her introverted husband, said, 'I don't think she was his first choice really - but apparently, he had to marry a virgin, you know, and there aren't many of those around these days - I wonder if it'll last? He was carrying on with a married woman called Camilla - whispers say he still is - well, who knows' she laughed as she lit another cigarette and greeted her adored trio of fluffy small dogs, vying to get the top licking position of their mistress.

Martin drove Isabelle around the Kent countryside and introduced her to his close friends - he always felt proud to be seen with such an exquisitely elegant young lady. The time passed much too fast for him, and soon they had to say goodbye. He was invited back to Belgium the following year, and he gladly accepted. He would accept whatever Isabelle was prepared to give him - but he felt pained about her boyfriend.

Chapter 5 - Coup de Foudre at Exeter

It was early October 1981, and a very nervous Beatrice was dropped off at her red brick hall of residence by her parents in their purple Citroen 2CV car. They couldn't fail to notice much smarter cars rolling up - Volvos, Range Rovers, and other large estate cars. Bea's youngest sister insisted on coming along, and the little car jallopied along with a packed boot of Bea's belongings. Bea's mother Therese was heavily pregnant with her 5th child - which in 1981 was considered dangerous at her age. She was 42.

'Gosh, look at that father carrying a crate of sherry in for his son,' said Robert while he parked. The halls of residence were single-sex, and the boys' halls were across a lane opposite the girls' hall. Beatrice's younger sister Tessa was crying as she was going to miss her sister badly. 'I'm only in the next county, Tess - not too far, and I'll come home often as the train station is just up the road.'

Robert handed Bea a brown envelope with a copy of Jackie magazine and some bars of Crunchie chocolate. Therese reminded Bea to find the Catholic chaplaincy, which was within walking distance of the hall. That was the last thing on Bea's mind, but she kept that to herself.

After their goodbyes, Bea started to unpack in her little brown room with a basin, desk, and single bed. It was spartan and unwelcoming. Her heart was beating with nervousness as she didn't know anyone there. However, she soon learnt that some of the girls on her course were on her floor. That meant she could walk to lectures and to the dreaded supper hall with them.

Bea was a bit too slim when she started at university and promptly put on a stone in that first term - the food was mostly brown food and a lot of chips. There was also a burger van that used to park by the halls and a petrol station opposite where Bea bought chocolate cakes. She also took up smoking and bought packs of 10 cigarettes.

One day she was invited to a fellow student's tea party to meet some of the boys from the halls opposite, and she was glad to go - she wore her favourite navy dungarees and pixie boots, which suited her henna orange cropped pixie haircut. She looked rather ethnic compared to the classic English rose girls with their long flowing blonde hair, crisp shirts, and regulation pearls.

The tea party was hosted by a kind girl with very long dark hair in her bedroom, and there wasn't much room for all the guests - Bea sat on the desk, which was at the back of the room, with a mug of tea while they waited for the boys to arrive.

Martin had made friends with his next-door neighbour - Michael Oak - they were both reading law. They were looking forward to the tea party and wore smart trousers, shirts, and ties. Michael already knew the host from a family connection, and the young men arrived with beaming smiles. As Martin entered the room, he immediately rested his gaze on the girl with cropped orange hair, orange lipstick, large brown eyes, and olive skin - he thought she looked French. He said to himself as he walked diagonally across the room to her - I'm going to marry that girl one day. He didn't know why he had this inner voice - it was like a coup de foundre.

'Hello - Martin Charmer,' he said in his most charming voice and held out his hand.

'Beatrice Eclectic, but most call me Bea' as she shook his hand firmly, and he promptly sat on the table next to her.

'Are you French by any chance - you certainly look it?'

'No,' she laughed loudly - but many think I am - I'm half Welsh, and a lot of Welsh have Italian roots - hence our Southern European looks.'

Martin was fascinated by her choice of outfit, which he felt was very unflattering, but she had a certain bashfulness and grace about her. They got on very well and spoke about the usual things one talks about when meeting new people, and Michael Oak came along with some others to join in the conversation.

Although shy, Beatrice was an extrovert and very direct in her conversations and immediately asked the men if they had girlfriends.

'Not at the moment,' smiled Michael while Martin replied, 'I have a girlfriend in Paris, but it's going to fizzle out as I don't see how we can keep in touch - also, I have nothing really in common with her. As his voice changed to a slower, softer tone, and he looked wistful and sad, 'My one true love lives in Belgium, but unfortunately, it wasn't requited. I was literally lovesick in her garden - it was awful. But we're very close friends, and she came to visit us, and I'll go to Brussels next summer - I know all her family now - They almost regard me as one of the family.'

'So you're dropping the French girl as you can't keep in touch, but you can keep in touch with the unrequited Belgian girl? Said a puzzled Michael drawing his mousey eyebrows together.

'Oh, I have more in common with Isabelle - she's educated, and we write to each other about everything, plus her English is very good.'

'Is your French lady happy about you dropping her?'

'No, of course not - she's trying to hang on - she loves me - and what about you, Bea? As he angled his head sideways towards her.

'Bit of a disaster, really. My first boyfriend was in the 6th form, and I stupidly went out with him for over a year - I tried to finish it many times - he kept buying me presents - including this gold ring', as she showed her little finger to the men. He wanted to marry me! - trouble is - it meant I couldn't go out for tea with other boys as he was always hanging around. I really wish I'd been able to just go out for tea with many boys, and then I would have got to know them - rather than tying myself down. Then I made the mistake of going out with younger boys, which lasted only a few weeks. Oh well - I don't intend to have a boyfriend here as I don't want the same thing to happen. I want to go out with a lot of men platonically, and that means I can meet a variety - why tie oneself down at this age? Bea wanted to make that quite clear to them in case they had other ideas!

Michael changed the subject quickly and suggested they watch the new ITV television series based on a book by Evelyn Waugh called "Brideshead Revisited."[5]

'There's a television room above the dining hall - have you read the book?' As he looked wide-eyed at both of them.

'Oh yes, I've read the book - good idea Michael.'

'I haven't read the book, but I love costume dramas - did either of you watch the "War and Peace" series and "The Pallisers"?' Bea asked.

Michael said he had, and Martin only "War and Peace."

In 1981 in the UK, there were only 3 TV channels, and for students, it was free entertainment on the campus. Brideshead Revisited was very popular that term, and Bea was quick to note that some of the men started dressing like one of the main characters - the gorgeous Sebastian Flyte - in white cricket trousers and stripey blazers and adopting foppy hairstyles.

Martin wanted to be good friends with Bea and found out where her room was and would often drop in and sit on the bed while she sat at her desk, and they would talk a lot. He often talked about Isabelle and Florence, and she was a good listener. He said he would like to get married and that his wife was going to wear knee-length skirts and fawn tights and have a Jaeger account - his mother's favourite shop. He didn't want a career girl for a wife, either.

---

[5] Published 1945.

‘Presumably, you don’t like girls in dungarees then - like mine?’

‘Well, do you want an honest answer, Bea? She nodded. ‘Those er…..may I call them sacks? - well, you have a lovely figure Bea, and it’s hidden by your ethnic sacks.’

Bea laughed, ‘Well, I’m not going around like a green welly, frankly - I like unusual clothes, and I happen to like my sacks, as you call them.’

Bea quizzed him about the Exeter girls and did he and Michael fancy any of them - yes - there were some very attractive girls. Very. Martin was a good flirter, she noticed.

Bea made firm friends with Martin and Michael, and they often met up in the great coffee hall, where Bea would often introduce them to her fellow language students if she thought they might be a good match. Occasionally her strategy worked.

The ideology called “Political Correctness” had not yet reared its ugly head, and the students were free to say what they thought. Some of the men Bea met used to say things like, ‘A woman’s place is in the bedroom, the kitchen, and the nursery.’ No one was offended by it - it was regarded as quite funny.

Bea’s new friends were intrigued that she was about to have another brother or sister, and they wondered at the 19-year age gap. One evening in the supper hall - it was pasty and chips night - Martin asked her if she was Catholic - as Catholics often had large families due to the papal ban on all forms of birth control.

‘Yup…but I don’t like the modern churches, and I haven’t even gone to the chaplaincy here - which makes me lapsed. But I *do* believe in the Church Martin’ as she gave him and his companions a serious look.

‘It’s ingrained in me - part of who I am - I can never escape it even if I wanted to - I sometimes want it not to be true, but it is true - every bit of it - the saints, the miracles, transubstantiation - everything', her big eyes glistened as she spoke emotionally about her religion.

'Oh gosh, you sound just like Julia in Brideshead. Isabelle is Catholic too - and they're very strict over there - I think probably Florence must have been, but I never asked her. She certainly wasn't the innocent sort', as he raised his eyebrows several times with a knowing look.

One Saturday, Martin challenged Bea to a game of squash at the campus sports club - she had been captain of the girls' team at Truro school. She enthusiastically accepted the challenge. Luckily she had some tennis outfits - she was very proud of them as they were quite chic - Bea admired the American tennis star Chris Evert - who wore a different dress every time she played a match at Wimbledon - and the dresses were beautifully stylish - very fitted and very feminine.

It was a few weeks into that first term, and Bea had decided to try and grow her hair again - it was difficult wavy fine hair, and there was a lot of it. She also hated the orange colour, which never washed out. It needed to grow out. She was determined.

When she met Martin at the squash courts, he was wearing very creased whites, and she noticed how very hairy his limbs were - she almost blushed. He was well-built and taller than average. The white of his squash kit set off his rather striking blue eyes - something Bea hadn't noticed before.

He didn't give her a chance and beat her hollow while he laughed, and she was annoyed immensely, '*You* did that on purpose, didn't you? You didn't tell me how good you were - I don't want to play you again.'

'Oh, don't be silly - you weren't that bad - you just need to get a bit fitter, that's all - tell you what - why don't you let me take you out for supper - I've got a car so we can drive to the countryside.' Bea thought about it and wondered why he was suggesting it.

‘Do you mean a date, Martin?’

‘No - just a friendly meal, that’s all’, he said, trying to sound casual. ‘Ok, that would be fun - I need to get some work done for an essay, so why don’t you knock on my door at around 7 - and… is it a smart place we’re going to?’

‘I’m sure you have something suitable, Bea - other than a sack?’

Martin decided to wear his smart cotton trousers, a slightly ironed shirt, tie, and navy blazer - and his very well-looked-after brown penny loafers.

When he collected Bea, he noticed that she was wearing a shiny jade green knee-length skirt, a crisp white shirt, and black pointed court shoes with kitten heels. It was the first time he saw her in a skirt. She wore bright orange lipstick, her cheeks had a hint of blusher, and her eyes had black eyeliner and black mascara. Her hair was tidy except for her very curly fringe.

‘Oh, you do look nice, Bea - you really suit skirts - I can see your legs now!’ He beamed, clasping his hands together.

‘Thank you,’ she smiled, ‘My father’s like you - he doesn’t like women in trousers, and also my granny never wears trousers. You look very smart, Martin - those slip-on shoes suit you - they look French’ as they walked to the car and set off into the damp Devon countryside. Martin drove fast. He knew the way as he had studied the map carefully. They arrived at an old pub with a cobbled car park.

‘Oh, this is a very cosy pub Martin’ as she walked towards an open fire.

They sat at a table near the fire and studied the menu, and ordered. As the evening progressed, Martin was pleased that it was going very well indeed, and there was a lot of chatter and laughter between them. Martin was finding himself attracted to this interesting woman, and he wanted to quiz her on her religion.

‘So tell me, Bea - are you a practicing Catholic?’

‘Well, yes and no - I don’t go to mass here at all - only when I go home. I don’t like the modern Catholic Churches, and I hate all the guitars and singing and ghastly modern hymns. But I believe it all - it’s part of who I am; I’ll die for my faith if I have to.’

Martin amusingly thought she was rather strange - but fascinating too. Bea was keen to hear how Martin’s romance was going with the French girl.

‘Oh, that’s over - how can I possibly keep up with her - she lives in Paris, and we have nothing in common. She’s very upset though - I think she thought it was going to carry on - she loves me and still writes to me- it’s all rather futile - I hope the letters stop and that she gets over it.’

‘But you keep in touch with the Belgian girl - Isabelle - don’t you? And she also lives abroad.’

‘Yes, but that’s different - I have much more in common with her. She goes into a lot of detail about her family, so I am getting to know them all, plus she’s coming to stay with us next summer. She will always be my first true love - but she turned me down - *not* once but twice - humiliating. I have to get over her - I really do.’

The coffee arrived, and Martin thought Bea looked very attractive in her white shirt, and he was waiting for an opportune moment as Bea was drinking her coffee. He looked intently at her, and suddenly his voice changed - it became very soft and a little more elevated than usual - with a slight wobble in it. Bea, who was very perceptive - noticed at once and thought to herself here we go. She glanced out of the window at the darkness outside.

‘Bea - you know - I think we get on quite well, and erm…. I like you’ moving his head sideways and looking deeply into her large brown eyes. His eyes were very blue and serious.

‘Er, I mean - do you think you would… like to er…’

Before he could finish the sentence, Bea had spluttered her coffee all over the table and tried to stop laughing.

'Oh well, that didn't go down very well, did it?' Martin was also laughing. 'My plans were scuppered by the coffee' as he reddened with embarrassment. 'I thought we were just friends, Martin - I didn't know you had other plans' as she gave him a mischievous look.

'I never miss an opportunity, Bea - no harm in trying - you have made it quite clear you don't feel the same way - oh well - it was a fun evening anyway, and I hope you enjoyed it too - and can we do this again?'

'Of course, I enjoyed it, and yes, we can - you are really very funny, Martin.'

Martin insisted on paying even though Bea offered to pay half - reminding him of what one of their male friends said,

'If the woman doesn't offer to pay their share - then I would expect something in return!'

'Well, I'm not like that, Bea - it was my idea to come here, and therefore I'm paying!'

Chapter 6 - A 21st Birthday Party in Kent

The Autumn term went very quickly, and Bea was anxiously waiting for the imminent birth in the family. Martin was falling for Bea and was determined she was going to come and stay over the Christmas holidays - a local friend had invited him to his 21st party, and he was allowed to bring a plus 1. He asked Bea and explained that the dress code was Black Tie.

'I would like to come - if I can - it depends on whether I'm needed to help out at home once my mother has had the baby.'

Bea had 2 much younger siblings, 9 and 11, and was used to looking after them.

'Oh well - do try and come - it would be great, and I know how much you like dancing', Martin pleaded.

Bea adored dancing, and she was definitely going to the 21st - her baby brother wasn't due for another week, and therefore she could go. She had planned her outfit and was going to borrow her mother's long black zigzag-edged skirt from BIBA and a black top broken up with a wide shiny belt. She had some red pointy shoes with kitten heels.

The train journey from Truro to Hersterlamb was long, and it involved going on the tube - Bea was not an experienced train traveller and managed to get the wrong train line. She got off and rang Martin from a phone box. He said he would go and collect her as it was already dark and she was at a lonely station. His parents were amused, and his chatty mother said,

'This one sounds a bit scatty, Martin - fancy getting the wrong train line.'

Martin loved driving, especially fast, and he jumped into his buttery Ford Fiesta and went to pick Bea up.

He spotted the lonely figure waiting in the drizzling rain - which had made her growing hair very curly all around her small head. He was so looking forward to her visit.

'How did you miss the wrong train line?' He smiled as he put her small Laura Ashley cotton holdall into the boot.

'No idea - honestly, I'm just not used to train travel - so sorry - what your parents must think of me!'

Martin drove above the speed limit, and eventually, they arrived at the charming 16th Century cottage in the middle of nowhere. Bea was full of apologies as she went into the kitchen and was greeted by Martin's mother, Anne - who was a short, slim woman with short blue hair. She had bright pink lipstick on and had the same intense blue eyes as her son. She was busy getting the supper ready with a cigarette in one hand. Bea noticed colourful horsey rosettes all along the beams and a lot of orange Le Creuset pots on pine cupboards. Three small fluffy dogs came bounding up to Bea, and she bent down to stoke them. Bea hit it off instantly with Anne - who, like Bea was an extrovert. His father Matthew was quietly spoken.

After supper, Bea was taken up to the top of the house to the spare room, which had 2 small beds with chintzy bedspreads and matching curtains. It was very cosy with the beamy sloping ceiling. The whole house was very tidy, Bea thought - gosh, that's where Martin gets his tidiness from.

'You may hear footsteps outside in the night - we have a friendly ghost. Or a baby crying.' Bea looked startled at Martin.

'When my parents were renovating the house, they found the skeleton remains of a baby in the inglenook. Very old - probably 100s of years old. But sometimes my mother hears a baby in the night.'

Martin's parents quickly realised that Bea was not a country girl - she wore ridiculously thin heels and had no Wellington boots or proper coat. However, they warmed to her as she was chatty and cheerful and helped in the kitchen.

Bea went to bed, and Martin sat on the other bed chatting.

'I'd better not stay long chatting to you - I got into trouble last time that happened when Isabelle stayed last summer.'

Bea slept well, and she heard no ghosts. After breakfast, Martin took her on a walk through the woods behind the house. He had a black and white cat called Noodle - which went with him on walks.

'I'm not used to cats as my mother's terrified of them - we were taught to shoo them away if they came near the house.'

Bea was keeping her distance from him on the uneven walk - in a pair of borrowed old boots. She saw him looking at her wistfully, and she didn't want to encourage him to come too close, so she kept her eyes on the ground.

'I'm looking forward to the party - do you know all the people?' 'Quite a few, yes - there will be a lot of young farmer types there. I wonder what you're going to wear?'

Back at the house, Bea was keen to know about the unusual little fluffy-headed grey dogs, and Anne was in her element when asked. She sat at the kitchen table and lit up a cigarette, offering Bea one - Bea lit up much to Martin's disapproving look.

'They are Dandie Dinmonts, and they are unusual Beatrice - as they're difficult to breed from - they have short little legs carrying long bodies - but I'm going to give it a go with "Crumpet," the girl. And I need to find a suitable male.

'Martin, I can see you're not really a dog fan.'

'And you're right - yappy things jumping up - I much prefer cats - you have to earn their love. They're altogether more mysterious and interesting than dogs, who are like doormats - and all that licking, ugh.'

The day was getting on, and the December darkness cloaked the cottage by teatime. Matthew had lit a fire in the sitting room and was reading a book. Martin had got out some photo albums to show Bea. In addition to the family photos, there were photos of Isabelle and Florence, who couldn't look more different from each other, Bea thought.

Bea got dressed into her black outfit with her bright orange lipstick and kohl eyeliner - the shiny wide belt accentuated her slim waist. She wore a simple gold chain around her neck. Martin was already waiting in the sitting room in his dinner jacket, white shirt, and plain black bow tie. He had very polished black brogues. He heard Bea's soft steps down the carpeted stairs and let out a silent gasp as he glimpsed her through the doorway.

'Oh, Bea, you do look dazzling! Is this your special disco outfit?'
'Yes, thank you - and you look very smart too.'

The party was in a private house with polished oak floors and heavily beamed. The disco was on a very large landing up a flight of stairs. It was a dark room with subdued lighting. Martin introduced Bea to the people he knew, and she took an instant liking to the young farmers - they had an earthiness and openness about them - and nothing pretentious about them - unlike some of the Exeter students. The music was loud and pounding.

Bea wasn't short of dance offers, and once she started dancing - she rarely left the dance floor - her favourite music was playing - disco - a popular genre at the time, especially songs by Diana Ross and George Benson. Martin tried to keep up with her moves but found it difficult. He watched her and was captivated.

'There's food downstairs, Bea. Shall we go and eat?' He had to almost shout as the music was so loud.

A huge buffet was on a long serving table in the dining room, with a choice of savoury dishes, such as tomato barbecue chicken and Moussaka, but it was the puddings that Bea feasted her eyes on. She was determined to save some space for the Black Forest Gateau and Strawberry cream cake.

A young swarthy farmer, in particular, took a keen interest in Bea - he had a thick head of curly dark hair and large hairy hands. His voice was deep, and he had a slight Kent accent. There weren't enough chairs to sit on, so he offered his lap to Bea, which she was grateful for. She didn't fancy him, so she felt quite safe. Martin smiled with amusement. He was enjoying this party and liked the effect Bea was causing.

Eventually, there was a final call for dancing, as the party was ending soon, and Bea was already dreading the slow music - she had been to enough school discos to know the format of the evening, and this was the worst bit. She remembered with painful embarrassment how girls huddled together in groups, waiting for some brave buck or two to dare ask one of them to dance.

Martin made sure he was with Bea as they went up to the dance floor, and the slow music was playing.

'Will you dance with me?'

'Ok,' she giggled with embarrassment - 'Im not very good at slow dancing. I much prefer the free, fast dancing.'

She put both her hands on Martin's broad shoulders covered in the heavy black wool jacket while he placed a hand on her shoulder and one on the small of her back. Her makeup had mostly melted off her face, and the eyeliner had smudged, giving her a dramatic ghostly look. The music was less loud, and they could hear each other speak.

Bea's shyness prompted her to speak quickly about the people in the room - who was with who, or who was going out with who - and did Martin like any of the girls' outfits? She realised with growing fear and alarm that she rather liked dancing with him - his intense blue eyes only looking at her, and for the first time, she felt attracted to him - but panicking, she thought - no, no, no - you're not my type - I *can't* fall for you - I really *can't*. Not on Bea. It really isn't!

Martin sensed her awkwardness with amusement.

'I hope you've enjoyed meeting some of my friends Bea. - I think you have a fan.'

'Oh yes - he with the manly voice and thick hair - he's very friendly', raising her dark eyebrows at him.

The next day was Sunday, and Bea asked to go to Mass at the nearest Catholic Church. Martin offered to take her and mentioned that they knew some of the Catholics who went there. Martin's parents joked about their son's seeming attraction to Catholic girls.

'Shall I drop you off and then collect you in an hour?' Asked Martin while Bea nodded with her overnight bag on her arm. She was wearing a brightly coloured skirt she had made with some Malaysian fabric her father had brought back from his travels and a black polo neck jumper.

'And then, if you can drop me at the station so I can get back to Cornwall, please? And I need to thank your parents - are they outside?' She went to the kitchen window. 'Oh yes, I can see Anne in a stable.' Matthew emerged from his study, and Bea thanked him and then went down some steps to say goodbye to Anne, who was mucking out, fag in mouth.

Bea liked the traditional church building as it wasn't a modern concrete monster like the one in Truro - it had a charm and a quaintness, and there were traditional paintings in the church and proper statues and wooden pews. The mass was in English, and Bea felt happy in that old 1920s church – her faith gave her a security and orderliness which she found comforting. She was blissfully ignorant of all the controversies of the Second Vatican Council, and when older people spoke of 'Vatican 2', she asked them blankly what that was, as though it was some object. She often heard her mother lamenting the overnight changes in the mass - how it went from strict Latin to ghastly guitars, hippy music, and bossy women. One day she would find out what happened, she thought, but not yet.

Martin took Bea to the station, and they looked forward to seeing each other next term. He was falling for her and hoped very slightly that his luck might be changing. He was very patient. Extremely.

Chapter 7 - Rebecca Prissy

Bea had made good friends with a fellow modern languages student called Rebecca Prissy. They went to lectures together and to the same social gatherings. She was a very neat-looking girl of below average height - almost petite, and she had a strawberry blonde wavy bob and hazel eyes. She spoke in one of the best Queen's English Bea had ever heard. Her voice was shrill and cut like a glass. She was always carefully dressed in good quality tailored trousers, pie crust stripey shirts, and fine wool cardigans. She wore sensible brown loafers. And, of course, she wore the regulation pearls. She and her many contemporaries at Exeter looked as if they had walked straight out of the recently published "Official Sloane Ranger Handbook."[6] Bea had already decided this look didn't suit her as she didn't have blonde hair and English rose skin. Rebecca was also keen on Martin and quizzed Bea about her chances with him.

'He's got striking blue eyes, hasn't he, Bea?'

'He's not really my type, Rebecca - but I could sound him out if you like. Not sure when I'm seeing him next as he moved out of the halls into the depths of some village near the sea - he just hated halls - plus he's got a car, so it's quite easy for him.'

'Hopefully, we'll see him in the coffee hall this week,' said Rebecca. 'Probably we will.'

Martin was still keen on Beatrice, but his energies were on his new abode, and it took him a good half an hour to drive to the campus. He decided to play it cool with Bea - thinking it might be a good tactic.

---

[6] By Harpers and Queen 1st January 1982.

A few weeks into the Lent term, Bea and Rebecca were sitting in the coffee hall complaining about the lecture they had just had on 'diphthongs.'

'Ghastly - why do we need diphthongs - I mean, how useless are they… ah just a minute, Rebecca, there's Martin coming this way' as Bea waved him over.

'How was your commute from the seaside?' Said Rebecca eagerly. 'Well, it beats halls anyway - and I like driving,' he said cheerfully. Bea spotted an opportunity to speak to Martin as they got up for their next lecture and told Rebecca she would catch up with her.

'Listen, Martin - you know Rebecca likes you don't you?'

'Um - well, she makes it fairly obvious - she will stare at me for long periods - rather disconcertingly, actually. I mean, she's quite pretty, I suppose - quite feminine, really. She can be a bit fierce, though, can't she?'

'Ok, I think there's a party next Saturday with the usual crowd - Rebecca and I are going - are you?'

'Oh yes, definitely, I love parties.' He was hoping it might make Bea jealous if he chatted up Rebecca.

A few weeks later, Rebecca confided in Bea that she and Martin were officially going out together.

'He's such a gentleman, Bea - and we seem to have a lot in common.' 'Oh, that's nice for you - no doubt you'll be invited to meet his parents - very nice - they live in the middle of nowhere with horses, dogs, and cats.'

'Well, if we get serious, Bea - I will invite him to meet my parents too.'

Martin liked having a girlfriend - but he found Rebecca quite twee, and she liked going into the city a lot - she liked shopping -

which he hated. He found time to confide in Bea one day after a chance meeting in the student bookshop.

'How's it going, Martin?' Asked Bea opening a large textbook.

'She's rather intense - and dare I say - a bit dull. She's a bit predictable, Bea - I'm not sure it'll last,' he said crisply.

'You mean there's no chase, no thrills?' Laughed Bea.

'Well, yes, I suppose that element is missing', he grinned, and his eyes sparkled.

'Oh dear - well, I'm afraid she's loved up on you.'

Rebecca was rather smitten with Martin, and Bea was worried for her friend - who was definitely in love with him - that was obvious by her body language - Bea thought - but Martin's body language displayed his not-so-keenness on Rebecca. Towards the end of the summer term, the romance was fizzling out, much to Rebecca's disappointment, who had hoped they would meet up during the long summer holidays - she found that he was unenthusiastic about most of her holiday ideas, and he was making excuses to *not* see her.

'He says he has a job in the holidays and won't have time to see me, Beatrice, and that he's going to stay in Brussels with his best friend Isabelle - who is this Isabelle that he talks about a lot Bea?'

'Ah yes - Isabelle - she turned him down when he first showed an interest in her before his gap year - he was devastated about her, as he fell in love with her the day he met her - first love and all that - you know? Then he tried it on again with her, when she came to stay with his parents - he got into trouble with his parents as he was in her room all night talking. I mean, he's pretty persistent with her - but she turned him down a second time.' Bea raised her eyebrows to Rebecca, who was listening with a doleful expression.

'I mean - he told me he had to be physically sick in her garden - hence the phrase "lovesick."'

‘I see. Maybe that’s it then - he’s always ever hopeful he’ll win her in the end - the ultimate prize.’

‘It’s called the thrill of the chase Rebecca - for many men, the chase is more exciting than the kill - well that’s what my father tells me’ - she looked sympathetically at her friend. ‘Look, I need to go to the library for a wretched essay - see you later?’ Rebecca nodded sadly as they parted.

A few weeks later, Martin saw Bea alone in the campus library and went over to her as he had received a letter from Isabelle - he confided quietly in Bea, who saw that he looked rather forlorn about it.

‘What’s the news then - you don’t look your usual happy self?’ She whispered.

‘Oh - Isabelle’s boyfriend is rather more serious than I thought. They met at the Cours de Danse - you know - the dancing lessons, where all the top-notch Belgians meet their future spouses. She’s really rather taken with him - he comes from a famous old family - he’s the sort of choice her parents want for her - from one of the top drawers of Belgian nobility. He sneaks into her bedroom at her parents' house - and is.. er.. rather demanding.’

‘Gosh - does Isabelle tell you every detail about her private life Martin?’ ‘Yes, absolutely - I’m her confidante of choice. She’s still planning to come and stay in the summer holidays and I’m going over there with an old friend for a few days only - as I have a job at a wine shop.’

‘Rebecca suspects you want to end it with her - you know she’s really taken with you - are you treating her cruelly?’ as she gave him a long questioning look.

‘Im trying to do it as gently as I can, and I was rather hoping she’d get the hint.’

‘You haven’t taken advantage of her, have you?’ Bea looked him straight in the eye.

‘No - I haven’t. I don’t... er find her that attractive. She’s also a bit too keen and keeps wanting me to meet her parents - must get to a lecture - see you around?’ Bea nodded.

The end of the first academic year was soon coming to an end, and students were maneuvering themselves into little groups of friends, as they would have to move out of the convenient halls of residence and move into shared houses, either in the city centre, or further out in the countryside. Those well-heeled undergraduates who had cars had the luxury of choosing where to live. Some had mopeds which gave them some independence, but a lot of the mopeds were bought second hand, and it was a lottery as to whether they would be a reliable means of transport - and not particularly pleasant in the Devon drizzly weather. Martin and his fellow law student Michael Oak needed one more person to share within the farmhouse they had found for the second year.

Michael and Martin saw Bea in the coffee hall alone - she was writing notes. ‘We’ve found a farmhouse - would you consider sharing with us, Bea?’

Martin looked anxiously for her to say yes.

‘I don’t have any means of transport, and for goodness sake, the house isn’t even near a shop,’ said Bea looking at them as though they were ridiculous to even think of asking her.

‘I can drive you both in.’

‘Or I could get a moped maybe - isn’t that what you’re doing, Michael?’ ‘Yes - until I pass my driving test.’

‘Ok, that’s settled then.’ Martin looked delighted. ‘Did I agree?’ As Martin nodded firmly.

The term ended, and the students went home to their families, their old flames, and their holiday jobs. Martin worked in a wine shop for most of the summer, and one day he received a letter from Isabelle - it was the letter he would rather not have received that hot sunny day in August. In it, Isabelle recounted how she and Étienne, her smart boyfriend, were caught in her bed by her father one morning - and as a result, her father told Étienne he must do the honourable thing and get engaged - he would not have his daughter taken advantage of!

Martin felt as if he had been winded in the stomach. His mother saw him reading the letter and asked who the letter was from.

In a depressed, low voice, he said, 'Isabelle isn't coming to stay now - she's just got engaged to her boyfriend. She wants to visit us next term, though, and bring her fiancé over. So I won't be going over there now - they plan to visit during the first weekend of the term.'

'Oh, you must be a bit sad then - isn't she very young to get engaged?' - his mother was folding up some laundry.

'Well, I was never in the running - not really. She's marrying a very suitable man from an aristocratic line going back centuries. He's exactly the sort of man they wanted for their daughter… it's a bit forced though, I must admit,' murmured Martin, thinking to himself - 'I really don't want to meet him - he who got the prize.'

Chapter 8 - Farmhouse near Crediton

Martin, Michael, and Beatrice arrived at the big old rambling farmhouse, the wing of which was for students with big tall draughty rooms, stone floors, and thin, tired curtains. The main part was lived in by the owners of the farm, who occasionally shared the big kitchen with the students. Raw milk swirled around in a big steel container in an outbuilding - and students were trusted to record how many pints they took. Bea's parents helped Bea with her cases, and her father put a slide lock on her bedroom door to keep "thieves and swains" away. Therese told Bea where the Catholic Church was and that she could easily get there on her moped.

'I don't know why you chose to live in the middle of nowhere, Bea - why couldn't you share with your other friends in the city - you've only that silly old moped, and it rains a lot here', said her mother while Bea's baby brother was crawling on the thin bedroom carpet towards the corridor where the staircase was, Therese quickly shutting the door to stop him.

'They didn't ask me to share - and anyway, Martin offered to drive us to the campus each day' while she got her big music system set up in the corner of her room and carefully put her LP records in a pile. There was a small single bed that Bea cosied up with a vibrant Mexican bedspread from her childhood. Robert was anxious to get off, and they said their goodbyes, 'No doubt we'll be seeing you soon and hope that moped works - and drive carefully - wear that helmet!'

Martin and Michael were at the house before Bea and had already sorted out their gin and wine supplies for the next few weeks. They agreed to do their own suppers during the week and planned to regularly host supper parties for their friends - all living in remote villages nearby. Martin had invited Isabelle and her fiancé Étienne to stay with them soon - over a weekend and asked Michael if he could share with him while the couple had his room, which had 2 single beds.

‘Gosh, we’re finally going to meet the famous Isabelle Bea,’ said Michael raising his eyebrows at Bea.

‘I know. It’s going to be intriguing, I think,’ as she was fastidiously sorting out the contents of her new canvas tote bag and making sure all her brand spanking new stationary was neatly inside. Bea’s biggest thrill every September was to buy notebooks of every size, shape, and pattern. The larger notebooks were for lecture notes, and the smaller ones were for her many lists on various topics, such as Accounts, Christmas present lists, Clothes lists, Diet lists, and so on.

Martin offered to take the others to campus on the first day of term, and they gratefully accepted - neither fancied taking their mopeds on that damp, drizzly day. If the first year at Exeter was a gentle introduction to undergraduate study - all one had to do was pass the year, the second year was much more serious and counted towards the final degree. The year ahead was an entirely new ball game for them.

When Isabelle and Étienne arrived at the farmhouse one late afternoon on a Friday, Michael and Bea were waiting in the big warmish kitchen - which had an ancient large white Aga and damp clothes drying on a pulley above, giving a faint whiff of detergent. They could hear laughter outside as Martin greeted the Belgians in the parking area. They were led into the kitchen and introduced to Bea and Michael, who were making a pot of tea, to go with the scones, strawberry jam, and clotted cream - all Martin’s idea, to show them a typical West Country tea.

Michael could barely hold his gasp as he held out his hand to the green-eyed tanned, tall woman with very long wavy mid-brown hair and wearing the Belgian version of the Sloane Ranger uniform. Her smiley fiancé was quietly spoken, and of average height and very slim, with almost black wavy hair, who simply introduced himself as,

‘Étienne De Tra-Vail-Dur - I am very appy to meet you’ while Martin hung his green Loden-style jacket on a peg. Bea too was mesmerised by Isabelle and thought she must have had ballet lessons as she moved with such quiet elegance in high stiletto court shoes too. As she shook Isabelle's hand, she felt very frumpy - although she no longer wore dungarees, she was wearing unflattering trousers, and her hair was short and unruly. Isabelle handed Martin an elegant carrier bag full of Côte D'Or bars of praline chocolate and bags of Chokotoff toffees - much to Martin's delight as he placed them carefully in the larder.

That evening they had a simple supper of Bea's granary flan, Michael's homemade raisin coleslaw, and baked potatoes. Bea was keen to know about their wedding plans. Isabelle was more talkative than Étienne, and she was more than happy to talk about it. They discovered they had a lot in common.

'Oh is a long time for that' - laughed Isabelle, 'I mus finish my stoodies to become a teacher.'

'And you - do you have a boyfriend?'

'Not at the moment - I had a boyfriend during the summer holidays, but he was a bit young and also a bit too keen - my parents are friends with his parents, and it's all rather awkward as he was cut up about us ending.'

Bea and Michael could see why Martin fell for Isabelle, and later when Martin was clearing up the kitchen with his guests, they had a long discussion in the sitting room about them.

'Well, I have to say I can see why he fell in love with her - I mean, she's so nice and friendly - very chatty, and she's got a certain demureness about her, hasn't she - she's so - well, she has that continental way about her don't you think, and that French accent, that soft voice?' Michael was crouching down to try and revive the fire, which was rather small for the size of the room.

'Gosh, yes… I think you mean she has a certain "je ne sais quoi." It's hard to define, isn't it? - I really like them - he's rather good-looking, I think - I wonder if he knows that Martin made two unrequited passes at her and that she writes and tells him everything that's going on between her and Étienne? I mean, Michael - don't you think that's inappropriate now that she's engaged to another man?' Said Bea holding her cup of tea close to keep warm and lighting a cigarette. Michael frowned,

'Actually, Bea, you've got a point. Hmm - if I were Étienne, I wouldn't like my fiancée telling another man what we got up to. Well, he's clearly bowled over by her still - I mean, he was dancing around her like a butterfly in the kitchen, offering her this, that, and the other - he puts that funny voice on, too - did you notice?'

'Yes, I agree he puts on that wincey voice - but equally, she laps up all the attention with that coy expression of hers. What woman wouldn't? - I'm sure her fiancé would hate it if he knew what she wrote to Martin, or maybe he isn't bothered. Who knows? I have to say I don't think Martin's future wife would be happy either with that level of closeness between them - it's almost as though they have this unbreakable bond. Have you heard the saying, "First love is the best love?" She's his first true love - but unrequited. I wonder… I mean… if she rejected him twice already, and yet she has this powerful emotional hold on him, using him as her confidant - do you think he's always going to be living in hope, being dangled by her heartstrings, that one day he may win her over? I mean, their engagement - isn't that all a bit forced? It's what her parents asked of him - almost like a shotgun wedding. Maybe they don't love each other really, and it's almost…well… like an arranged marriage? Maybe Martin is hoping it won't last and will always be there for her. Étienne doesn't seem that loved up over her, does he? - he's actually quite cool towards her - well that's what I think anyway - I'm tired now, so I'm hitting the hay - see you tomorrow - I wonder what they have planned for the rest of their stay?'

Martin spent the rest of the weekend showing his visitors the local attractions - he felt like a gooseberry, and it was starting to hit him that his dear Isabelle was really going to marry this quiet, reserved man. He had no doubt in his mind that Étienne was a gentleman and a man of his word, and the marriage really would take place between them. He knew he had to get over his fantasy, but all the time Isabelle was around - he fantasised about what the future could hold for them. He felt possessed. She was almost like a drug to him.

When the short visit was over, he and Isabelle made plans for the next reunion, and of course, they would continue to write to each other. He was her confidant, and she was his confidante. No one was ever going to break that.

Bea was still keeping her male visitor friends at arm's length - she enjoyed going out in the countryside to various parties with them and always had a lift. She felt safer going out with plain men - she found the good-looking ones could be very arrogant, and that put her right off them. Her mother used to tell her that ugly men were more interesting than handsome ones, as they had to rely on their wit rather than on their looks. One of her male friends was rather keen on her, and he liked to show her his car, which he proudly called his "silver machine." He had a logbook where he wrote down all the mileage of his trips. She enjoyed his attentions and chivalrous behaviour towards her but made it clear she wasn't romantically interested in him. Soon he found a girlfriend, much to Bea's relief.

Martin decided it was futile to keep living in the hope of a future with his Belgian belle, and he was just happy to receive any letters she wrote, often sharing the information with Bea, who felt she was getting to know Isabelle really rather well. Martin thought it was time to try again with Bea, and he decided to use tactics. He could see that other men were keen on her, and it annoyed him. He was going to treat her with coolness and aloofness.

One day when Bea was on her moped to the campus, the moped broke down as it often did. It was raining, and she had a rather pathetic rain jacket on. She walked to the nearest phone box and made a call to the moped shop where she bought it and was told to wait beside it until someone came to repair it. As she waited in the drizzle, she saw

Martin driving by - he glanced over as he was driving by and just waved. Bea's mouth opened as he sped by. Charming behaviour thought Bea as she walked up and down the pavement trying to get warm, wondering why he didn't even stop to offer to help. She thought to herself - what good would stopping do - he's hopeless at mechanical things anyway, but he could have stopped to ask how I was. Really rude of him. Well, I'm going to pretend I don't care, and I won't even mention it when I see him, she thought. Two can play that game.

Chapter 9 - Martin and Beatrice

Bea had enough admirers not to worry about Martin's cool behaviour towards her, but she felt annoyed by it and thought he was grieving over Isabelle. She certainly had enough work to do to keep her mind occupied. All essays were written by hand - laptops and word processors weren't readily available in 1982. Bea made her bedroom cosier by putting up her Christmas decorations by the end of October, and the ceiling was covered in shiny dangly shapes and paper chains diagonally across the room.

One day an admirer friend came for tea at the farmhouse and asked Bea if she might consider marrying him at some point in the future, at some unspecified time. She asked Martin and Michael what they thought.

'How very absurd,' said Martin, his intense blue eyes looking sharply at Bea, 'And how did you answer?' Asked Michael pushing his dark eyebrows together and making a frown.

'I just said I would think about it when the time of the proposal came - maybe he was sounding me out as he didn't want a rejection and it was safer to put it some way off in the future - it was neither a yes nor no answer.'

'I think he's obviously keen on you, Bea - maybe you're a bit naive, that's all.'

Martin wondered if his coolness was having any effect on Bea at all - he didn't like her getting proposals, even future ones - no, no, it wouldn't do at all. He couldn't tell what she was feeling as she treated him as amiably as she treated everyone else. He decided he didn't enjoy being aloof - it wasn't in his nature, and so he became friendlier towards her - he was sorry about going past her broken moped, but he wasn't going to let her know that! He was going to make an effort and find things to discuss with her. Isabelle temporarily left his mind - his mind was now on Bea - he saw a glimmer of hope - just. He liked the way she put much care and attention into what she wore - although he loathed her trousers - he thought her thighs looked "thick" in them. He noticed she wore more skirts now, revealing her slim ankles - always in feminine-heeled shoes. Bea did indeed love clothes but didn't follow fashions unless they suited her. She liked experimenting - mixing vintage pieces with new ones. Her hair was her biggest cross, and she used temporary dyes to colour the greys - and it was prone to look wild and unkempt with a mind of its own.

One day in early November, Bea asked the others if they were going to stay up and watch the new TV channel called "Channel 4?"

'Yes, I'll watch it for a bit,' said Michael, 'not sure I can stay up all night though - we've got lectures tomorrow.'

'Friday, I only have afternoon ones,' said Bea, 'I'll see how I go.'

The opening night of Channel 4 saw the start of the Comic Strip series, with the first episode being "Five go mad in Dorset", with the very young actresses Dawn French and Jennifer Saunders. It was a parody of the Enid Blyton books and featured very strong themes.

It was a night they would never forget, as no words were spoken - Martin and Bea were alone on the very old lumpy sofa enjoying the new channel, and Martin was slowly moving up closer to Bea - it was the early hours of Friday, and he very tenderly put his arm around her - she could resist his charms no longer, and it was an unspoken agreement that they were boy and girlfriend from that day onwards. Bea didn't love Martin, but she enjoyed his company and found him attractive. Martin fell in love with Bea, but it would be months before he told her. Bea was still strict and would on no account have marital relations unless she was married. She wondered if she could marry Martin, and she thought it a strong possibility. He would sound her out in a roundabout way about marriage until he felt confident she would say yes. Martin had given up flirting with other women - he only had eyes for Bea.

After 6 months of what was a blissful courtship, Martin sounded Bea out about thoughts of marriage. He was no longer worried about her Catholicism being a stumbling block as he could see she wasn't really practicing - she hardly went to church, for goodness sake! But he was more concerned that Bea's degree required a year in Spain, which was in the next year, and he dreaded the thought of it - losing Bea to another country with all those swarthy Spaniards.

It was a warm day in May, and they were in the overgrown garden - Bea clutching her usual mug of hot tea writing in her favourite notebook - supremely happy just being with Martin, who was lying sideways on the dry grass staring intently at Bea. He felt his heart beating faster than normal as he quizzed Bea - trying to sound casual.

'What do you er think about marriage, Bea?'

'Well, now you ask, I definitely want to get married, and when I do, I would like at least 5 children, and I plan to look after them myself, and they'll go to Catholic schools.'

'Ok..er…em…what would you say if I asked you to er… marry me?'

Bea looked at Martin's strikingly blue eyes, hardly blinking, and his glowing cheeks. His voice was in that same love-struck tone that he had when speaking to or about Isabelle. She wondered if he was joking and decided he was not. She put her notebook and mug on the knackered garden table and put her sunglasses on her head while she pondered what to reply. She felt a quickening in her heart.

'I would say yes…providing you agree to allow any children to be brought up as Catholics, and I want quite a few,' she looked at him seriously.

'Really?' His eyes looked yearningly at Bea, 'I love you - you must realise that - I don't like the thought of you living abroad next year and meeting Spanish men - you don't need a degree if you marry me. Oh... and I can tell you now - I'm properly over Isabelle - I really mean it. The day I saw you across the room at that tea party - I knew I would marry you - don't ask me how - 6th sense or something.'

'Yes I know - I…er …I..love you too', she blurted in a very low voice as it was the first time in her life she had told a man those 3 words, and Martin sat up and held her hands in his.

'Well, you do need to be over Isabelle; otherwise, I can't marry you - I just can't. The other thing Martin, is that Catholic marriage is for life - and you need to be of the same mindset - otherwise, if you think you can just get divorced if you get bored or whatever - believe me, you *will* get divorced - so that's why you really have to believe it's for life - you're protestant, and they can get divorced.'

'Of course, I believe it's for life - why wouldn't I?!'

'Well, non-Catholics can divorce - and you're agnostic, aren't you?'

'I am on the same page, Bea - regarding marriage for life. And I need to do it properly so we'll drive down to Truro, and I'll ask your father for permission to marry you - don't tell anyone!' As he grabbed her hand in his two hands and kissed it, looking up adoringly at Bea.

Bea was very close to her grandmother, and she simply *had* to write to her at once. She was the happiest she could remember.

June 1983

Dear Granny

I have some top secret confidential exciting news that must not get to Ma or Pa or anyone. I trust you with this secret, very exciting news. I am unofficially engaged to be married in the summer of 1985 - as soon as my degree is finished - it's Martin - always been him, but it took me over a year to realise it. He's got everything I look for, and also, I love him very much - he's not against the Church - and I think he may convert. Don't worry about the fact that we live in the same house - he's the perfect gentleman and very old-fashioned. He knew the minute he met me that he would marry me. I won't be going to teacher training college now.

You'll be pleased to hear that we're living in London for the first year and then in Sussex or Kent in a big enough house for our many children - which we intend to have soon after we get married. He's agreed to Catholic schools for them. We've already discussed the names of the children. God must have given me a sign that He wanted me to get married and have children - and I've found the right person. You know when he was being ghastly towards me? Well, it was his ploy to get me. Well, it worked.

Do you know whether we will be allowed to have a Catholic marriage in a church other than the Catholic one - as I don't like that modern one in Truro - I want a traditional church building - or a little chapel? Please find out if it's possible. It has to be above board and properly valid.

Love Bea XXX

The elated couple soon went to see Bea's father - Martin took him to the pub, and Robert was delighted with the proposal, after which Martin surprised Bea as they drove to a cloudy Land's End, where he led Bea down a rocky path to the sea. The waves were noisily crashing against the rocks, spraying them with sea drops. Bending down on one knee, he handed Bea a rose while he fumbled in his old Barbour pocket for something, while gazing up at Bea in adoration - her tiered skirt blowing in the wind, her hair going gypsy wild in the damp air.

'Beatrice, will you marry me?' Handing Bea a small box.

'Yes, I will,' she said while opening the box and putting on the simple engagement ring, her face lighting up as she proudly held out her finger.

'It's a temporary ring - until I can afford to get you a proper ring.'

But not everyone was happy at the news of the young couple - Martin's family and especially his father Matthew was aghast and wrote his son a letter with a long list of "why nots" to marry.

'You've got a beer pocket and champagne tastes - you will end up with a van full of screaming children before you know it - she's Catholic, you know - and they're not allowed birth control - what are you thinking of Martin - it's madness at your age - you've not long come out of nappies. I will ring Bea's parents as this is utter madness - are you in your right mind?'[7]

Matthew Charmer duly made the phone call to the Eclectic household and was very polite but firm in his reservations. Therese was equally firm, 'We know Beatrice is ready - we know our daughter. We're planning to put it in the Telegraph announcements.'

'I'll get off my bike then,' said Matthew, graciously bowing out of the fight and knowing how determined his son was.

Their university friends thought it was reckless madness too - and joked that it was Martin's ploy to "have his wicked way" with Bea. The second year came to an end, and Martin was relieved that Bea had decided not to continue with her degree - she didn't enjoy it particularly, hadn't done particularly well - and she knew he didn't want her to go to Spain and meet Spaniards.

'What will you do instead, Bea - you have to get some sort of qualification if you don't get a degree?' Robert asked her - 'although you've got a meal ticket now - more useful than a degree,' he laughed loudly, rubbing his hands together.

'Well, I like cooking, so I'll train properly as a cook - I've looked at St Austell College of Further Education, and they do a course there' - it means I'll have to live at home and get the train there.'

---

[7] See Appendix re Catholic teaching on birth control.

During the 2 year engagement - some admirers tried to persuade Bea not to marry so young - her unavailability made them try harder - it was futile though she had firmly made up her mind to marry Martin.

Part 2. Marriage and Family Life

Chapter 10 - Two Weddings in 1985

Like their Belgian friends, it was to be a long engagement for Martin and Bea. Martin decided he needed a decent degree to get a good job, and he studied - just enough. Bea was no longer a distraction as she lived with her parents while doing the cookery course. Bea would go and stay with Martin during the weekends of his final year, and they would discuss wedding details.

Bea pretended that she was already married and lived like a married woman - throwing all Catholic teaching out of the window[8]. She trusted Martin that he was an honourable man and would still marry her. He would drive her to her college in Cornwall on Monday mornings and get back in time for his lectures. During the holidays, they wrote long letters to each other or telephoned after 6 pm - which was the cheaper rate.

There was no marriage preparation with her parish priest - and he was relaxed about the marriage taking place in a non-Catholic chapel. He didn't ask Bea if she was going to mass on Sundays or living a chaste life prior to marriage. He didn't instruct the couple on the teaching of birth control - he just told Martin that he mustn't be an obstacle to any children being brought up as Catholics. In the chaotic muddle of the post-Vatican 2 era, he was typical of many priests.

In the summer of 1984, Martin passed his degree with a respectable grade, and Bea qualified as a cook. Martin went to live with his parents while he looked for a job, and Bea found a job in a wine bar on the Pantiles of Tunbridge Wells as a lunchtime cook during weekdays and cooking on Friday and Saturday evenings.

She found a bedsit in the attic of a large Victorian house within walking distance and had to put money in a meter for the electricity. The bathroom was shared with the other residents. She found the

---

[8] The Catholic Church teaches that it is a mortal sin to have marital relations outside of marriage.

hours at the wine bar very antisocial, as did her fiancé. On Bea's days off, she would often go to Martin's family home for the day - she loved the peace and calm and cosy atmosphere - Martin's parents were fully accepting that their youngest son really was getting married, and they could see how happy she made him. One day at their kitchen table, Bea announced, 'I've had enough of the wine bar job, so I've found a live-in job in Birmingham through an agency. I'm going to be cooking for an elderly couple in Solihull. And then I'll go and live at home until the wedding - there's so much to organise, and the bridesmaids seem to be a growing list! - we just want a simple wedding, don't we? - but even simple weddings need a lot of planning - don't they?'

'We're doing the cars and flowers,' said Martin - 'Oh, and I've decided not to go into the law. It doesn't pay well enough for years - and I need a better-paid job. So I've been shortlisted for a job at Lazards - if I get it, we'll have to rent something in London after the wedding. And by the way - we've been invited to Isabelle and Étienne's wedding, which is soon after our wedding - and no, they can't come to ours for some reason.'

Bea couldn't wait for the big day to arrive, but the nearer it got, the more nervous she got about things potentially going wrong. The day finally arrived on Holy Saturday in April. Ordinarily, it was not permitted to get married during Lent, but the afternoon of the vigil of Easter Sunday was allowed, so the ceremony was due to start at 1 pm.

The flowers were late, and a panic set in. Bea was inwardly anxious about the day - and looking forward to the honeymoon. It was a cold and typically Cornish drizzly day.

'I need the flowers for my hair,' said an anxious Bea as she was applying some makeup with Lucy, 'and we need the flowers for the bridesmaids.'

'As long as they get here by noon - but I will ring them anyway,' said Therese's mother - who was busy sorting Bea's siblings out.

Eventually, Bea was dressed in her wedding dress - it was her mother's dress and was a vintage ivory brocade dress from Harrods. The veil was a simple short one. The flowers arrived just in time, and some cream orchids were hastily arranged in Bea's short hair. Her many bridesmaids were all in sailor dresses, and her brothers wore sailor suits. The wedding cars arrived to take them to the Methodist chapel at Truro school, and Robert walked a glowing Bea slowly up the aisle while the organist, gowned in a black cape, was playing Wagner's Bridal March. The Marriage ceremony started after the hymn "Jerusalem."

As a delighted Martin slipped his late grandmother's wedding ring on Bea - it had been altered to fit Bea's slim finger - Bea's fine complexion was flushed with happiness, and her eyes radiated serenity. It was her vocation - this was her career now - all she ever wanted. She thought her husband looked so handsome in his morning coat and white shirt - the black-suited his beautiful eyes and pale skin. The organist began to play, "I vow to thee, my country."

After the final hymn, "Love Divine," the jolly organist belted out Widor's "Wedding March" as the happy couple went out into the cold grey day for the traditional photo session, which Bea found the most tedious as she didn't like being photographed and it was cold.

'It's the line up next, Martin - in the big hall - I'm freezing out here.'

The Charmer couple led their guests towards a large dark panelled hall, where they stood at the entrance to do the traditional "line up" - where the 100 guests had to queue to congratulate the newly married couple. On a long side table, there was an array of food, including Galantine of chicken and other traditional fare, overseen by a smiling army chef wearing his tall white chef's hat. The 2 tiered wedding cake was made by a Catholic parishioner.

Robert decided to serve Champagne at the start of the reception, followed by a French sparkling wine called Veuve du Vernay. Bea had found a good offer from Victoria Wine, at the special offer price of £2.99 per bottle.

'We need the top tier of the cake for our first child's baptism,' Bea explained to Martin as they went to get some food.

'Will it keep til then? He joked, 'it'll be speeches soon, and then we can get away to the lodge I've booked for tonight - I'm dreading what they're doing to my car' he grinned.

When the speeches arrived, Bea was glad there was a large post to hide behind. When the best man started his speech, she wanted to sink into the floor - it was all about Martin's past conquests accompanied by cringingly lewd language. Martin had a straight face, while the best man's parents were visibly mortified at their son's coarse speech and could hardly speak to him after the wedding.

'It'll be a talking point whenever our wedding is mentioned,' Bea whispered to her embarrassed husband.

'I can't believe he did that speech - wait til I do his speech - if we're still friends then!'

Therese came up to her daughter and new son-in-law, beckoning them to cut the cake.

'Nearly time to go, Bea,' he whispered as they went to the cake table. Weddings were simple affairs then - the bride and groom were expected to leave soon after the reception so that their guests could get away.

It was finally time for the couple to get changed into their "going away" outfits, and Bea had bought a Laura Ashley two-piece sailor suit in white - reminiscent of the 1920s. Martin always told Bea that white was her best colour.

At around teatime, the newly married couple went onto the terrace to say goodbye to guests and family, accompanied by some emotion and tears. Bea had one final job as a bride - she threw her white orchid bouquet into the grey, damp cold air above a group of women - some but not all wanting to catch it.

When they got to their little cream Peugeot 104, it was covered in shaving foam, loo paper, and trailing tin cans. They didn't care - they were just happy to be off on their honeymoon - it had been a long engagement - too long, they thought.

At the lodge, Bea was shattered - and much to Martin's dismay, she cried.

'Sorry, so sorry - it's been a long day, and I'm so glad we got through it - the lead-up and all the organising was stressful - then the flowers not arriving on time, you know - then your best man's awful speech - you know,' as tears ran down and her mascara ran down with them.

'Anyone would think you regretted marrying me.'

'Oh, don't be silly - I'm quite an emotional person, and it's a release, I guess - I find crying helps.'

'I hope you don't cry when we get to Spain tomorrow.'

'I won't - and it won't be so cold there - gosh, it was cold today. The poor bridesmaids were cold in those cotton dresses, especially the little ones.'

Bea's parents had a studio in the new golf resort in Spain called "La Manga," and it was their honeymoon destination - as neither had much money saved up. Bea soon discovered that Martin was not very good at managing his money, and he had used his credit card to the maximum limit.

'Someone has to sort the bills out when we go to our bedsit next week - so do you want me to take charge of bills and the accounts?'

'Yes, do it - I hate doing all that.'

After their honeymoon, they found out that the real excitement of the wedding was after they left.

'We missed the best bit - apparently, some wedding guests went to their hotel, and there were a few dramas there - one of my contemporaries was showing off a hand gun - and then your farmer friend held him against the wall thinking it was real. It wasn't, of course - it was a fake pistol, but a very good fake, and they all thought he'd gone mad and might shoot them. And they were all discussing that infamous speech - oh dear.'

Martin had started his new job with a merchant bank and had secured them a bedsit in a tall, elegant old terraced house in Cranley Place - South Kensington - which Bea was astounded to find out was next to her grandmother, who was in a ground floor bedsit which opened into a wild overgrown back garden.

'Gosh, that's such a coincidence - I mean, how on earth did that happen, Martin? - look, we'll be able to wave at granny from the balcony?'

'I had no idea - I hope she isn't going to try and convert me.'

'Well, she'll always try, and she'll have masses said for you, I'm sure.' 'Well, hopefully, we will have found somewhere to buy very soon – I certainly don't want to share a bathroom longer than necessary,' he said firmly as they were unpacking wedding presents and making the large bedsit homely.

'Yes, it's not great for your commute, but it's fine for me as I can pick and choose where to cook with the agency - and it's so nice I only cook during the daytime now. Oh, and I was just thinking - it's only 2 months to Isabelle and Étienne's wedding - what am I going to wear?'

'Well, I don't have to worry as I can keep the morning coat indefinitely - so that's me sorted - why not your sailor suit? Oh yes, I had a letter - we can stay with Isabelle's family in the countryside, as the wedding is at the castle of one of her aunts.'

'Undoubtedly only people in "High Life de Belgique" will be there - we don't count as we're foreigners, aren't we? OO…How nice is this brand new duvet Martin, and bedlinen' as they opened more wedding presents.

The day for the Belgian wedding arrived just two months after the Charmers' wedding - and it was a full Catholic wedding with nuptial mass - the groom was in a traditional morning coat, and Isabelle was modestly dressed in a high-necked dress with long sleeves and a floral crown of white flowers. It made her look even taller and ballerina-like than usual. Isabelle was one month away from her 22nd birthday, and her youthfulness meant she didn't need makeup. She still possessed a natural sense of demureness that had captivated Martin on the day they met five summers ago.

The reception took place at a disused old castle - which was run down but still had an old charm and faded grandeur. The food and drink were served from stalls in the garden with canopies over them. Bea didn't leave Martin's side as she didn't know anyone apart from the bride and groom and the bride's family, who she had met the summer before when Martin took her to Belgium.

'She's radiantly happy, isn't she?' 'Yes - I can see that.'

'Her parents must be pleased with Isabelle's catch - he's quite reserved though, isn't he? I don't think he enjoyed the lineup small talk - but she definitely loved all the attention.'

'I'm sure they're delighted with Étienne - he's got her father's hard work ethic - we'd better go and mingle with the guests.'

Chapter 11 - Young Marrieds

Martin was anxious to leave the bedsit as soon as possible, and in the autumn of 1985, the Charmers bought a 1 bedroom garden flat on Wandsworth Bridge Road near Clapham Common tube, which was part of a tall Edwardian house. It was newly converted and had new carpets, a new bathroom, and a kitchen complete with the original tiled floor. The sitting room and bedroom had original panelled shutters and the original open fireplace. The walls were painted in "Magnolia" - seen as *the* safe off-white. It cost £35,000, which was based on three times Martin's salary of £9500 plus once times Bea's salary of £5500 - now that she had a permanent job cooking lunches for the directors of a large catalogue in Stockwell. Martin was able to get to his City job on the Northern line. It was regarded as an up-and-coming part of London, but they soon discovered it had an unpleasant side, as they were burgled of all their silver wedding presents, and Martin was mugged on an evening walk from the tube.

There were no wardrobes in the bedroom alcoves, so one Saturday, Bea went to MFI and bought two cupboards that had to be assembled.

'These cupboards should fit exactly the alcoves - and they look easy to assemble - can you do it?' She smiled sweetly at a disconcerted Martin.

'I'll try' in a resigned tone.

Bea soon discovered that assembling things was not her husband's strength - unlike her practical father-in-law - so they decided to ask a practical friend to help.

'Don't worry. I won't ever buy anything that needs assembling.'

Married life agreed with them both, and they loved having their own flat - with a long garden. They could afford to take themselves out to dinner sometimes - Martin loved good food and good restaurants - he was quickly climbing the corporate career ladder and was ambitious.

On their first year anniversary, they went out to celebrate - and Bea broached the subject of children.

'Well, it's a year now, and didn't we agree we could try for a child?' 'Oh really?' He had a pained expression.

'It takes on average six months, apparently.'

'Does it - well, if you're sure?' He said nervously, looking at the other tables while he was secretly appalled by the idea - I'm only just 24, far too young. Why's she so keen we're having fun together? Did I really agree with this? Yes, I did in a moment of madness - madness because I wanted more than anything to marry Bea, but this is the last thing I wanted; maybe it won't happen. It might take months and months. He took a large sip of red wine.

'Of course, I'm sure,' she said, beaming at him as he poured another glass. 'Happy Paper Anniversary, Beatrice - I do love you, you know.' Bea picked up her glass and held it up while Martin clinked it.

'Happy Anniversary, darling Mab.' Bea started calling Martin by this pet name shortly after the wedding.

Bea elatedly came off the "pill," and it would be many years later that she realised it was only then that their marriage was properly consummated, one year after the wedding. For Catholics, consummation means that the marital act must be open to new life.[9] All birth control devices frustrate the act, rendering it sterile.

---

[9] See Appendix on Catholic teaching on regulation of births.

Chapter 12 - Young Parents

Six weeks later, Bea felt queasy, and her monthly event didn't happen. She thought it couldn't be possible, surely - it was far too soon. On her way to work, she bought a pregnancy kit and would do the test after work. She had a spring in her step and felt her heart racing while she was hoping it was going to be good news. It was.

As Martin came through the front door, Bea was waiting in the sitting room - the table was laid for supper, and the room was tidy as always - Bea liked order. He could see she had a wide grin, and her eyes were gleaming.

'Good day, Mab?'

'Yes - and you - why have you got that funny expression on?' 'Well, you'll never guess what…'

'What?'

'I felt queasy this morning… and so I bought a… well, you know, a test kit and - well… it's positive - I'm pregnant' she could hardly contain her excitement as she searched in vain for some reaction from Martin's steely eyes. He stood like a statue - motionless - and voiceless. Then he went to change into casual clothes and poured himself a gin and tonic, and sat heavily down on the very uncomfortable MFI foam sofa bed.

'How do you know it's accurate - did you follow the instructions?'

'Of course, I blooming did - it's totally accurate - and anyway, I have some of the signs.'

'I don't want to know,' he said quickly - his voice was elevated and tense. 'You told me it takes six months - I believed you - you've tricked me.'

‘I said the average was six months - so some couples can take 12 months and some immediately, which makes the average 6 - I had no idea it would be this soon either.’

Bea looked aghast at her husband’s unwelcome reaction, and anger was soon welling up inside her, which Martin sensed, and never liking any sort of confrontation, he smiled and held out his hand.

‘Look, it’s just a shock, that’s all - I need time to process it - look, I can’t pretend to be elated like you - I don’t get worked up about children - unlike you. Look, I’m sorry - of course, I’m happy if you’re happy.’ He was deeply unhappy, and it showed. Bea was horrified at his attitude.

‘I haven’t told anyone yet - but I may tell our parents in confidence. It’s safer to wait 12 weeks, as miscarriages are quite common before that.’

‘Yes, don’t tell anyone else - so when’s it going to be born?’

‘It, Martin, is a baby - *not* an alien - and I worked out that he or she will arrive around the 19th of February. This means I can work until Christmas as I’ll be too large to cook and serve lunches.’

‘We’ll have to move - we can’t stay here - and it’s too expensive in London now - we’ll have to move out into commuter land.’

‘Can’t say I’m too sad about that - we *were* burgled, and you were mugged. I’ll need to learn to drive - I can’t have a baby and not drive, can I? - I’ll look into getting lessons ASAP - before I get too big’ as she noticed Martin cringing at the thought of her getting big, and springing up she said in a flat voice ‘I’ll get supper.’

As she got the food out of the oven, she thought - well, he did agree he should’ve thought about it. What’s his game? He’s behaving like a spoilt child, well, too blooming bad!

Martin begrudgingly came round to the idea, but he had another surprise in store for Bea. Once the bump started to show, he stated, ‘I can't come near you - I have a phobia of pregnant women - sorry, but I can't help it.'

'Funny, you never told me that when you asked me to marry you and to agree to many children - how on earth did you think you would cope if you have a phobia of pregnant women - I mean, when did you know you had this phobia? - or is it because you're furious with me for getting pregnant? It takes 2 you know!'

'I'm phobic of all pregnant women.'

'Do you think there's an alien about to break out and get you?' 'Stop it - that's awful.'

Bea felt abandoned by her husband, but she grew close to her older sister Lucy - who volunteered to be her birthing partner. Her happiness was too much to be a dampener on their situation, and she accepted his phobic behaviour and kept at arm's length from him. She also deliberately disguised the neat bump with baggy jumpers. She was just thankful she felt very well - she was fit and healthy, and things were progressing as they should when she attended antenatal appointments. The grandparents were all happy for them, and the senior Charmers started looking around for a house for them on the commuter line.

Bea started saving all her maternity pay to buy baby stuff - and she passed her driving test - much to her relief, and the biggest treat was driving to the big Sainsbury's at Nine Elms.

1986 was a time of growing house prices, especially in Clapham, and the little garden flat was a good investment - Martin's parents found a modern little terraced house in the commuter village "St One Gate," which they snapped up and planned to move into after the birth.

Five days after Bea's due date, her waters broke in the bathroom - and it was the start of a fast and furious labour lasting just over 6 hours. Martin made sure he shaved and drove them to University College Hospital and parked illegally.

'You don't have to come in the room, Martin - honestly, I wouldn't expect it - my father never attended our births. You'll only get put off seeing me in that awful state - I'm sure I'll manage with the midwife.'

'No, I must come - I don't have to watch, though.'

As the 6th hour of labour progressed, Bea was furious at herself for not learning the breathing techniques - and as a result, she got into distress, hugging the gas and air tube for dear life. She saw the midwives muttering about a man in white, and the next thing she knew, a pair of forceps appeared.

'Mrs. Charmer - you're very tired and distressed. The baby's head is too large, so we need to use forceps. Can we ask you if you mind having some students watch the procedure, Mrs. Charmer? as she saw a queue of white-clad eager fresh faces hovering at the door.

'I'm past caring who watches,' cried Bea in desperation, who then started praying Hail Marys out loud - much to Martin's horror.

As they heard the scream of the infant cry out - the emotion was all too much - Bea was shattered but alert - Martin felt brutally traumatised.

'You have a healthy boy - just below 8 pounds' as Bea's weary eyes enlarged - wanting to hold the boy immediately - impatient that they were doing tests on him.

Bea forgot the pain quickly - a phenomenon that happens to most women as though by design - in order not to put them off having more children. She was hardly aware of the after birth coming out and being stitched up with her legs in stirrups in such an ungainly fashion.

Baby Frederick was a lusty boy and very alert - he had bright brown eyes and much dark hair. He was also very hungry, and Bea couldn't feed him - her sensitive skin meant she had shooting pins every time the baby sucked – and nothing came out - or so she thought. Luckily there was a nursery attached to the ward, and some babies were bottle-fed. Freddie took to the bottle and fed often, not sleeping much.

They stayed in the hospital for 5 days, which was normal in 1987. Martin visited every day after work and was kinder to Bea than he had been for months - he actually looked lovingly into her eyes. He nervously picked up his son for brief moments.

When they returned to the flat, Freddie slept in the sitting room in a big new pram with large wheels, which the Charmer grandparents bought. Bea often slept with him as he wasn't a good sleeper, and Martin couldn't have a disturbed night.

'Why are you sleeping in here?" A disgruntled Martin said one early morning. Bea had Freddie sleeping in her arms on the sofa bed.

'He wasn't settling down, so it was easier if I slept with him,' said an exhausted mother - now wide-eyed at her husband's annoyance.

'He'll expect that all the time now.'

In desperation, Bea gave into the dummy - it helped. Bea's rose-tinted glasses fell off once she was in the flat alone with a demanding baby - it shattered her sense of order - she was tired from disturbed nights and the business of sterilising bottles, changing bedding, and all that goes into looking after a small baby. In those early days of trying to get into some sort of routine - making sure supper was on the table - looking presentable for her husband - keeping the flat tidy - keeping nappy paraphernalia out of sight - it was like a never- ending treadmill of physical labour. Even trying to have a bath was difficult - she snatched moments when Freddie was asleep.

The young family moved out of the flat when Freddie was seven weeks old, and friends and family helped them move to Sussex - they didn't have much furniture to move as the flat was hardly big enough to house many large items. Bea had regained her figure very quickly and bought some new clothes.

Bea had made the decision that once she had a baby, she would resume the practice of her faith - it was now her responsibility to bring the child up as a Catholic - so she was anxious to book his baptism in[10]. She hadn't been to the Catholic Church in Clapham but knew that moving to East Sussex would mean going to the local parish - which was in Hurstwad.

On the first Sunday after the move, she took Freddie to Mass - armed with a bottle. They saw many friendly faces, and she introduced herself to the elderly priest - who had an air of severity about him - and asked about baptism.

'Yes, of course, I can baptise him, but you first need to do a course - see that tall lady over there - that's Miss Gracie - she's in charge of baptisms, and she will go through it all with you.'

Bea spoke to the very efficient Miss Gracie, who offered to come and visit them and conduct the lessons there. She also asked Bea if she had Catholic godparents for Freddie?'

'Oh dear, the godparents aren't Catholic,' said Bea. 'As my husband is Church of England, and I don't know of any practising Catholics amongst my friends.'

'Ok, that's fine - they're really just witnesses - as long as you have at least one practicing Catholic godparent - that's fine. The non-Catholic witnesses can't be expected to help with the child's Catholic faith, and that's why you need a practising Catholic, ideally two, for that.'

---

[10] Before the disastrous Second Vatican Council, it was a serious obligation for babies to be baptised within 2 weeks of their birth. Baptism is necessary for salvation.

Bea approached the subject of the Catholic godparent to Martin.

'I don't want to ask family to be godparents as they're already involved in Fred's life - so we need a non-family practising Catholic to be a godparent - and you know - I don't know any.'

'Ok, I'll ask Isabelle - she's practising, and I'm sure she'll agree.'

'Great plan - yes, she takes her faith very seriously, doesn't she - I mean, she wasn't allowed to date a non-Catholic, was she?' Bea shot Martin an amusing look.

'I'll write to her.'

Bea's mother, Therese, had another idea for a Catholic godparent - one of her friends would be happy to be one.

The Charmers liked their new home - it had views across the fields, and they discovered how friendly the village was - some Bea had met at the church, local toddler groups, and some were introduced to them by Martin's parents. They soon had a busy social life with other young parents with small babies. Martin, however, didn't like having neighbours all around the house, and this irritated him.

'Why does Mrs. H keep coming into our garden to see us?'

'Oh, she's very kindly offered to look after Freddie when I do the weekly food shop - it's very hard carrying him in the sling as he's heavy now and restless in it, and he's too small to put in the trolley seat.' (Online food shopping was another ten years away).

'I'm sure my parents would be happy to do that, Bea.'

'Yes - they are - but good to have a backup, don't you think?' 'Not if she's going to keep coming over the fence to gossip.'

Bea was due to have her postnatal checkup in their new doctor's surgery in Herstwad shortly after the house move. Martin didn't want any more children yet, and Bea agreed to take the "pill" again. Since returning to the practice of her faith - Bea went to confession in her new parish, and when she mentioned the issue of the "pill," - the priest didn't give any opinion or advice. He gave her absolution with no conditions attached. Bea wondered why this was - the only thing she could think of was that the old priest was sympathetic to Catholics in mixed marriages and therefore felt more 'lenient' towards them, especially if they were being coerced into using artificial birth control, and therefore they were not fully consenting to this particular mortal sin[11]. In that case - she thought - why isn't the priest asking me questions about it, or does he not want to confront a new parishioner? She thought it a mystery all the same. She wondered if all priests were like Fr Laugter.

Bea was bathing Freddie one evening - as was his usual routine - and Martin appeared at the bathroom door waving a letter from Isabelle.

'She isn't going to be a godmother sadly, as she says she won't be any good living in another country, and how can she participate properly in Fred's life if she only sees him occasionally - I suppose we can't blame her, can we?'

'It's fine - my mother's friend is going to be godmother, and she's very keen - we have the minimum requirement now, no problems. We haven't got a date from Miss Gracie yet - I think she has to report back to Father Laugter to tell him how we're getting on with the lessons - to see if we understand the obligations attached to having Fred baptised - weekly mass as a minimum, that sort of thing - it is rather amazing though - that at one time you were made to have babies baptised as soon as possible after birth, and now the Catholic Church is more relaxed.' Freddie was kicking in the water - his eyes always alert for any happenings.

---

[11]Mortal sin so called as it kills the soul.

'I doubt he'll fit in the family Christening gown now as he's big for his age.' Martin was pulling faces at Freddie and waving his hands to get a reaction. Freddie smiled while moving all his limbs.

Freddie was baptised at eight months of age in the altar area during Sunday mass - which was the priest's preferred time - a departure from private family-only occasions. There was an old baptismal font at the entrance of the church - which wasn't used, so a portable stainless steel bowl was used instead, with holy water in, which Freddie's chubby hands grabbed as he tried to tip the water out. A celebration took place at Martin's parents' home.

Martin was headhunted to an American bank, and soon after Freddie's first birthday, the family spent some months living in Boston, America - before returning back home shortly before Freddie's second birthday. Bea was anxious for a brother or sister for him, and both agreed this would be a good idea.

'In that case, we'll have to start looking to move as the house will be too small for four of us - and the garden definitely too small,' said Martin - 'and not sure I can put up with the neighbours popping their heads over the fence - plus Freddie's now throwing balls over the fence and annoying the pensioners.'

'The housing market isn't great though - things haven't recovered since "Black Monday"[12] and anyway, it might take a while to get another child - so there's no panic to move yet,' Bea said as they were eating beef casserole while it was a dark January evening, and Freddie was in bed.

'What's Freddie done today?'

'He went for tea at Peter's, and they wore each other out, and tomorrow we go to toddler group in the village hall - there's a toddler

---

[12] 19 October 1987 - the worldwide stock market crashed.

group somewhere every day of the week - he seems to enjoy socialising.'

'You're looking particularly attractive, Bea - have you done something to your hair? - as Martin held her hand across the kitchen table - a habit he adopted regularly throughout their marriage.

'I use a hairdryer nowadays - it helps calm it down.' 'I miss the large flat in Boston - so much space.'

'It wasn't great for Freddie - no other children in the Navy Yard complex - but I will miss Filene's Basement.'

'Oh, I've had news from Isabelle - she's about to have a baby. They would like to come and stay at some point this year - and bring the new baby.'

'Ok - when did we last see them - was it their wedding? I think it was.'

It wasn't long before Bea announced that she was pregnant - and this time Martin was prepared for the news and was very happy. He still had his phobia of pregnant women and kept Bea at arm's length once the bump was showing -and it showed early now that the abdominal muscles were relaxed from the first birth.

'This time, I'll learn how to breathe properly and attend antenatal lessons,' said Bea.

Shortly before Cecily Charmer was born, there was a mini stock market crash on Friday, 13th October 1989, referred to as "Black Friday." It caused further turmoil in the UK housing market as the Charmers would soon find out - Martin being a natural risk taker, wasn't put off and was very impatient to move house.

Little Cecily was born like her brother 5 days late, and she was an easy birth - being under 7 pounds and a dream baby who slept most of the time.

‘She sleeps more the Freddie - she’s a gentle breeze! And we now have Catholic friends who might agree to be godparents,’ said Bea studying Martin’s handsome face - which got more handsome with age. This time Bea was anxious to get home after the birth and only stayed three days in the hospital.

Freddie was unsettled and slept badly once his sister was at home - and still needed a bottle at night.

One day Martin was anxiously waiting to show Bea something -

‘Bea… I think we should look at this house for sale - it’s not too far away - only the next village, Washber Wood’, as he showed her the details from that morning’s post. Bea was putting bottles in the steriliser.

‘Isn’t it a bad time to sell, though - don’t you think we should wait until things are more settled, Mab?’

‘I don’t think it’s going to get worse - I’m an optimist Bea - I hate living here with all these retired neighbours - knowing everything about everyone.’

‘Let’s go when Freddie’s at play-school - and I’ll take the morning off - Oh… and when do you think the Tra-Vail-Durs can come and stay - I said I’d let them know once you’d had the baby?’

‘Crikey Martin - do you think you can wait until I’ve had my postnatal check cup - I’m meant to be taking things easy, plus I do have two small children to look after - where are we all going to sleep? They’ll have to have Cecily’s room, and Cecily will have to sleep with us as Freddie’s not a great sleeper.

‘Ok, I’ll invite them to come in around two months' time - around New Year's time - we can have a New Year’s Eve party and introduce them to our new friends.’

‘Yes, Ok - as long as they don’t mind staying in a small house.’

'That won't be for long - I'm sure we won't be here in a year's time,' said a determined Martin, who had a spring in his step about moving.

The Charmers went to look at the house for sale in a neighbouring village and decided it might be worth buying, although it had everything wrong which could possibly be wrong, but their naive youthfulness couldn't see the negative aspects; it was on the busy main road, and the house was very old in parts, and in need of complete renovation. Martin was keener on it, as it was within their budget and it was detached - no neighbours would be able to pop into the back garden unannounced.

'I don't like the main road - it's noisy,' said Bea as they were driving home.

'But a nice project for us - and you're very creative, Bea - I'm sure you can do it up in good taste.'

'I'm really uneasy about it, Martin - and we need to go on the market ourselves.'

'I'll make a low offer as it needs a bit of work,' said Martin as he drove fast - they were in a new sporty Alfa Romeo Sportwagon - a company car.

The offer on the house was accepted, and their house went on the market - but it was a difficult time to sell, and prices were tumbling. There was no interest in their little house in the commuter village with one of the best primary schools in the area. It was also a bad time of year to sell, with the nights getting shorter and people not wanting to move over the Christmas period.

'Let's not be in a rush,' said Bea holding a very contented Cecily, 'We can look forward to New Year with our Belgian friends and our new village friends.'

When Isabelle and Étienne finally arrived with their baby daughter - it felt as though the gap of 4 years wasn't there at all as they greeted each other as though it was yesterday. Isabelle was still tall and slender, and her long wavy hair was now tied back. She was modestly dressed and had a quiet elegance, while her husband had filled out a bit and was still very quietly spoken. Isabelle and Bea got on extremely well as they were both young mothers and had much in common, mostly their exhaustion from looking after small children and everything that went with running a house with no outside help.

When New Year's Eve came - the Charmer's friends from the village came and met the Tra-Vail-Durs.

'Marion and Philip, let me introduce you to Étienne and Isabelle.'

'And who's that over there?' Marion said, walking over to the placid baby in her chair.

'Hélène - she's nearly 1 year old,' said Isabelle stooping down to undo the chair strap.

'Ah, that's the same age as our second.'

As Isabelle took her daughter out of the chair and up to her travel cot, the men were having drinks in the sitting room, and Bea was getting things ready in the kitchen. Freddie was in an all-in-one fleecy dressing gown running from room to room, not wanting to go to bed, unlike Cecily, who adored going to bed for the night. Marion offered to help Bea.

Bea quickly said in a low voice, 'Oh, by the way - that's Martin's first love…well, he got over her eventually, and they've stayed very good friends ever since,' laughing at Marion raising her eyebrows.

'Gosh, I'm not sure I'd want to be friends with Philip's past loves,' she said, frowning.

'Oh, he's definitely over her - and she loves Étienne - she does everything he says.'

'Well, you're very relaxed about it all - and Martin's lucky you don't mind being so friendly with them.'

As the couples sat down for the celebration meal of Beef Wellington - and Martin's carefully chosen wine selection - the Tra-Vail-Durs spoke about their life in Brussels and how they were renovating their house. Isabelle gave the news of all her family and close friends, as Martin knew them all.

'We're hoping to move once we sell this,' said Martin.

'If we sell,' said Bea, 'It's a very bad market at the moment.'

The evening was very enjoyable, and Bea observed happily that Martin didn't pay too much attention to Isabelle - the men spoke amongst themselves, and the women did the same. The countdown to midnight had started, and the new year was about to begin - 1990. The three young couples would all be celebrating five years of marriage.

When it was time to go, the Tra-Vail-Durs insisted that the gap mustn't be four years and that the Charmers must come to Brussels next time - when they would hopefully have their second child by then.

'Yes, of course, we'll come,' said Martin kissing Isabelle goodbye and shaking Étienne's hand - as they walked to the estate car.

'Yes, I'd love to go to the TinTin shop when we next come,' said Bea.

The two families kept in touch and saw each other regularly over the next few years.

Chapter 13 - Busy Parents

Unable to sell their house in 1990, Martin, the optimist, arranged a bridging loan to purchase the house that needed everything done to it - and they lived in the little house while Bea took charge of renovating it. Eventually, the house in St. One Gate sold for a loss, and they moved into the bigger house with a back garden on a slope and on a busy main road - the road that killed their first cat.

Freddie was accepted at St. One Gate primary school - which wasn't Catholic, so he attended catechism lessons arranged through the parish. Bea took them to mass every Sunday and Holy Days of Obligation - and they made their first confessions and First Holy Communions. It was a time when Bea felt alone at church trying to keep her children in order, and she often envied the Catholic couples, who had each other to help with misbehaving children. On such occasions, she thought to herself - you made the choice to marry a non- Catholic - you take full responsibility, so don't complain - why didn't you think of the difficulties which might arise…but no-one warned me, not even the priest.

Her children noticed that their father had no religion, and they often resented being taken to mass while he stayed at home. Bea wasn't a particularly devout Catholic - she did the bare minimum. Martin was happy with her lukewarmness towards her religion. He also liked the peace on Sundays when they were at mass - he liked listening to The Archers while cooking lunch.

When Cecily started school, Bea was restless and wanted something to do, so she contacted a catering agency to get part-time work as a cook. When Martin came home that evening, she said, 'I'm going to do some part-time jobs with a catering agency.' Martin wasn't amused.

'What?! No, please don't, Bea - I don't want my wife to be a skivvy.'

'OK - but I need to do something - I'll see if they need Spanish tutors at the Adult Education.'

'Yes that's better.'

After 8 years, they decided to get off the main road - and the house was difficult to sell as a result. They found a big project nearby in Washber Green - a listed 16th Century farmhouse, which needed totally gutting. But it was in a quiet location and had land. It was safe for dogs and cats. They bought it, gutted it, and over the following years, extended it and converted the stable block into a self-contained annexe.

At the age of 10, Freddie went to an all-boys Catholic boarding school, and Cecily would go to a Catholic school in due course. Martin worked long hours in the City, did a lot of business travelling, and was extremely successful. Bea had some time on her hands during the school day, so she got a part-time job at an auction house. The social history behind antiques fascinated her so much that she decided to study for a degree in antiques. In 2000 she started a distance learning degree through Southampton Institute.

Bea found it tiring looking after the children and running a big house - and she and Martin decided that they didn't want any more children. Bea was on the "pill," and one of the side effects was the loss of libido - so she discussed the idea with Martin of him having "the snip."[13] He was squeamish about it but was happy to consider this permanent solution to not having any more children.

When they went for the appointment to discuss the procedure, Bea was told she had to sign her consent to it, which she found troubling - and decided to do some more research. It also troubled her conscience as this was totally against the Catholic Church's teachings. It was a mortal sin.

---

[13] Slang term for vasectomy.

‘Look, I’m not that happy with signing this form for you to have the snip - and I know you’re squeamish anyway.’ They were seated in the winter sitting room in the oldest part of the farmhouse - with the fire going in the inglenook. One of the cats was sitting on Martin’s knees and was being stroked as though it were a princess. This cat was his favourite - it was a Korat, and the breed is known for its close interactions with people.

‘I’m prepared to go through with it,’ he said resignedly, gazing at the grey furry princess on his lap.

‘Well, I’ve decided not to sign the consent form. I can’t in conscience sign it as a Catholic. So - you don’t have to go through with it’ as she sipped some more white wine.

‘OK.’

The next time Bea went to confession and mentioned the “pill,” - the locum priest said,

‘You can’t permanently close yourself off to new life.’

This really troubled Bea - this was the first priest to say something negative about birth control. It was the first priest to actually “call her out” on this issue, and it made her stop and think. She had justified the use of birth control by telling herself she was in a mixed marriage and, therefore, it was OK. What she hadn’t realised was that she was possibly being selfish by not obeying the clear Catholic teaching, and just because “everybody’s doing it” didn’t necessarily mean it was OK. The priest had made her feel very uncomfortable and spurred her to do some research on the topic.

During this period, the Charmers continued to see their Belgian friends and watched their children grow up. Bea got on very well with Isabelle, and they both had solid marriages. The opening of the Channel Tunnel in 1994 gave them more options for travelling to one another’s homes. The mid-1990s saw electronic mail - aka email becoming widely used. Mobile phones were now commonplace - and they were capable of sending text messages, and by the year 2002, Europe's first camera phone was launched. The TomTom car navigation system started in 1991. The digital revolution showed no signs of slowing down.

Part 3. Beatrice's Religious Experience

Chapter 14 - The Ritalin Episode - May 2001 Onwards

Bea was busy revising for her law exam, which was part of the antiques degree, and she was finding it difficult to concentrate. She thought she might have the same problem that her son suffered from - ADHD. She was also praying a lot and asking God if it really was His will for her to be studying for an antiques degree. The priest calling her out in the confessional had made her start praying a lot. He had made her feel bad about the "pill," and she was praying about that too. She also started praying for the conversion of England to the Catholic Faith. It was something her grandmother always prayed for.

One Sunday in May, she thought it might help if she took some Ritalin pills - she had read that it focused the mind - and she needed that right now if she was to pass the exams that summer. She found her son's supply and took two pills in the morning before going to Mass.

Bea was fairly involved in her local parish and had a number of voluntary roles - she was a catechist (one who instructs others in the Catholic faith) and a sacristan (one who looks after church linen). On the morning of taking the Ritalin, she went to Mass with Cecily as usual, but she felt slightly odd. She felt a strong sense of alertness and energy, and she was rather more gregarious than usual.

When she got home, she was still feeling full of energy. Martin had cooked the Sunday lunch as he always did, and Cecily was playing with her beloved cat.

'You're very wide-eyed and lively, Bea,' commented Martin while he was carving the joint.

'Am I? - I do feel full of energy, I must say.'

After lunch, Bea went off to pray in the garden, and while she was asking God if she was doing His will and for the conversion of England, she started hearing interior locutions as though a supernatural force had come over her. A voice inside her said, 'Will you do anything for the conversion of England?' 'Yes, of course, I will, Lord - what do you want me to do?' 'Will you offer up your life for your country?'

Bea's heart was racing, and a sense of terror gripped her as she answered with some trepidation,

"Er… yes - if that's what you really want, Lord… is that what you want me to do?'

'Yes - it is.'

'Ok, Lord - you want me to die for the conversion of my country, so you're going to take my life…can I at least say goodbye to my family?'

In a blind panic, she went quickly to the house to find Martin and Cecily. As though gasping for breath, she said, 'Martin, Martin - my love - I need to say goodbye to you - as God is taking my life - where's Cecily, and I need to ring Freddie.'

'What the hell's going on, Bea - are you completely out of your mind?' As he made her sit down on a sofa. She was breathing deeply and seemed suddenly exhausted.

'No… no… I'm not mad - God spoke to me in the garden…well, I mean interiorly,' she said slowly and quietly as she felt all her energy draining away.

'Don't be absurd, Bea' Cecily ran into the sitting room and sensed something was terribly wrong.

'Darling Cecily, I need to say goodbye,' Cecily started having hysterics and hugging Bea frantically as she lay on the sofa.

'I need to ring Freddie to say goodbye.'

'No, you won't - I'm ringing the doctor,' said Martin firmly while he promptly rang an out-of-hours number which the local surgery had on the answerphone. Bea lay on the sofa calmly and felt her life was ebbing away - she spoke in whispers. She was holding her crying daughter closely. Martin was nervously pacing around the sitting room, waiting for the doctor.

The doctor came to the house and sat opposite Bea, who was still lying on the sofa with her navy velour dressing gown on and wearing the hood. Bea told her what had happened. The doctor told Martin privately that she thought Bea may have had a manic episode and she would refer her to a specialist immediately.

That day Bea was taken to a mental health doctor at the hospital, and she strongly advised Bea to spend some time at The Priory voluntarily to be observed. Bea agreed. In the car on the way home, Bea was quiet and subdued.

'I didn't die.'

'No - they think you've had a manic episode - and you've agreed to spend some time at The Priory.'

'You mean the "nut house" - well, I won't have to cook and do chores, but who's going to take Cecily to school?'

'I've asked your mother to come and stay.'

Bea spent ten nights at The Priory, and all sorts of tests were done. The diagnosis was that she was possibly a manic depressive and needed to take Lithium, even though she told the men in white coats that she had taken Ritalin just prior to her 'turn.' Whilst they thought it likely that the Ritalin could have caused the episode, they still wanted to prescribe drugs for manic depressives.

While Bea was in The Priory, she had a few visitors, including her parish priest, who wanted to know why she was there. She told him about the interior voices, and he was very concerned. She asked him to hear her confession.

'Father, I have thrown the "pill" away.'

He made no comment but gave her absolution and then left.

Bea stopped taking the Lithium after a few months, but Martin was more worried about her throwing the "pill" away.

'They aren't good for my health, but more worryingly, I don't like how they work, Martin. They make the womb hostile to the embryo, so they're actually abortifacient - they *don't* halt conception. Women are sold this lie that they are contraceptives, but they don't stop conception, so this is a misnomer, which is disingenuous of the health authorities. I'm 38 now and don't want to take hormones indefinitely, so I'd like to learn the natural methods - I need your cooperation too', as she prayed that he would agree. He saw her pleading look and relented.

Martin noticed a sea change in his wife of 16 years - she was more religious than at any time he had known her - he saw her taking a rosary when walking their dogs - she was going to church more often, even on weekdays - whatever happened on that day in May changed her. 'She's done a Brideshead on me,' he thought. Just like Julia Flyte in Brideshead Revisited, who emerges out of her lapsed state and decides she can't marry the divorced Charles Ryder as it would put her outside of the Catholic Church. Martin felt crushed by his wife's newly found Catholicism.

One day he asked her something he wanted to ask for months. They were sitting outside on a sunny warm early autumn day.

'So tell me, Bea - who's more important to you these days?'

'What a strange thing to ask Martin…', as she looked intently at him through her sunglasses while the sun was disappearing at sundown.

'Well, obviously, God is first - and that's how it should be - He made us! Then you, of course - after all - God gave me the vocation to marry YOU and no one else!'

‘I see…but you used to put me first…you’ve changed…I can’t quite understand.’

‘People can and do change as the years go by. But we’re closer than we were, aren’t we? I mean, now that I no longer have those horrible hormones in me, you now respect my natural cycles - I’m no longer ‘available’ all the time, and we both have to work with nature - I feel it’s a vast improvement. Remember how I told you that the “pill” suppresses desire?’

‘Ok, yes, yes, that is a positive thing to come out of your funny turn,’ as he removed his sunglasses.

‘And what’s happened to the antiques course?’

‘I’ve had to stop - I was in no fit state to do the exams, so I’ve missed the boat this year. I’m still working at the auction houses, though - and I learn a lot there - and I enjoy it immensely.’

Bea had become more religious, and she discovered that the day she had her religious experience was the Feast Day of Our Lady of Fatima. Her late grandmother was devoted to this and had a statue in a wooden box that had the Fatima prophecies on it. Bea started devouring Catholic books and began to study the controversies which started with the Second Vatican Council - why was the Latin mass banned - who was this French Archbishop Lefebvre who was excommunicated by a pope - why were Catholics so divided? Scandals were emerging about priestly abuse, and the Vatican started an investigation from 2001 onwards. She was shocked at the can of worms coming out of the Vatican.

Bea’s reconversion to the Catholic faith also brought home to her all the difficulties of being in a mixed marriage. Her decisions, even about little things such as what TV programmes to watch or books to read, were determined by her faith. Was this a suitable film to watch or a book to read - was there pornography in it etc? If Martin wanted to see a particular film, Bea would research it first and then decide if it was Ok to see - it created tension at times. She understood why the church discouraged mixed marriages - there were so many areas of potential conflict. 'No one warned me about this,' she thought, 'I was so wrapped up in love that these things didn't occur to me.....I knew the children had to be brought up as Catholics, but I had no idea about all the other issues.....why didn't the priest who married us say anything?'

Bea also joined the pro-life movement with "Life Charity" and volunteered as a counsellor in her nearest centre. However, as with many centres, the number of women coming in for help diminished fairly rapidly once the "Morning After Pill" became readily available from pharmacies in 2001. This inevitably led to the closure of the centre.

One day while Bea was helping in the sacristy, a locum priest was going to say mass, and he was a well-known Jesuit priest. He had moved to the Benedictine community and was more than happy to say masses while priests were away. He was in his late 80s and needed help with the vestments. While Bea was helping him, he was very chatty, and he asked Bea,

'Do you go to the Old Rite Mass at all?'

'No, Father, I haven't been - do you mean the Latin Mass? I've read about it, and I would be interested in going - but I don't know where they're held.'

'I say it daily in the little care home chapel for the residents - you're more than welcome to come - 10 o'clock daily.' Bea noticed his sparkly blue eyes, and he exuded a holiness she hadn't come across before - he clearly loved the Faith.

'That would be great - I visit some of the residents twice a week so I could come to mass.'

'I'll introduce you to some of the people who come.'

Bea found out that the priest was a convert from Anglicanism and converted during the Second World War. Like many converts, he was more devout than cradle Catholics.

Bea went to her first Latin Mass and noticed the women wore head-coverings such as scarves and lace mantillas. Bea recalled that her late grandmother always had a headscarf for daily mass. The requirement for women to wear head coverings was in force until 1983, when the new Code of Canon Law had no mention of it. However, the requirement was still in force for the Latin Mass and is still the case today.

Bea gradually became attached to the Latin Mass and met new friends as a result - she would drive the Jesuit priest to other churches as he was in great demand for the Old Mass. Bea was curious about why the Latin Mass was suppressed by the modern popes, and she read the biography of the late Archbishop Marcel Lefebvre, which was an eye-opener. If it hadn't been for this holy French Archbishop and another bishop, the Latin Mass would have died a death. Bea was impressed by his courage and shocked at his treatment by post-Vatican 2 popes. This was the start of her many years of investigation into Catholic church history - leading up to the murky waters of the Second Vatican Council with its deliberately ambiguous documents.

Much to Martin's horror, he discovered that Bea was going to a strange Catholic cult-like organisation that one of his parents' acquaintances had introduced her to, called "Ocpus Dei." There was a centre near East Grinstead - an area known for its strange groups, including Scientology and the Rosicrucians. Bea went there for monthly confession and to meet other women to socialise with.

One evening after supper Martin broached the subject while they watched television.

'I don't like you going there, Bea - they're very odd - so I've heard.'

‘I like going as I’ve made some nice friends - I don’t think they’re odd - they seem very normal to me.’

‘You’ve changed so much since that strange episode of yours three years ago,’ he said briskly with an impatient sigh. Bea sat up, slightly agitated.

‘People can and do change after years - oh, and I’m not a manic-depressive - they’ve signed me off’ as she mentally decided to move her religious books to somewhere which wouldn’t annoy him. It was no point discussing religion with Martin - it was a taboo subject. She knew this issue was her cross and of her making. She had willingly married a non-Catholic and, therefore, must accept the difficulties that inevitably arose.

‘And now you prefer Latin Mass to your own Catholic parish.’

‘I go to both - I’m still instructing children and helping in the sacristy.’ ‘Isabelle and Étienne don’t go to Latin Mass or our other friends.’ ‘Many don’t, Martin - because they don’t know about it, and they like hearing the vernacular. I adore history, and I’ve been researching the Catholic controversies surrounding the 1960s when all the radical changes came in - it’s a bloodbath of horrors, and it’s compulsive reading’ as Martin’s expression glazed over while he changed the channel. She knew he didn’t want to know anymore - she knew that telltale expression of his. He promptly changed the subject to a lighter topic.

‘By the way, Isabelle wants her daughter to do an exchange with Cecily in July - and we can drop her off and stay for a night in their new house - and then they’ll drop both girls off here and stay a day or two.’

‘Good idea, let’s hope they get on - they’re quite different characters.’

The summer of 2004, when the girls did their exchange - was not particularly successful, and Cecily didn’t want to do another exchange. She was dropping French for Spanish anyway. It would be another nine years before the two families met up again - and apart from the annual Christmas cards, which Bea always sent, they completely lost touch with each other.

Chapter 15 - A Gift from God

It was early spring in 2006, and Bea and Martin had moved into a spare room as their bathroom was being redecorated in the beloved hotel style which Martin loved - with pale neutral colours. Martin was a restless man and always wanted to make improvements to the house.

Bea was now 43, and she left her fertility charts in their bedroom - she had become rather lazy about it for months now, as she felt that at her age, it wasn't going to happen - she found out that a woman's chance of getting pregnant at her age within one year dropped to 1.2%. Also - the church teachings were very clear about when natural methods could be used - and they had to be serious reasons. Pope Pius 12th cited four serious reasons; medical, eugenic, economic, and social.[14] Martin didn't notice that the charts weren't in the spare room. He hadn't been paying much attention to them of late and didn't ask questions. He hadn't seen Bea taking her temperature either recently - one of the indicators of the natural method.

Bea thought there were no serious reasons to avoid another child as Martin was by now quite wealthy, and they had three spare bedrooms and plenty of outside space. She was also fit and healthy with no known inherited medical conditions.

One day as she was doing her daily prayer - she said to God.

'Lord, if you were ever to send me another son, I would like him to be a priest.'

A few weeks later, Bea's monthly didn't happen - she thought it might be menopausal - as she was at an age when menopause symptoms could be present. However, she bought a pregnancy kit, and it was positive - she could not believe her eyes and thought it was a mistake - she felt her thudding heart, which had quickened. Sixteen-

---

[14] Allocution to midwives - by Pope Pius XII, in 1951.

year-old Cecily was nearby playing with the two cats in her bedroom, revising for her GCSEs, and it was Mother's Day. They were all due to take Martin's mother out for a curry lunch, still raw and shattered from her widowhood of seven years.

'Cecily, you won't believe this,' said a very breathless and shaking Bea. 'I've done a pregnancy test and…well…It's…er… positive!'

'Oh wow,' shouted Cecily, 'Oh, that's fantastic - have you told Dad?' 'No - where is he?'

'In the garden, I think - his favourite place.'

They waited for Martin to come inside, and he looked at their faces with wide grins and smiled at them - waiting for them to speak.

'What's the joke?' As Bea looked at Cecily, who burst out, 'Mummy's pregnant.'

'What?!'

'It's true, I am.'

'Oh - how on earth - aren't we a bit old?' He laughed. 'It's still very early days.'

'Well, well,' said Martin pacing up and down the kitchen. 'Dad, isn't that amazing?'

'Well, I'm quite surprised, really - well, yes, that would be nice, he said, trying desperately to sound positive, yet inwardly he was dreading it - another screaming child - his insides were churning around in knots while he forced a smile, and Bea and Cecily were showing delighted expressions - oh the hideousness if it all.'

'*Of course*, it's nice daddy - I'm going to have a brother or sister.' 'Well, I suppose you are - you can tell granny later today.'

'It might cheer her up,' said Bea.

‘Apart from immediate family, we’d better keep the news to ourselves until three months have passed.’

‘When’s it due mummy?’ ‘The day after my birthday.’

That night in the spare bedroom Martin appeared concerned, ‘Is it going to be OK?’

‘What do you mean?’

‘Well, given your age - you know - isn’t there a high chance there’ll be something wrong with it?’

‘I’m sure it’ll be fine - I need to let the surgery know - no doubt they’ll want to do blood tests as I was anaemic with the last two.

‘Just when we were getting our freedoms back - Cecily nearly finishing her schooling and Freddie going to University - and now we’re starting all over again - look, it’s just a big shock, that’s all.’

‘Unlike last time, we’re in a better position - a bigger house, big garden - and a new excuse for you to get a new car - you know how you love your cars,’ she grinned.

‘It’s fine - but please make sure you have help sorted and babysitters so we can go out.’

‘Yes, I’ll sort that out - plus, we should convert the stables before the permission runs out.’

‘I’m still phobic of pregnant women, so I won’t be able to come near you when you… you know… show.’

‘I know that - I’ll try and get clothes to hide it.’

When Bea went to see her doctor, she was startled when he simply asked her, ‘Do you want to keep it,’ ‘What do you mean - do I want to keep it - it’s a gift from God!’ ‘Oh, I see - well, that’s fine then.’

As the months went by, Bea was blooming and in very good health. She had no signs of sickness and ate a lot - she also went to antenatal classes. She made the nearest spare room into a nursery and kitted it with new things - all the old baby things had been chucked. The work on the stables had begun, so she was dealing with builders and making decisions on a daily basis. It was an intensely busy time for the Charmers, but at the same time, it was exciting - even for Martin.

Bea's weekly visits to Ocpus Dei stopped, and Martin was very happy with her new interest in the building project. He hoped she was never going back to that cult.

'I'm glad you aren't going to that place in East Grinstead - I would like it if you never went there again.'

'OK. '

The stables came together into a two-bedroom annexe - which Freddie was going to move into during the university holidays.

In late November, Bea's mother came to stay as Bea could no longer drive to her appointments and take Cecily to school. The due date came, and no sign of the boy (Bea found out at the ten-week scan that it was a boy - she wanted to know the sex so that she could get baby clothes and decorate the baby room accordingly). Therese encouraged her to pick the late apples as that might start labour.

Two weeks later, and no sign of the child - so as it was getting near Christmas, Bea was strongly advised to go into hospital to be induced. She told Martin he didn't need to attend, but he insisted on it. The labour was very slow, and the doctors decided it was because there was such a gap between the last baby; therefore, it was like having a first baby all over again, but much harder at 44 years old. She accepted every means of pain control, including an epidural - all her plans for a natural birth firmly out of the window.

At one point, Bea was gowned up for a Caesarian, but baby Rufus arrived with the help of the ventouse - 15 minutes before midnight on

18th December and was healthy. They stayed one night in the hospital as Therese needed to get home to Bea's father, who wasn't well.

'I'll sleep in the nursery so I don't disturb you, Martin - I can't feed him myself, sadly, so he'll be on the bottle.'

To say Bea was overwhelmed was an understatement - she felt her age keenly during the night feeds - but it was such a joy to have this tiny placid bundle in her arms.

She took him to mass, and the Jesuit priest told her that Rufus was born on an old feast day - "Our Lady's Expectation."

'Father, I would like you to baptise him in the Old Rite - in January if you can?'

Bea had found out that before the disastrous Second Vatican Council, it was imperative to have one's baby baptised as soon as possible after the birth - and certainly within a few weeks. Without baptism, the church teaches that a baby who dies won't go to Heaven and instead goes to Limbo - which is a place of perfect happiness - but still not Heaven.

'Yes of course I will.'

As the chapel emptied after mass, Bea knelt in the aisle with Rufus facing the tabernacle and said to God,

'Lord - here he is - this is the son you sent me - I consecrate him to You.'

On the day of the baptism - Rufus was agitated and cried while it was going on. He had three Catholic godmothers and three Anglican sponsors as co-witnesses.

After their six-week checkup at the surgery, Bea had a lot of weight to lose - far more than she thought. Martin remarked on it as Bea was feeding Rufus in the new rocking chair.

‘Thank God you aren’t wearing those ghastly pregnancy dresses anymore - you really did put the weight on this time,’ he sniggered.

‘Yes, I know - I really did eat much more this time - don’t worry, I’m constantly on the go now - so it’ll fall off - as soon as I reach my acceptable weight, I’m going to get a new wardrobe - I can’t wait - and I need to grow my hair - I hate it so short, here do you want to wind him?’ Martin was very taken with Rufus and was more relaxed about holding a small baby.

‘Don’t worry - you don’t have to change his nappy.’

‘I should *hope* not - I didn’t do the others’ nappies, and I’m not starting now!’ ‘I know that - but you don’t mind giving him a bottle occasionally, do you?’

‘As long as I don’t have to deal with sick’ - as he put on a fake squeamish expression. ‘Don’t get cross, but I think you should try a different hairdresser - they don’t cut it that well.’

‘I only went there as they do safer hair dye.’

‘I bet you’ll find other salons are doing the same now.’ ‘I’ll find out.’

Bea was the sort of woman who needed structure and order in her life - if there was disorder, she panicked and couldn’t cope, so she had a weekly routine with Rufus, taking him to different baby groups, going to Latin mass, and visiting people in the Catholic care home. She had a regular cleaner and someone to do the ironing. Cecily was a good babysitter, and she loved having a baby brother.

Deaths of Robert Eclectic and Anne Charmer

A few weeks after Rufus's birth, Bea's father had a fall in his kitchen, and Therese called for an ambulance to take him to A&E. He hadn't been well for a few years and had lost much weight. Therese was in a shattered state, 'I shouldn't have left him for such a long time,' she lamented.

Robert was born on Christmas Day and was baptised in the Church of England, but he favoured the agnostic position throughout his adult life. He wasn't an anti-Catholic and cooperated in his childrens' upbringing as Catholics.

It looked as though Robert wasn't going to leave the hospital anytime soon, so the family started praying for him and sprinkling holy water on him. Bea was also praying for his conversion. Therese asked the local parish priest to pay a visit. But before the priest came, a mysterious nun in a brown habit paid Robert a visit - no one knew where she came from, although there was a convent in Hayle.

The priest came and asked to be alone with Robert, who had no objections - he was weak and in much pain. He spoke quietly to Robert and asked him questions.

When the priest left the bedside, he told the family that he had performed the Last Rites - he explained that Robert had received an extraordinary grace and wanted what he was offering.

'I felt a supernatural movement from Robert.'

'Do you mean he's had a deathbed conversion Father?' asked Tessa. 'All the signs were there - I believe he did - yes, I believe so.'

Beatrice was reminded of the famous deathbed scene of Lord Marchmain in Brideshead Revisited, lapsed Catholic who, on his deathbed, makes the unmistakable sign of the cross while the priest is present.

Robert died on the feast of Candlemass - 2nd February. He had a Catholic funeral.

Less than two years after Robert's death - Martin's mother Anne was nearing death in her nursing home - she had been diagnosed with Vascular dementia - a cruel illness with seven stages of decline. She had the classic symptoms of not recognising some family members, and she even forgot that she smoked and drank Gin.

Martin was very close to his mother, and he was her great delight - being the youngest after a six year gap. Beatrice got on with Anne since the day they met - both extroverts and having much in common.

The nursing home was in Herstwad, and the Charmers were regular visitors. Towards the end of her life in December 2008, Bea started praying for her. One day Anne said something very profound while her children were by the bedside.

'God did all this.'

When Martin told Beatrice this, Bea regarded it as a public act of faith. Anne was not religious by any means, but she was often searching for answers to the meaning of life.

A few days later, she died. Her funeral was just before Christmas, and she was buried in her husband Matthew's grave in Hersterlamb Church.

Chapter 16 - Martin the Flirt

Chambers dictionary defines "flirt" as "to play at courtship, to indulge in light-hearted amorous or sexual banter with someone."

When Bea first met Martin, he was very charming, and he loved women - that was blatantly obvious. He didn't have a type - he loved all women with regular features. He flirted with Bea and with many others. Some flirted back, and some didn't. Once he and Bea were engaged, all his flirting stopped. He had only eyes for Bea.

A leopard doesn't change its spots in a hurry, and when Bea was pregnant for the first time, Martin resumed his flirting. It usually started with him complementing the woman on some aspect of her appearance - always with a dazzling smile and a racy look - he would wait for their reaction to gauge whether to continue with silly banter. It led to their first row. He thought Bea was being unreasonable. She thought he had overstepped the mark and was quite annoyed.

The flirting resumed when Bea was pregnant the second time - and it led to another serious row. It was after a supper party.

'Here I am, very pregnant, and you're doing it again - it's so embarrassing and humiliating, Martin.'

'Oh, don't be so silly - I don't fancy her - it's just fun, that's all.'

'You don't realise how you can lead women on - they might take you seriously, and then what?'

'Oh, for goodness sake, Bea - they don't take it seriously.'

'Hmm - you'd be surprised - I saw my parents' generation, and it was not harmless at all - actually, sweetheart, it's very dangerous,' turning her face and giving him a stern look.

'That's my nature, and I can't change,' he said with a sigh of impatience as he was putting his pyjamas on.

They slept well apart as he had his phobia of pregnant women. It made Bea feel very sad and vulnerable, and unattractive.

Bea often thought to herself - I didn't marry him for his looks, but he seems to get better looking with age. Two people thought he looked like Richard Gere - he's a magnet to certain women. He once said jokingly to Bea when he was very senior, 'Powerful men are an aphrodisiac to women - you know,' raising his eyebrows several times.

'Gosh, you're really getting quite vain, Martin - and that wasn't very funny.'

Bea often wondered what he was like with women assistants at work - she didn't want to know. She did know he got quite close to some of his PAs and often stayed friends if they moved jobs. He even went on a dinner date with a former PA - while Bea was visiting her family in Truro and hadn't told Bea. This fact she discovered many years later when she was playing 'detective,' and seeing that he had invited the former PA out for "din-dins," as Bea was away, as was the husband.

Some of his flirting behaviour went too far, and Bea had to drop friendships. When he asked her why they hadn't seen so and so, she would say,

'How many times have I told you about your inappropriate behaviour, and yet you still carry on - and now *even* your children notice - *my* family notice - *your* sister notices, sorry but I'm sick of being humiliated in public like this so - that's why I dropped them as friends. And I'm sure their husbands don't like it either. Sorry hun, but there *are* consequences to your bad behaviour. It was different when you were single, but you're not single - you're married with three children, and you need to show them a good example - I mean, Cecily was quite shocked the last time. I dread going to certain parties now - as I don't know how you'll behave.'

‘OK....OK.....I’ll try..... but will you stop saying that French phrase to me ”Il y en a toujours un qui aime et un qui est aimé”[15]. I never know what you mean by that anyway.’

‘You’re the one who is loved, Martin,’ she smiled wickedly. ‘You’re being sarcastic.’

Mostly the arguments ended with Martin affirming his love for Bea and looking at her pleadingly, often on his knees while she sat on a sofa.

‘There’s only one woman for me, and it’s you, Beatrice.’

And Bea believed him and trusted him completely for then. But his flirting had a cumulative effect.

Bea was conscious that she was getting older and therefore had to make an effort to look good for her husband - as St Paul exhorted married women to adorn themselves lest their husbands run off with other women. She had had her colours ‘done’ a few times - and it was a different season each time!

‘I’m now an autumn Martin - so I need a new wardrobe.’ ‘I’m sure that won’t be a problem for you,’ he laughed.

---

[15] There is always one who loves and one who is loved.

Chapter 17 - Beatrice and Catholicism

In the same way that Bea was perturbed by Martin's flirting episodes, he was disturbed by Bea's Catholicism, which he perceived as getting more rabid - ever since that extraordinarily odd episode in 2001 - leading her into the Priory for a brief spell. He thought the only good to come out of it was that they were much closer physically since that episode led her to bin the pill. She was more affectionate towards him than before - which was new. She was not by nature a tactile person and was more shy and reserved than Martin.

Shortly after her religious experience, she took Freddie and Cecily to the famous pilgrimage site in Ireland - Knock Shrine, and to another shrine on Achill Island. Then some local Catholic friends asked Bea and 16-year-old Freddie to go to Lourdes as helpers - which they did. While in Lourdes, on the Feast Day of Our Lady of Mount Carmel (16th July) - Bea asked to be enrolled in the Brown Scapular, and she found an elderly Benedictine monk who followed the instructions on the enrolment pamphlet. Her late grandmother had worn the large brown scapular and was buried in the Carmelite nun's habit.

As a result of going to Lourdes, Bea fantasied about becoming a nurse - even applying to become one, being accepted, then turning it down as the hours were too long and she was squeamish.

'How on earth did you think you could become a nurse, Bea - you can't stand the sight of blood, you can't watch hospital programmes - what possessed you to think you could become one?' Martin asked while they were on their family holiday near Pompeii.

'Oh well - it was a fantasy - it's not going to happen' - she laughed.

After the birth of Rufus, Bea started going to Ocpus Dei again and formally joined it. She didn't tell Martin - who had asked her not to go anymore. When she felt the time was right, she would tell him.

One evening after supper, when Rufus was in bed, she told him. A huge row followed.

'Why did you go back when you said you wouldn't - that's deceitful.'

'I missed the people - and they have a creche, so I can leave Rufus in it while I listen to the priest's talk.'

'They're very odd - and they give you strange advice.'

Troubled by this, her advice from the organisation was to pray for her husband and to keep going even though he had asked her not to go. Many years later, she thought that was very bad advice and not Catholic. But it would be her public writings that led to a simmering row with the organisation, and she left, helped by two Latin Mass women. She felt as though they were sent to her for a reason, as she didn't see them afterwards. She told Martin,

'You were right all along about Ocpus Dei - they *are* strange - I've been doing some research. Also, I don't know if it's true, but apparently, they bailed out the corrupt Vatican bank in return for the sainthood of their founder. And I don't like the way they try to control my writing. There's something not quite right, and I'm sorry I went against your wishes - I won't be going back - please forgive me.'

'Good. I'm glad to hear it. Has the Latin Mass replaced it - is that your latest thing now?' He asked.

'Well - yes…I'm only going to Latin Masses - that's true. My research is leading me to the shocking conclusion that modern popes went against all their predecessors by suppressing the Latin Mass and making a new vernacular rite - rather like the protestant service. I mean - when you go to a protestant service, it's very similar to the modern Catholic Mass.'

'It's not something that worries me - I have absolutely no interest in any of it,' he said, sighing with indifference.

Bea loved clothes and mixing styles - as a child, she and her siblings had a dressing-up box that fuelled their love of fashion. She didn't know that the Catholic Church had a lot to say on the subject, especially on the topic of showing off too much flesh. She stumbled on a book by Colleen Hammond, a former model, beauty queen, actress, and now image consultant, called "Dressing with Dignity."[16] The book was an eye-opener as it had quotes from the Bible, popes, saints, and private revelation.

A quote from the Bible which startled Bea was from Deuteronomy chapter 22, verse 5; "A woman must not wear man's clothes, or a man go clad like a woman; all such things are hateful to God."[17]

When she read that verse, she consciously made the decision not to wear trousers - after all, both Martin and her late father didn't like women in trousers. It was an easy decision as she felt trousers did zilch for her - they made her feel hot and unhygienic. She happily binned the very few pairs she had. Women wearing trousers was a relatively recent trend; before the 1950s, it was considered unacceptable for women to wear them as everyday items - as they were considered men's clothing.[18]

As for the Latin Mass, Bea started going to the SSPX[19] masses, taking Rufus with her - after reading about the late Archbishop Lefebvre's doubts concerning the new episcopal rite of consecration. The Archbishop felt that the new rite introduced by Paul 6th in 1968 - was, at best, doubtful. This meant that if bishops were consecrated in the new rite, they were possibly not valid, which meant that any priests they ordained might not be valid as a result. Bea felt safer going to the SSPX, knowing that the priests were properly ordained

---

[16] See Bibliography
[17]See Bibliography, the Knox Bible - 2nd edition 1956.
[18] Google also Cardinal Siri's pastoral letter on "men's dress worn by women" - 1960.
[19] The Society of St Pius X.

in the old rite and not the dubious new rite. Some of the priests ordained by the Archbishop went even further - they felt that no real pope could do what the modern popes did - that of introducing the new mass, along with ambiguous teachings, and they fell into Sedevacantism[20]- that is - they believed the chair of Peter to be vacant. This position was also adopted by the late Father Luigi Villa, who had been given a mandate by Pope Pius XII[21] to investigate and flush out masonic clergy who had infiltrated the Church. This was a very dangerous mission, and several assassination attempts were made on his life. His investigations in 2012 led him to call Benedict XVI out as a heretic, making him a sedevacantist.[22]

All these difficulties in the Catholic Church disturbed Bea horribly - and she often regretted going down the "rabbit hole," but she felt compelled to continue and prayed that God would intervene and sort His divided Church out by divine intervention. She was thoroughly torn by all these positions but would only attend the Latin Mass if it was said by a validly ordained priest.

Bea's faith spurred her to write articles for the Catholic press, and they were published. She would interview local well-known Catholics and supply articles. She rediscovered her love of writing after Rufus was born and started blogging and tweeting on Catholic issues. This is what got her into hot water with Ocpus Dei, who asked her to stop. They reasoned that she was being too controversial and, therefore, this would look bad for the organisation.

After a phone call from HQ and a polite but firm 'telling off,' 'Is the writing on the wall?' she asked the person calling her while she was walking around the kitchen, 'I think I'll have to leave.'

---

[20] Sedevacantism started from the mid-1960s onwards.

[21] Reigned from 1939-1958.

[22] See chiesaviva.com

'Just have a think about it please - if you do decide to leave, you need to write a letter with your decision.'

Bea wrote her resignation letter, and that was the end of her involvement with Ocpus Dei. She soon discovered that when a person left the organisation, other members were instructed to have no more to do with the person leaving. She concluded that the friendships were not deep - and were really a form of 'grooming' just to get more members to join.

Beatrice becomes a spiritual daughter of Padre Pio[23]

After Beatrice's Ritalin episode, she became a spiritual daughter of Padre Pio - the famous Italian stigmatist priest from southern Italy. After the death of her father, she used some of her inheritance money to have a statue made of Padre Pio by a local sculptress.

She had a great admiration for this holy priest, much persecuted by the Vatican mafiosi led by John XXIII. She discovered that he knew about the famous Third Secret of Fatima, which John XXIII refused to disclose to the world, thus disobeying Our Lady.

---

[23] Born 1887, died 1968.

Drawings of St. Padre Pio

One day Tessa came for tea with her children, and she commented on the new statue nestling in an elevated wild part of the garden. Bea saw her questioning look, and before Tessa asked, 'Oh, that's the statue of Padre Pio I had commissioned.'

'Oh, I seem to remember that granny used to talk about him a lot.' 'Yes, she did - but I don't think she knew about his knowledge of the cover-up of the Fatima secret.' 'What secret?'

'The secret that was meant to be disclosed to the world in 1960.'

Tessa looked confused. The children went to look for their cousin Rufus.

'In 1960, Padre Pio told the future chief exorcist - Fr Gabriele Amorth, that the Fatima secret was about the apostasy in the Catholic Church and that a false Catholic Church was emerging - ruled by Satan.'[24]

'Oh well, I have enough on my plate to even think about what's going on in the Church,' sighed Tessa, who was busy with a house move and looking after small children.

It was on occasions like this that Bea missed her grandmother - who could talk for hours about the Catholic faith.

---

[24] See Dr Taylor Marshall's utube, "Padre Pio on Great Apostasy Within the Church."

Part 4. Heartstrings

Chapter 18 - Reunion with the Belgians

One day Martin received an email invitation to a joint 50th birthday party for July 2013. It was from Isabelle De Tra-Vail-Dur. He forwarded it to Bea.

'Well, that's a sign of the times,' said Bea as she was emptying the dishwasher while Rufus was having his supper - the cold dark wintry days were starting to get lighter, and spring was around the corner. Martin was opening an above-average bottle of red wine - over the years, his knowledge of wine grew considerably, and he was more fussy over his choice of everyday wines.

'Well, I mean - after 9 years of *not* seeing the Belgians, and out of the blue, we get an email invitation to Isabelle's 50th party - you know.... what happened to paper invitations? - so sad everything like that is electronic.'

'Is it really 9 years that we haven't seen them - can't be, surely?'

'Well, yes - the last time we saw them was when we did the exchange for Cecily and Hélène, and it wasn't that successful - remember?'

'Oh yes, I do. Have you looked at the invitation?'

'Yes - it looks like a huge party as she has a joint one with her 2 best friends - and it's going to be a pizza party in Étienne's family castle. I honestly don't want to go all that way for a party where we'll only know a handful of people - and we're already doing something on the Friday of that weekend, so we can't really go. Anyway, we've lost touch with them - we exchange Christmas cards, and that's it.'

'That's a pity - I'd like to go - we haven't seen Étienne's family castle before - it looks rather impressive.'

'Rufus do you have to eat so slowly - you need to have your bath.'

Martin replied to the invitation lamenting the fact that they wouldn't be able to attend the party and it was very kind to invite them. When Isabelle received the reply, she was very sad. Her email said, 'Oh, you mus come, Martin! It will not be the same without you - please, please come - are you really sure that you cannot come - I am too sad!'

'Really sorry Isabelle - but we are committed to something else that weekend. Maybe another time.'

'OK - but you mus come and see us this summer - is too long without seeing you - will you come and stay in our holiday house in Knokke - and we want to meet Rufus - how old is he?

'Isabelle, that would be a super idea - and yes, time flies - Rufus will be 6 and a half in August - we could come before he goes back to school. He will want to bring a bucket and spade.'

The following evening - Martin discussed the invitation to Knokke that August. Bea's face lit up.

'Yes, fantastic - Rufus would love the beach there - how nice - presumably we'll drive there? Oh, how nice to see our Belgian friends again - nine years is such a long time not seeing them - how did that happen!'

By the time the Charmer family went to Knokke - smartphones were gaining popularity globally, and the free messaging app "WhatsApp" was quickly replacing the old BBM messaging service, which many "Blackberry"[25] owners used. The WhatsApp service is very quick and safe - calls to other WhatsApp numbers are free - even to other countries, and it is free to send photos, videos, and documents. As a result, many users of smartphones with WhatsApp and other messaging platforms have become addicted to their phones - always waiting for the next message and checking the 2 little blue

---

25 The Blackberry was a popular mobile phone until Apple's iPhone 4 overtook it.

ticks informing them that their message has been read. It has also led to a type of virtual reality where people become totally involved in other people's lives - through a little rectangular device. Couples are often seen in restaurants not engaging with each other but on their phones - in their own little lands of make-believe.

Before Martin had an iPhone, he used a Blackberry phone - which was his work phone - as it could send and receive emails. On their holidays, the Blackberry had to accompany them as Martin would need to be on "call" for any work emergencies which may arise while on holiday - which they invariably did. Bea could see that he was on his Blackberry a lot.

On the day of their journey to Knokke, Martin wanted to drive his new Aston Martin - which had room for Rufus in the back. Martin's love of fast cars was inherited from his late parents, who both drove fast cars. Martin drove it fast - pleasing Rufus - another fan of fast cars. SatNav got them to the house in Knokke, which was in a smart leafy quiet location.

'Are we going to she seaside' - shouted Rufus in great excitement and jiggling in his seat.

'We certainly are,' said Bea opening the door to feel the warm breeze on a hot Friday in August. Bea was wearing a red and white cotton dress - fitted at the waist and flaring in an A shape below the knee. She had summer canvas wedge shoes - as flat shoes didn't suit her, she felt - and a white sun hat.

As they took their luggage to the front door - Martin was studying the garden, which was very formal with little box hedges and flower beds in geometric patterns. It took his breath away. This house was no ordinary holiday house - it was a very substantial house - with a very heavy smart front door - and as the door opened - a very dazzling Isabelle appeared - a totally different Isabelle from the Isabelle they had known all those 9 years ago. There was a tall slim 50-year-old woman - very tanned, in a very short slinky dress in a bright orange-pink pattern - and high-heeled stiletto sandals. Her wavy hair was below her shoulders and was no longer the mousey brown of her youth but highlighted blonde. She gave the air of someone on a mission - Bea thought quickly - whatever happened to the modest Isabelle from the old days?

As they greeted each other - like long lost friends - Martin could hardly speak - this dazzling woman rendered him speechless - and Bea felt like a complete frump with her far too short curly hair and pale skin.

'Ello ello Rufus - I am Isabelle - we will go to the beach - do you want?' 'Yes, pleeeeeease,' shouted Rufus.

Isabelle greeted the Charmers warmly, and they all lamented the fact it was 9 years since they last met.

'We will ave some food first - you mus be ungry - yes?'

As they made their way into the marble hall - Étienne appeared - he had filled out since they had last seen him, and he still had a full head of very dark hair.

'Allo Rufus…. I am Étienne - and I will show you the swimming pool in the cellar - it has a wave feature.'

'Your English is so much better than our French,' said Bea, 'And this house is so incredible - do you only come here in the Summer?'

'In the main, yes', Étienne said - 'But we pay a lot of taxes to ave it', he sighed with a resigned expression - in his quietly spoken voice.

'We will eat now - and then we take Rufus to the sea - on Sunday, Isabelle's parents will come for lunch.'

'Oh, how nice to see your parents again Isabelle - did we see them 9 years ago too? Asked Martin.

'Yes, I sing so,' answered Isabelle in her soft, slinky voice, looking earnestly at Martin.

On Saturday, Isabelle wanted to show Bea the chic shops in Knokke - both women shared a love of fashion and formed a deeper friendship over that weekend. The men were going to take Rufus to the seaside again, and in the afternoon, they were all going to see the old castle, which Étienne was about to do up as a major events venue. The castle had been the family seat since the 13th Century.

On Sunday morning, Bea came down early to give Rufus breakfast, and Isabelle was getting things ready for an al fresco breakfast. She asked Bea if she was planning to go to mass. She was dressed in another short, brightly coloured skimpy dress with a low neckline. Her hair was tied in a loose ponytail and swung from side to side every time she walked, accompanied by the clickety-clack of her high heels.

'Well, yes, I usually only go to the Latin mass, but I don't think you have any around here?'

'No - I don sing so, only in Brussells - we can walk to the church.' Rufus ran excitedly outside to play with a small dog.' Isabelle began to tell Bea about the huge project they were about to undertake - not something she was looking forward to - the complete renovation of Étienne's family castle - so that it could be used as an income generator for weddings and corporate events.

'Sounds exhausting,' said Bea, 'but quite exciting too?'

As they were taking bowls and plates to the table outside the kitchen - Isabelle said flatly out of the blue while looking seriously at Bea, 'You know Beatrice - I could not ave Martin for boyfriend as he was not Catolic - I could not marry a man not catolic - you know dat?'

'Oh really...hmm...Well, I did marry him, and I didn't really think it was a problem at the time, but now I know there are real conflicts if you aren't of the same religion,' while puzzling over why Isabelle was telling her this completely random piece of information. Bea thought Isabelle sounded slightly bitter about this - was this sour grapes after all these years of knowing her? Years later, Bea concluded it most probably was.

Bea took Rufus to his bedroom with instructions to get dressed in his church clothes - while she went into her room to see if Martin was awake yet. He was already getting dressed into his red cotton trousers and a long-sleeved shirt - preferring them to shorts and T-shirts due to getting sunburnt easily.

'Oh, guess what,' she said in a jokey tone - 'Isabelle gave me the following random piece of info - that she couldn't go out with you, let alone marry you as you weren't Catholic - I mean - fancy coming up with that after all these years. Of course, that implies that she would've gone out with you - so you were in with a chance, darling - did you know that? - does your heart skip a beat on hearing that?' She giggled loudly, raising her eyebrows in an exaggerated fashion at him, not realising that it was *indeed* stirring up a fluttering in his heart.

'Well, I sort of did know that - my friend Chris also told me that when we first met - so that wasn't a total surprise.'

'We're all going to Mass soon, so what will you do?'

'Oh, I'm sure I'll relax in the garden - I'll offer to do any lunch preparations - don't worry about me.'

Étienne was getting impatient to get to Mass on time, and he saw that his wife was in a fluster with the preparations for her parents' visit later.

'Isabelle - we need to go.'

'Étienne, you take them - I don sing Martin should be lef alone - yes you go - we can get everything ready for the lunch.'

Étienne sighed in annoyance and bade Bea and Rufus go with him to Mass - a short walk away. As they arrived, an already annoyed Étienne was worried about what the parishioners would think of him arriving without his wife and with a strange woman and child, so he quickly instructed Bea and Rufus to take the side door and sit in a different pew from him. Isabelle's mother was near the front of the church - and Étienne went to join her, while her husband Édouard was one of the altar servers - he always volunteered his help when they visited Isabelle. Bea eyed the parishioners and thought how smart they looked - it was clearly an affluent part of Belgium.

Alone together in the house - Isabelle offered breakfast to Martin at the table, and she had an air of slight unhappiness which Martin thought she must be in a panic as her parents were due for lunch after mass. While he ate a Pain au chocolat, she sat on one of the sun loungers by the grass and put on some big sunglasses.

'I can help you with the cooking,' said Martin, 'I'm used to cooking the Sunday lunch anyway.'

'Oh, is OK - it can wait' - as she lay on the lounger, her long tanned legs outstretched - which Martin could hardly believe his eyes. He, too, like Bea, saw a different Isabelle from the old. This was a new re-invented Isabelle - sophisticated and glamorous - but still with her gazelle-like movements of always.

'Étienne showed me the plans for the castle Isabelle - how very exciting isn't it?'

'No - I don like it - is too much for me, Martin - ee expects me to do all the work with no pay! - I am not giving up my teaching job, and I'm keeping the pay.'

'What do you mean - if he's expecting you to do a proper job, he should pay you, surely?'

'Yes, but he thins is my castle too - so I don need to be paid.'

'Oh dear - that sounds a bit harsh Isabelle - and this house is so beautiful, and did you design the exquisite garden - and is it true you may be selling it?' In another pained expression, she said, 'Maybe yes - is true - all my work here going - I love this ouse.'

‘Sorry we missed your party - but it’s so lovely that we’re here now - and I’m so looking forward to seeing your parents again - are they well?’

As the pair forgot about lunch, Isabelle saw that look in Martin’s eyes - that brooding look that told her the bond was still there since they first met as teenagers. He was the only man she could talk to who wasn’t family.

The pair were deeply engrossed in conversation - and weren’t aware that the others had arrived and were in the kitchen - only to see that very little had been done for lunch, putting Étienne in a very bad mood. He could see what Isabelle was up to, and he was always a little worried about Martin, the English man who met her before him. Isabelle’s parents went to greet their daughter, who jumped up quickly, kissed them hello, and quickly started doing food preparation - Martin also jumped up and went to help with whatever job was needed. Bea also joined in - while Rufus ran outside, throwing a ball at the dog.

‘How was church, Bea?’

‘The same as the English Novos Ordo really,’ and she lowered her voice and said, ‘but I had to sit in another pew lest people wag their tongues - you know, about Étienne arriving with a strange woman plus child - he’s very well-known here’ - she said with a wide-eyed grin.

It was time for lunch outside, and as they were jointing the chicken tarragon at the table, Isabelle’s mother was curious as to why her daughter was not at mass. Paulette had looked after herself over the years, but frequent sunbathing had not been kind to her skin - nevertheless, there was a knowing sparkle in her glinting blue eyes, and she was a sharp bird who knew her daughter very well. Extremely in fact.

‘Isabelle - why weren’t you at Mass?’ She said teasingly.

‘I didn’t want to leave Martin hall alone - and ee elped in the kitchen.’

Paulette looked directly at Martin, ‘Ahh Marrteen, you are blushing… look…! you are blushing’, in a loud voice as she looked directly at Bea, who simply smiled. And the whole table erupted in laughter at the joke - except Étienne, who didn’t find it in the slightest funny. He raised his eyes and sighed with annoyance.

‘Rufus, it’s nearly time to go,’ said Martin as they were finishing lunch with a huge fresh fruit tart.

‘Can we come again?’ he pleaded.

“Yes, of course’ said Isabelle, ‘nez time, we will take you to Waterloo.’ ‘Yaay,’ cried Rufus jumping up and down.

‘And you must come and stay with us,’ said Martin as he said goodbye. ‘Ah yes - we will do dat,’ said Isabelle with a determined voice.

Back in England - and in bed - Bea was curious about what her husband and Isabelle talked about, which was so important that they forgot to prepare the lunch.

‘Oh, she was telling me that she’s fed up with the castle project, and he’s expecting her to drop her job and work at the castle for no pay - he doesn’t sound very kind to her, Bea.’

‘She also told me that when we were shopping - he sounded quite mean.’ ‘Yes, I think he is - he’s far too serious - and quite hard work to talk to - don’t you find? Also, she’s upset that they probably have to sell the Knokke house - the taxes don’t make it worthwhile having. And I think he wants the money to pay for the castle works.’

In the deep of the night, Martin churned over why Isabelle told that piece of information to Bea - it did seem odd - maybe she hoped Bea would tell him, and it was her way of telling him she still had feelings for him - a sort of coded message. He also pondered that the

Tra-Vail-Dur marriage was having difficulties due to the castle business, and there seemed to be tension between the pair. After all, Isabelle had done nothing but complain about Étienne while they were there. We have this deep bond. Still, he thought, I will always be there for her - in her time of need.

Chapter 19 - The Pearl Wedding Anniversary Party

In the spring of 2015, the Charmers were going to reach a milestone wedding anniversary - 30 years. Bea was completely besotted with Martin and wanted very much to have a celebratory party for their immediate family and close friends. Bea's devotion to her husband prompted her to write a Haiku poem to him;

I ONLY HAVE EYES FOR YOU

Only eyes for you
The one true love of my life
Thirty years married!

When I first met you
You said No to career wives
And No to trousers

You said, "My wife will
Wear tweed skirts and light fawn tights
And Jaeger account."

You are so funny
So generous and loving
Rarely getting cross

You never complain
When I buy clothes, shoes, and bags
You say "Carry on!"

You cook a good roast
While we go to Sunday mass
A good curry too!

You belong to me!
My love for you hurts at times
Like a love-sick pup

You, loving husband
I love it when you hug me
So tactile are you!

Your mischievous eyes
Making women melt and swoon
Giving them false hopes

My handsome husband
George Clooney, the nursie said
When Rufus was born

Don't let your head swell
While women are chasing you
Giving me heartache

Great father to three
Freddie, Cecily & Rufs
We all love you lots

I can't convert you
With scripture quotes & doctrine
I can only pray

I love you more now
Then the day we got engaged
My heart skips a beat

Thirty years married
Happy Anniversary
Darling Martin

'Yes, we'll have a party Bea - a good excuse to declutter the barn and clean it - I'll sort the wine out, and we'll need caterers' - Martin was smiling as the cat was in a playful mood and chasing a feather in the winter sitting room. This clever Thai cat knew she was being watched and loved the attention.

‘I think we’ll have proper invites too,’ said Bea as she was writing party notes in her notebook, ‘Not email invites. And I’ll put a wedding photo on it. We’ll need to post them in good time.’

Martin was crawling on the floor where Prada the cat was wriggling on her back. He started tickling her soft grey furry tummy.

‘Of course, we’ll invite Étienne and Isabelle - I mean - now we’re properly in touch - you know - and I’m sure they’ll want to stay for a few days?’

‘Oh definitely - and what about the dress code - I presume you’ll want Black Tie won’t you?’ said Bea.

‘Oh yes, we definitely need Black Tie.’

‘Actually, the theme for 30 years is pearl - I know - why don’t we have a choice of dress code?’

‘Pearl and 30s’ that kind of thing?’

‘We could add the 80s too - as we met in the 1980s.’

‘Pearl, 30s, and 80s - that gives people a bit more scope, and it’s not as rigid as Black Tie - a bit more fun?’

‘Excellent - I’ll wear my 30s tails.’

‘And I’ll definitely buy a new outfit,’ said Bea.

Over the news few weeks, Bea was busy planning the party like a military operation - Martin wanted to have some wedding photos blown up into posters to put on the barn walls and a film screen with a slide show of general photos. The barn was slowly being cleared of rubbish, ready for their handyman to come and steam clean it. Bea loved dancing, so they hired a dance floor and a music system.

‘It’s like planning a wedding, said Bea. ‘On a much smaller scale, though.’

Bea and Cecily went shopping for outfits as Cecily was keen on fashion and wanted to see what was available. They went to an occasion dress shop in Tunbridge, Wells, and Bea started trying on dresses. Martin loved Bea in white, and there was a Spanish white silk-tiered dress with a sparkly bolero - it was the one! It was also reduced at a bargain price. As she was paying for the dress, she spotted a small pearl tiara in a glass cabinet, tried it on - and bought it.

'I'll wear my pearl choker, so that's me sorted - just need some shoes to go with it.'

'Don't get them without me!' Said Cecily.

Bea thought it would be a good idea to have a WhatsApp group with Isabelle so that arrangements for their arrival could be communicated quickly - it was just Isabelle, Bea, and Martin.

The weeks flew by, and the party was imminent - all the spare rooms were prepared for the long-distance guests - including Bea's widowed mother and sister, Lucy. Seating plans were made for the six tables, which were named after places they had lived in, and Bea was determined that a certain friend - Natalie, would be seated away from Martin and with her back to him as she had made a pass at him at a dinner party, witnessed by several people, including her poor husband. While the Charmers were having supper, Bea mentioned the seating plan.

'I think we should put the Belgians on our table, Martin - they will have travelled the furthermost of anyone - and not only that - I'm putting Isabelle on your right and Étienne on my right - the guests of honour… oh and I think we'll put the Oaks on our table too, as Michael has known Isabelle as long as I have. Bea felt happy with the seating arrangement as she knew there was nothing going on between her husband and Isabelle. She felt very safe with that decision. Sorry, Natalie - find someone else.

'Excellent,' said Martin.

It was the night of the party, and the guests started arriving for the canapés and champagne - all dressed in the various themes. Michael Oak and his wife were also staying and had hired Pearly King and Queen outfits. Philip and Marion were in shimmering black 1930s outfits. Natalie arrived in a Kate Bush-style velvet green dress - long and vampish, with vampish black heels. Her meek husband was always with her and always seemed scared of her. She was working her way around the guests to get to Martin, who was talking to his mother and sisters-in-law.

Isabelle and Étienne were dressed in the 1930s - Isabelle had a stunning cream Gatsbyesque floaty dress and a feather headband with stiletto sandals. As Isabelle and Étienne made their grand entrance into the room, Bea quickly looked at Natalie and saw her jaw drop and face fall a thousand miles as she realised she had been upstaged by Isabelle. Bea felt inwardly amused at Natalie's reaction.

Natalie sidled her way to get into Martin's circle of people and introduced herself to Therese and Isabelle, who was already in this group as she didn't know the other guests. Therese complemented Natalie on her velvet dress.

'Thank you, Therese. I found it in a vintage shop. And you look very smart in your sparkly jacket', while Martin clasped his hands together with his most charming smile and said,

'Can I say…you girls look absolutely marvellous.'

While Martin held court in these few minutes, Therese could not help observing that both Isabelle and Natalie were hanging on Martin's every word - and how he relished their girly reactions to his small talk. Therese thought what silly women they were and couldn't wait to circulate amongst the other guests. Bea's sister Lucy, who was wearing one of her signature red dresses with killer heels, like their mother was sharp in her observations, also watched Isabelle with interest and she thought privately, 'Hm - I wonder if Isabelle's trying to outdo Bea - hmm?

The party was going supremely well, and soon the black and white chequerboard dance floor was begging to be danced on - there was an anniversary cake to cut, and a slide show was on the gallery upstairs - the disco lights started darting around the room, lighting up the pearly balloons, and the music was playing - a compilation of all the family's favourite songs, old and new. The photographer was busy weaving stealthily among the guests, and the waiting staff was quietly pouring more wine and clearing things away. Martin went over to Bea to get the dancing started. She gazed adoringly at him in his 1930s tails outfit, and they opened the dancing.

After a few minutes, Bea started solo dancing, and she got lost in her dancing. If she hadn't become a cook, she would have liked to become a professional dancer. As the guests joined in, Martin went surreptitiously over to Isabelle for a dance, and they started dancing. Within minutes a serious-looking sober Étienne strode over and politely swept Martin away while he and Isabelle gave a display of Ceroc dancing. Isabelle's face glowed with happiness as Martin was mesmerised by her skill and ballet-like gracefulness. She knew he was watching her, and she loved it - oh, how she loved it.

Someone was feeling left out - the woman in the green dress. Martin wasn't paying her any attention, and she knew her time was up. She knew his attentions were no longer on her but on this elegant Isabelle from Belgium - the flirting had been sweet while it lasted, but it was over now - game up. She knew a wily woman when she met one - after all, it takes one to know one - she thought. She suddenly felt as green as her dress, and her eyes glowered as she tossed her long chestnut hair back and fumbled with her bracelet. Her long-suffering husband took her arm, and he knew what her thoughts were while he led her onto the dance floor.'

'You'll just have to put up with *my* dancing sweetheart - sorry, I'm not that good a dancer or as interesting as our host. Do look happy, Natalie - smile for the camera, dear.'

Natalie scowled at him - while he pecked her on the cheek and whispered, 'You'll get over him darling' as she gave him a withering look.

The party was coming to an end, and the happy guests started leaving as their taxis arrived. Finally, the Charmers fell into their bed in the early hours.

'Well, I think it went well, don't you?' 'Yes, it was good - and no rows.'

'Oh - did you notice when I danced with Isabelle how Étienne told me where to go?'

'Yes - I did see that - it was quite funny.'

'I think he's jealous of me - hm...always has been, I think.' 'Maybe he sees what others don't?'

'Oh well - it was a great evening' as they held hands until drifting off to sleep - it was going to be another busy day with lunch to prepare for the guests who were staying.

In the morning, Isabelle was already dressed, exploring the garden - she shared Martin's passion for gardens. Bea came down to make her cup of tea to take up to bed and, noticed Isabelle on the terrace, and waved hello. Isabelle was wearing a Chanel-type spring jacket over the tightest jeans Bea had ever seen her wear - and her customary stilettos. Bea wondered what Martin thought of tight jeans on Isabelle. He probably didn't care.

'Bonjour,' breezed in Isabelle - 'nice party laas night - yes you sing so?' 'Yes... it went well...I'm so glad you enjoyed it - can I make you a coffee?'

Isabelle nodded and sat down while Bea started making the drinks. Prada was under the table eyeing up the tassels on Isabelle's jacket and started lifting her paw to try and grab one.

‘You are reely lucky - you know - Étienne never has party for our wedding anniversary - never!’ she sighed sadly. ‘And we are also 30 years zis year.’

‘Oh, we always celebrate the big numbers - we had a silver party too - sorry we didn’t invite you as we’d lost touch with each other - 9 years Isabelle - we didn’t see each other - can you believe it!’

‘Yes is true - we mus never do dat again - is a too long time,’ as Prada was grabbing a tassel. Bea saw sadness in her expression and voice and felt sorry for her.

‘Maybe Étienne isn’t a party man?’

‘I don know why ee doesn't like party.’

While they were busy talking about what their grown-up children were up to, Lucy joined the gathering and made her customary cup of Earl Grey tea. She greeted Isabelle warmly while thinking that Isabelle wanted to upstage Bea again with her alluring outfit.’ Lucy, in her fleecy leopard onesie, took her tea outside and had her first fag of the day. Bea and Isabelle joined her.

‘Well, that was a good party. What time is Mass, Bea?’ ‘11 - and will you and Étienne be coming to Mass?’ ‘Oh I sing so - yes.’

Martin cooked his usual brilliant roast while the rest of the family was at the local parish for Mass, and then it was finally time to say goodbye. Isabelle was determined that their meet-ups were to be more regular now, and Martin agreed.

A few days later, Bea decided the WhatsApp group was no longer necessary, and not thinking about it, she removed herself from the group, not realising that once you remove yourself from a group, there is no going back. She naively assumed that Martin and Isabelle would do the same. They didn’t.

In July of the same year as the Charmer party - an internet dating site called “Ashley Madison” was in the headline news for a breach of data on 1000s of its users. It was a dating site for married people to start extramarital affairs. Users were terrified that the hackers would inform their spouses about their cheating.

'Gosh - I've never heard of a dating site for married people to have affairs - have you, Martin?' As they sat in the pool area.

'No' said Martin.

'I mean… this would never be possible without the internet, would it?' 'No, I guess not' while trying to concentrate on reading the Telegraph. 'Apparently, 85% of users worldwide are married men.'

'Really?'

'And people use the Ashley Madison App on their phones - gosh how easy it is to have an online affair - just with a smartphone and the click of a button - how ghastly.'

Chapter 20 - EU Referendum Fallout

On 20th February 2016, David Cameron, the Prime Minister, shocked the country when he called for an EU referendum - the people were going to be given a say on whether to stay in or leave the EU. The vote was to take place on the 23rd of June. Two camps of people quickly formed, and it became a nasty few months of hostility between the "Remainers" and the "Brexiteeers." Friends fell out over it, marriages broke up, and many regarded Cameron's decision as a disastrous political earthquake. Strangers even fell out in supermarket queues.

'What the heck is Cameron doing?' Said an annoyed Martin while they were watching the late news - Prada was startled and jumped off his lap.

'He's letting the people decide…finally,' said Bea.

'It's completely absurd - why's he taking such a huge gamble - is the man mad?' Prada went to hide under the coffee table.

'I disagree.'

Bea had followed in her late father's footsteps when it came to politics - he had been proved right on so many issues, she felt. He was one of the first to join UKIP - having voted conservative all his life but felt they had abandoned conservative values.

'So - I can assume you want to leave the EU, Bea - what good reason can you give me?'

'I'm frankly fed up with the corruption and bureaucracy in Brussels, and why should they decide all our laws?'

'Oh, I know it's corrupt and imperfect, but we're still flipping better off being part of the EU than not. I mean, really!' Martin got up and went to get himself a stiff whiskey. 'I hear you listening to Farage a lot in your study - he's completely nutty and confused.'

‘I suggest we don’t discuss it or we’ll end up in separate bedrooms - we have 4 months of this. On another subject, what are we doing when Isabelle and Étienne come to stay in May - you know how they love visiting gardens?’

‘I’m sure we’ll find a garden they haven’t visited before.’

It was a tense few months in the Charmer household, and Martin was more annoyed that Bea was so passionate about it that the two eldest children were starting to agree with leaving the EU.

A few weeks before the vote, the Belgians arrived for a flying visit - joyful to be in Sussex again. They were also excited to tell them the news that Hélène, their daughter, was getting married the following summer - and the Charmers must come to the wedding at the castle. They even had accommodation sorted for them. Martin thought it was splendid news.

Of course, Isabelle and Étienne were intrigued about the referendum and naturally wanted to know how the Charmers would vote. Bea answered - ‘It’s not a topic we discuss anymore, Isabelle - we’re on opposite sides on this - I’m a leaver, and Martin wants to stay.’ Isabelle and her husband both looked sad. Isabelle swiftly said with disapproval, ‘Marrteen, you are right - UK mus stay in EU - oderwise will be difficul to do zings - yes?’

‘I quite agree with you, Isabelle - and I’m confident the vote will go the right way,’ giving Bea a triumphant look - and knowing this would annoy her immensely.

‘Let’s not predict results - it may be a total surprise,’ said Bea, giving Martin and Isabelle one of her glittery looks.

All was calm on the day of the vote itself - Martin and Bea spoke little about it and voted separately. They didn’t stay up to watch the news and had an early night - Martin was confident the vote would be to stay in the EU - his bank was relying on it - they had gambled on it.

Radio 4 came on automatically every morning at 6.30, and the earth-shattering news that the British public had voted decisively to leave the EU by a margin of 4% - 52% wanted to leave, and 48% to stay. Martin gasped in horror, and Bea shouted with elation, jumping out of bed, 'We won - we're out!'

'How dare you vote to leave - the bank was relying on us staying,' Martin was puce with rage. Bea went down to make her morning tea - thinking it best to avoid her husband in this black mood.

Their adult children came to stay that weekend - something they did during the warmer months, and explained why they voted to leave, 'Dad - Ma was so passionate about it, and you said nothing to try and change our minds,' said Freddie.

'It's true, Dad,' agreed Cecily.

'I didn't think I needed to,' said Martin begrudgingly, 'People are more stupid than I thought.'

'Oh - wow - my…you're just so arrogant, Martin', said an angry Bea, flashing him a disdainful look, 'No use complaining now - it's done - let's all move on.'

Martin was 54 when the vote took place, and he was toying with the idea of reducing his workload in his city job - he would be able to draw on his pension at 55, something the government had introduced - apparently to allow jobs to filled by younger workers, and to stop older workers claiming benefits.

Bea was a volunteer at Citizens Advice and enjoyed the variety of different problems that she had to try and resolve face to face or refer the issues to more experienced advisers. It was mentally stimulating.

One day - soon after the disastrous Brexit vote, Martin was sitting at the family iMAC computer when he received an email from Isabelle with her formal garden plans for the castle gardens. He was starting to think he had so much more in common with Isabelle than with Bea, and he was still smarting at the Brexit vote. He and Isabelle thought it was terrible that Bea voted to leave. Martin emailed back that they were magnificent plans. He also mentioned his plans to semi-retire the following year, something she approved of, and he said it would mean having more free time - time to go and visit her more often, and of course, she must visit them in England. He sent the family love to her and then signed off, "And with my special love to you, Martin."

The Charmers muddled on fairly happily, and Martin got used to the Brexit vote and became more positive about it. But like Catholicism, it too became a taboo subject amongst the Charmer family. Bea was also starting to make annoying noises about moving to a smaller house. It irritated Martin - he wanted to die in this house with the garden and woods he so loved. Why didn't Bea take any interest in his garden? Why did she disapprove of him spending a fortune on *his* garden - always complaining about the cost of it? Where would the cats go if they moved? They needed a big garden and fields to run around in. Martin sometimes regretted the day Bea took on the household accounts when they returned from honeymoon. But I've never been good with budgets, he thought, and someone has to do it...hmm...It's annoying all the same.

Martin was born with a faulty heart valve, only detected after a check-up in his 20s. One day, it would wear out, and in 2010, the valve was replaced with a pig valve. The operation was traumatic, giving him permanent "white coat" syndrome. Every year, he had the valve checked out, and he was due for his annual checkup in November. He had never felt better and was confident that the heart consultant would sign him off for another year.

One dark November, he came home earlier than his usual time, and Bea was in the kitchen getting supper ready. Rufus was playing with a remote control car. As he came into the kitchen, he had a frightened look, and his face was an ashen grey colour.

'Earlier train today - are you OK?'

‘No, everything’s not OK - I had a phone call from the heart specialist - the valve hasn’t lasted as long as he’d hoped…I have to have it replaced with a permanent metal one as soon as possible - another pig one will wear out, and I won’t survive another operation. It’s too ghastly for words,’ he sighed, sitting down and putting his face in his hands while Prada pounced on his lap.

‘But you’re so fit - this is shocking news!’ exclaimed Bea.

‘You know… he said - if we do nothing… I could just drop dead at any time! - it’s too awful - the first time I thought I was going to die and then that excruciating pain of having my lung drained - I can’t bear the thought of going through that again - I never thought I’d have to do it again, Oh Bea - it’s my worst nightmare all over again.’

‘That’s too awful, Mab - when are you having it done?’

‘10 day's time. They have to open me up again - I don’t know how I can survive another op like the last one.’

‘Do you think all the commuting has put stress on your heart?’

‘Well, yes - he said that was a contributory factor - and he said it was probably time to reduce my workload and go part-time - well, I was planning to cut down anyway – I’m nearly 55.’

‘You’re going to need weeks to recover too - I seem to remember from the last time. I’ll stop doing CAB[26] so I can visit every day and look after you when you come out.’ Martin held out his left hand for Bea to take while he stroked Prada firmly, making her purr loudly.

---

26 Citizens Advice Bureau.

Part 5. Of Human Bondage

Chapter 21 - A Near-Death Experience

Martin packed a very small bag for the hospital - with just the bear minimum. He had no intention of staying for longer than absolutely necessary. He knew it was quite a risky operation - but he hadn't told anyone - what was the point? There was a risk in whatever he did. Have the op and risk it going wrong, or not having the op and having a high chance of a heart attack at any time. He had decided the op was worth the risk if there was a good outcome in the long term.

Bea travelled with Martin to the hospital and helped him settle in. He was in low spirits and not saying much.

'Hope it goes well tomorrow - will pray it does. I'm assuming they'll ring me up after the op?'

'Yes - I think so.'

'Shall I set up a WhatsApp group to let family and close friends know how it went?'

'Yes please,' as Bea went to hug him goodbye.

On the evening of the operation, Bea was anxiously waiting near the phone - and it was getting quite late. At around 11 pm, the phone rang - it was the heart specialist.

'Mrs. Charmer - the operation was completed, but Martin had a bad reaction, and his immediate recovery is going to take a little bit longer than normal. He's in ICU, and you'll hopefully be able to speak to him tomorrow sometime.'

Bea thanked God he was alive, and she put the news on the group.

Martin rang Bea the next evening and was very drowsy with drugs. His voice was hoarse.

'I'm still in ICU - the op took much longer than they thought as I had some allergic reaction - it was a close run thing, Bea - I think I nearly died.'

'You're alive, Martin!! - When can we visit?'

'Can't cope with lots of visitors, Bea - please just you and family at the moment. Maybe tomorrow? - oh, and I hate these gowns - please bring my pyjamas.'

Martin updated the heart group - but he was so drugged up that he didn't notice that the predictive text was in overdrive, and as a result, the messages made no sense. He was beyond caring and in too much discomfort to worry. Isabelle was the most vocal in the group, with a lot of crying emojis, beating heart emojis, and emotional language. Bea found her a bit cringing but put it down to European ways.

When Bea arrived at the hospital bed - Martin was looking grey and shellshocked. He was wired up to monitors, and the heart rate lines were moving all over the place. He saw her look questioningly at the monitor.

'I'm not stable yet - I'm here for a while until I'm more stable. Can't eat - it's ghastly seeing that monitor. I didn't think I'd ever get out of ICU alive.' 'Are you able to move yet?'

'Not really - I'll have to see the physiotherapist soon - they won't let me leave until I've walked around the block - I mean on this floor.... not sure I can see too many visitors either - just the children maybe.' The door opened, and a jolly nurse came in - her plump arms did the necessary checks that had to be done.

'Every half hour, someone comes in - there's no peace here - always checking this, that, and the other,' said Martin wearily and drifting off to sleep.' Bea made herself comfortable and had a book to read or watch the news and worried about the wavy lines on the monitor.

Bea continued with the daily visits to St John's Wood in North London and helped him in the bathroom sometimes - his mobility was shaky and, getting up from the loo was difficult, and he was short-tempered. She continued to put updates on and photos of the patient.

When he trawled through the get-well messages, he loved reading Isabelle's comments - 'Oh how she cares for me - what heartfelt emotion she shows,' he thought privately, 'Bea never shows emotion like that - oh well - it's not her way really - never was.'

'You'll lose weight if you don't eat,' said Bea after the first week. 'I don't care - probably need to anyway.'

'Do you want any wine or brandy?' 'No thanks - can't taste anything.'

Three weeks after the operation, it was early December, and Martin was discharged from the hospital with strict instructions to take it easy and not to get stressed. A family member drove him home. When he walked into the dining hall at the farmhouse, he saw a huge box that Bea said was for him.

'Oh, what's this? oh… a wine advent calendar.'

'Yes - I thought you'd like it, but I don't think you will now.'

'You're right - I can't stomach any alcohol - my sense of taste has deserted me. I might try Sherry - you can drink the advent calendar, Bea.'

Martin's recuperation took many months, and he didn't go into the office until well into the new year. He was traumatised by the whole experience, and a nasty side effect was the noise of the metal valve. It was audible to others within a metre away - he found it hard to sleep at night with the pounding noise inside - it always seemed noisier at night as there were no other noises. It was better in the daytime when it could be masked. The specialist thought it was unfortunate, too. It was pretty bad luck. Bea looked after him and didn't go back to CAB, but she started volunteering in the local internet cafe - helping locals with digital queries and iPad problems.

While recuperating, Martin thought about his near-death experience - and decided it was a life-changing experience - it made him view his life differently - what his priorities were now - but more importantly - who were the most important people in his life? He decided that there was only one true friend in his life - but she lived abroad - sadly. His dearest Isabelle was shining like a shooting star on the heart WhatsApp - with her beating heart emojis and tearful emojis and her emotional gushing words. He dreamed of his Isabelle and thought over and over again - she's my best friend - I'll do anything for her - my angel sent from Heaven - my dear goddess - and that dulcet accent of hers - she really cares for me. After all, Beatrice puts God before me, so why shouldn't I put Isabelle before Bea? Martin thought this was perfectly reasonable and fair. When the heart group had run its course - Bea removed it. Isabelle and Martin continued their own little private WhatsApp relationship as they were now mutually best friends. They confided in each other about everything. Martin felt a deepening bond - as though their two hearts were knitted together… of human bondage - with the help of smartphones and WhatsApp.

Bea often thought of Isabelle's dulcet voice and found it too wincey pussycat. But she could see why men could fall under her spell - men liked feminine, soft voices, and Bea knew she didn't have a dulcet voice. It did not occur to her that her own husband had fallen under Isabelle's alluring spell - let alone that she was now the most important woman in his life. To say that Beatrice was quite naive was an understatement. Had she an inkling, however small, of the "special" close friendship between Isabelle and Martin, it would have been a dagger through her own heart.

Chapter 22 - A Very Belgian Wedding at the Castle

Martin made a fairly good recovery from his heart operation and went to part-time work, as strongly recommended by his cardiologist. He was doing as much exercise as possible to build up strength - he would walk to the small lake at the bottom of the garden and feed the ducks - followed by Prada with her little dance displays common to her breed. Apart from the irritating noise of the metal valve and bad shoulders as a result of having his ribcage opened, Martin was in good spirits. He enjoyed only having to go to London 2 or 3 times a week, and he was investigating the idea of learning how to fly. Bea thought this was stark raving mad and decided he was a restless man - always needing to be doing something and not able to relax.

The Charmers soon received a stiff triple invitation to Hélène De Tra-Vail-Dur's summer wedding - eldest child of Isabelle and Étienne. It was to be the first wedding at the now-revamped castle.

'Gosh, what a posh invite - in 3 parts,' said Bea, 'How wincetastic is that - all that flowery pink and green writing and little illustrations' as she laid them out on the dining room table, 'ah look…they're using their formal titles now - Vicomte and Vicomtesse.

'That's the Belgian way, I think - not everyone's invited to all three events - but we are,' said Martin gleefully.

'They even have a theme for the dress code - that's a new trend, surely?' 'We've been offered accommodation in one of the converted farm buildings on the estate - for two nights.'

'Well, the castle does look pretty amazing on their website - I'll look forward to sorting my outfit in the theme of "a touch of pink and green" - it looks as though I'll need a change of outfits for the evening, do too' said Bea happily - she loved putting outfits together.

'I'll have to take my top hat - I can get away with it as an Englishman.' Bea picked up the main invitation to see where the ceremony was taking place,

‘Oh, the marriage isn’t going to take place in the castle chapel - that’s a shame - maybe it’s too small?’

‘Far too small, yes - it’s taking place in the local Catholic Church.’
‘Do they like the groom?’

‘Oh yes - he’s very suitable - Catholic, of course, and a Knight of Malta - a fair bit older though - not a looker, I’m told.’

‘We’ll have to arrange someone to look after Rufus as he isn’t invited - I think I’ll ask one of the school mothers to have him.’

‘It’s something to look forward to, Bea - after the horrible months I’ve had all winter.’

The Charmers travelled to Belgium in Martin’s favourite toy - his new Aston Martin. He drove it fast and with purpose - wanting to arrive as early as possible. When they arrived at the castle estate, it was hot. They were taken to the converted farm building.

‘Crikey, it’s massive,’ said Bea in wonderment - ‘hardly an old shed, is it - it’s a proper building - and look at the formal garden - they do like their geometric flower beds don’t they?’

‘Yes, I agree - it must have had an important function at some time, when it was a full working farm,’ as they stepped inside - to find an immaculately presented home - in good Belgian taste, or as they liked to joke - in very “High Life de Belgique” taste. Their bedroom had an ensuite bathroom - with a deliciously deep bath for Bea. It had been a long day getting there, and Martin plonked himself on the soft, enormous bed while Bea hung up their wedding outfits. Bea had decided on a fairly plain outfit, not wanting to attract any attention - a pale green dress with a plain pale pink fitted jacket, a formal brown straw hat, and her high cream LK Bennet stilettos. The next day was going to be very long and exhausting.

The ceremony took place in the large Catholic Church near the castle and was packed with high Belgian society in traditional dark morning coats and fancy hats - Bea noticed that there was a lot of loud talking inside the church and hardly anyone genuflected anymore before getting into their pews. She put the lack of reverence down to the changes in the liturgy since the Second Vatican Council. She sat with her arm in Martin's - secretly, she was dreading the reception and not knowing many people - her French was lousy, and she had made no effort to brush up on it - hoping desperately she would be sitting next to people who spoke decent English.

The champagne reception was on the castle grounds with views of the moat, where a rowing boat was waiting for the bride and groom to have their photos taken. The sun was shining, and it was pleasantly warm. Bea had got to know Isabelle's family pretty well by now, and some of their closest friends - she was at ease in their company and deliberately sought them out.

They were all instructed to go into the huge new Orangerie overlooking the moat - purpose-built especially for large reception parties. There was a large easel with seating plans. Bea scrutinised it, looking for their places until she looked startled at Martin,

'Wow, Martin, you, my dear, are in pride of place - next to the mother of the bride - I mean, that's pretty amazing, isn't it? But where's Étienne sitting? He's not at the same table as Isabelle - how odd.' Martin seemed surprised by the table plan. But secretly, he was elated.

'Maybe it's a Belgian custom - not to sit with one's spouse at weddings - I don't know,' he said, trying to suppress his delight, 'Étienne is on a different table.'

'Where the heck am I?' said Bea as they tried to find her place.

'Oh look - you're on the other end of the table - next to Isabelle's brother Benoît - at least you know him, and he speaks good English.'

'That's a relief,' said Bea as they walked towards their table with sumptuous floral arrangements - Martin at one end and Bea at the other end. As Martin beamed at the pride of place - he stood behind his chair, waiting for the other guests to arrive. When Isabelle arrived, he pulled her chair out for her to sit down and did the same for her close friend Anne-Marie on his other side. Isabelle was in a shocking pink and green silk shift dress and a shocking pink hat - adorned with flowers and big gaudy earrings. Her Valentino stiletto heels made her as tall as most men in the room. In contrast, Anne-Marie had on a plainish masculine suit and flat shoes.

Bea thought the seating was so unusual it was incredibly funny - and on the spur of the moment, she took her iPhone out of her clutch bag and, with a big smile, went to take a photo of Martin and the Viscountess. Martin was smirking like the Cheshire Cat that got the cream. Isabelle was putting on a wide-eyed, innocent look.

'Who's the cat that got the cream, Martin,' Bea said as she took the photo, then went to sit in her place - greeting Isabelle's brother by her side. Luckily, the man on her other side spoke brilliant English too.

Bea was grateful she was sitting next to Isabelle's brother - a charming man - rather plainer than his sister and not very tall. He ~~is~~ was a hard-working man with a well-endowed matronly wife and five beautiful children. Bea often thought that plain-looking parents often produced beautiful children. They chatted about Martin's love of fast cars - as Benoît also had a weakness for cars, especially MGs. Bea could see that he thoroughly enjoyed speaking English, as did the other man.

One little snippet of conversation escaped Bea - she was too busy studying the guests' wedding outfits. Benoît is looking towards his sister and Martin, and he casually mentioned, 'You know Beatrice… Martin is the only man Isabelle speaks to - yes, it's true - the only man. He's her best friend - she tells him everything, yes.'

'Oh, that's nice for her,' said Bea as their first courses were whisked away by efficient staff, and she drank more wine. It would be five years later that Bea realised what he said was pregnant with meaning. Loaded in fact.

The meal wore on, and it was finally time for a rest and change of clothing before the evening party, where there was going to be dancing in the castle ballroom. Bea was glad she had survived the formal sit-down meal, and she was glad for a rest before the final dance-fest to come. As they walked back to their accommodation, Bea slyly looked at her husband.

'Do you want to see the photo - here - look at your smirking face, Martin - honestly - I still can't get over you sitting in the top seat - I mean, what will the "High Life de Belgique" people think? They might think you're her English trophy boyfriend,' and they both laughed. Bea sent the photo to a close friend, who was deeply shocked and surprised at Bea's possible naivety - thinking that if it were her, she would have slapped Isabelle.

The bride and groom started the dancing off and were joined by new guests, who were only there for the evening party. Bea and Martin joined the dancing, and Bea was in her most comfortable place - the dance floor. Martin had not brought a change of clothing and was still in his morning coat, while Bea had changed into a casual summer skirt and top - in the pink and green theme.

'Men are so lucky the way no one notices if they haven't changed or not,' said Bea loudly.

'Étienne hasn't changed either - oh, there's Isabelle.'

And waiting for the appropriate moment, Martin swiftly went over and asked his goddess to dance - knowing that Bea was happy alone on the dance floor, although one of Isabelle's relations asked her for a dance. Bea watched Martin dance with Isabelle and then saw Étienne waving him away - as he did at their pearl party two years before. Martin smugly returned to Bea and suggested they get a drink from one of the stalls outside.

'Good plan.'

'Did you see Étienne moving me away? He's jealous of me - always has been.'

'Hmm - I wonder why? I mean - does he know she turned you down twice when you met her?' Shrugging his shoulders, Martin said, 'I don't know what he knows, actually - he's probably too busy to care.'

After a few hours, the Charmers grabbed their moment and crept away unnoticed back to their bedroom - they had an early start in the morning. Breakfast was going to be another smart catered affair at the castle, by the moat.

After a gourmet breakfast, it was time to say goodbye. Martin asked Isabelle to keep him up to date on their next renovation project at the castle - which was the huge carriage block. It was going to be converted into their new final home and two other dwellings.

'Where did Étienne get all this money - I mean, it must be costing millions all these projects?' Asked Bea.

'Remember, he sold his technology business for a huge amount.'
'Oh yes.'

As they walked to Martin's big boy toy - Isabelle caressed the car lovingly and made noises with her dulcet voice. Étienne liked it too - but he was not a car man - preferring big estate cars, which were like workhorses at the castle. They were capable of transporting things.

'We think our son is going to get married next year - you mus come,' piped Isabelle.

'Give us the date when you have it,' said Martin excitedly.

Martin started up his big boy toy, and it made a roaring noise - he looked at Isabelle while she waved at them. He spun the wheels on the gravel - on purpose, as they sped off towards the channel tunnel.

'Well, that was some wedding… and a half,' said Bea. 'Magical I'd say.'

The following spring, the Charmers received an invitation to the son's wedding. It was another stiff triple whammy invitation - this time the writing was in peach - and it was a peach theme for the wedding.'

'I can't face another Belgian wedding quite so soon, Martin - sorry, I really can't.'

'Ok, I'll go alone - there must be a Charmer representative there!' Said Martin firmly.

The topic of the Belgian wedding came up when they were at a supper party with very old friends, friends who had met the Tra-Vail-Durs over the decades.

'I've told Martin I'm not going to the wedding as I just can't face it - I really can't.'

'So I'm going alone,' Martin said matter of factly.

One of the friends - a high-powered city woman, gave Martin a knowing look and said very quietly but enough for Martin to hear,

'It's not appropriate.'

Bea heard her too and mentally agreed - she was getting mildly irritated with Martin's growing obsession with Isabelle. Much as she admired the graceful Isabelle - she was beginning to think that she and Martin were much too close - and she thought their city friend thought so too - otherwise, why did she make that comment, "It's not appropriate" with that knowing look - squarely at Martin. After all, Isabelle never sent Bea messages or emails - only to Martin.

Much to Isabelle's annoyance and Martin's sadness, the Charmers turned the wedding invitation down.

Chapter 23 - Covid and Lockdowns

The growing rift between Beatrice and Martin was subtle but simmering. Bea didn't know why she and Martin were so distant - it was a mystery. She felt his mind was somewhere else - some fantasy place perhaps. They only spoke about house and family problems. Their cuddles were a bit fake - not quite right. She disliked him, and he disliked her - she felt unloved and ignored and didn't know if she even loved him anymore. She concluded that she didn't love him anymore. A great chasm opened in their marriage and grew ever wider throughout the whole of the lockdown period.

During the final months of 2019, Bea embarked on a teaching course - it got her out of the house and back to studying, which she loved. During this time, the global news was about some terrifying virus called "Corona" - which was highly contagious. A lot of people in white Hazmat suits were on the television - with their heads and faces covered up. They were shown with spray guns spraying the virus. Countries were locking their citizens down - in order to stop the spread of the disease.

Princess Prada cat was an elderly 17-year-old when she ate a whole rabbit. It made her very sick, and she couldn't move. The vet had to remove the rabbit, and she lived for a few more months before dying. Cecily was devastated -

Prada had been 'her' cat since she was 12. Martin was also desolate and wanted another Korat. A few months later, they acquired a female kitten and named her Fendi.

One of Bea's friends - Liesel, was advertising kittens on Instagram. Her designer cat - a Ragdoll, had been bedded by a local feral cat. Bea immediately wanted to see the kittens, and when she got to the farm - one of the kittens jumped into her hand and curled up into a little bundle of purring fur - with its alert eyes on Bea. It was love at first sight. The Charmer family wanted this kitten. It would be a companion to little Fendi. They named the half Ragdoll - Furla. The cats would prove to be a great comfort to the family when the lockdowns started.

Just before Prime Minister Boris Johnson locked England down - on March 23rd, 2020, Bea obtained her teaching qualification.

'Well, I won't be teaching now as the schools are closing,' said Bea, 'but there's a job going on Facebook to be a personal assistant to a lady in her 90s within walking distance - I'm applying for it.'

As the two adult children came to live at home during the lockdown, Bea was desperate to escape for a few hours and was relieved to get the PA job. Rufus' school had arranged for all his lessons to be online, and he needed the main study. Martin moved all his work computers to the top floor of the house and spent many hours on Zoom meetings. The weather was sunny, warm, and dry - nice for people with gardens - but not so nice for people stuck in flats.

One day, Bea found herself unexpectedly elected as a parish councillor for Washber Village. Martin encouraged it, so she accepted the role.

'You'll find it interesting, Bea, and you'll be good at it.'

While he was at the top of the house, Martin found solace in looking through his old photograph album of his teenage trips to Belgium. He found it comforting. He found himself escaping into them - into a make-believe world.

That's me lying on the grass with Isabelle gazing down next to me - and there we all are, sitting on a park bench in Brussells. Why did I let you get away, Isabelle? I didn't try hard enough, did I? He thought. We have so much in common - far more than Bea and I have.

Isabelle was also locked down, and all the booked events at the castle were cancelled - she found she had a lot of spare time, as did Martin. They mutually agreed to do a morning meet-up each day to talk about how they were coping with the lockdowns and difficult family members, including their spouses, and then they did an evening meet-up to tell each other how their days went.

Isabelle found time to WhatsApp photos to him, mostly of herself. Some of the photos were quite titillating, of wistful looks and, slightly open mouths, and low-cut tops. She also started to complain about Étienne. And Martin also started to voice criticisms about Beatrice and some of his children. It was their secret time together. It was the start of their emotional affair, started by the not-so-coy - Isabelle[27]. They justified their special meet-ups as perfectly innocent, as nothing physical was happening.

Bea noticed that Martin was spending more time than usual on his walks - he spent much time in the woods he loved. She joked with herself that he might be having an affair as he spent so much time away from the family. It became a growing unease with Bea - and she wondered what he was up to during all those long periods alone. Her gut feeling told her something was desperately wrong - but what?

The bond between the pair deepened, and Martin fell madly and deeply in love with Isabelle - and it hurt him terribly. He was that 18-year-old teenager all over again and as lovesick and desperate. He told himself that Isabelle was the most wonderful human being that ever lived and that she was the love of his life. Does she know how much I love her, he thought - too too much. His heart - with its two major operations was hurting again - and it was a horrible feeling. Was his love reciprocated or not? - that was the question he asked himself over and over again.

'She clearly needs me - that bully husband of hers - always bossing her - do this, do that - don't complain - your work is in the castle - you're my wife, and I'm the big boss.' Martin told himself that she needed him as much as he needed her - they were each other's

---

[27] Kathy Nickerson PHD, asserts that 99% of emotional affairs "begin the same way", when relationship details and difficulties are shared with someone other than your spouse. The mutual support causes an emotional attachment.

support - in a time of crisis - the covid crisis - Étienne and Beatrice, their annoying, nagging spouses. Martin's emotional energy was no longer towards his wife.

Martin daydreamed of being Isabelle's knight in shimmering armour on his chestnut charger - all puffed up with the steel breastplate on and lance in his right hand - the English flag flying. Martin fantasised himself, ready to rescue his damsel in distress - his Isabelle lamenting at the castle window with arms outstretched with a pile of bed linen filling up the room - there she was, her hair cascading down like Rapunzel - waiting for her knight in shining armour. In his fantasy, she's crying, "Marrteen elp me please - save me from my usband - ee is orrible to me - all this laundry ee make me do."

"Here I come to the rescue Isabelle - I'm flying over the channel on my chestnut charger with wings - to the rescue my love - my one true love - to the rescue - we'll sort your bully husband out - you can rely on your Martin, my sweet lady - my angel - I'm coming to the rescue - on my big horsey."

One day, at the height of the lockdown, Martin composed a private little love voice message to Isabelle to send via WhatsApp. He felt a little sensation of riskiness - he knew he was crossing a line. In his nervous excitement, he accidentally sent it to the family WhatsApp group and not to his lady love. He didn't check it had gone to the person he intended it for.

When Bea clicked on the message - she heard a voice she had not heard since Martin declared his love for her all those years ago. It was a quavering voice in a higher octave than usual and simply said in a very slow, measured tone, "You are the most beautiful person."

Bea felt a sharp pain in her stomach - she knew immediately it wasn't for her - she knew she wasn't the intended recipient, and she was quite annoyed. The children also thought it was not for their mother, but they had no idea who it was for. They hoped it was for their mother. When he emerged into the bedroom after his long walk, she asked him about the voice message. The look of panic was revealed on his reddening face - he did not know he had sent it to the family group.

'Oh, oh um yes… it was for you, Bea,' he said unconvincingly and looking very guilty as he was nervously pacing around the bed. He put on a false smile, but his eyes were in panic mode. Martin, deep down, knew he had crossed a line with that love message - he was horrified he had sent it to his family group. How could he have been so careless and stupid? He thought.

'You know it wasn't for me.' Bea's eyes widened, and she stared directly at him, her mouth tightened in a straight line.

'Of course, it was for you,' trying to sound convincing.

'It blooming well wasn't - you never speak in that wobbly voice to me - you haven't used that voice since you chased me - many decades ago.'

'Ok - sorry… sorry… it was for Isabelle - look, Bea, I'm worried about her - you know Étienne is such a bully - making her do too many jobs.'

'Oh yes - oh dear - what's going on there?' Said Bea, suddenly feeling remorse for her friend in Belgium.

'He's - he's not nice to her - you know - she just wants to please him and be loved by him, but he's never really pleased with her. She's having such a hard time, Bea', as he slumped on the bed and looked pleadingly at her.

'OK…OK… I understand,' said Bea, 'but explain that to our children, who all heard it.' Martin thanked his lucky stars that Bea was being understanding.

A few days later, instead of resending the voice message to Isabelle, Martin determinedly went to the lake with his cats, rang her up via the free WhatsApp audio, and declared his feelings for her, 'I love you.'

Isabelle already knew how he felt about her, but this was the first time he had vocalised his feelings for her. She knew he was in the palm of her hand - she had won him - it gave her delicious feelings of power. She knew he found Beatrice annoying and that he didn't like her anymore and had fallen completely out of love with her. Isabelle felt empowered. She did not feel like Étienne's wife - she felt belittled by him, and she loved him and was always trying to please him. Martin loved her and always had - she knew this. He would do anything for her.

Martin, in his love sickness, forgot his marriage vows - he was committing emotional infidelity with another woman and stabbing Beatrice in the back.

There seemed like a long pause on the phone while Martin waited in agony for a response - any response, and then Isabelle laughed coquettishly like a temptress. He felt a blow to the heart. She hasn't reciprocated, he thought - a little bitterly - third time unlucky - love is so cruel….oh so cruel. She needs me, yes - but does she love me in the same way I love her - I mean, does she have any idea how much I love her? Maybe not, he thought. Maybe I'm reading into this relationship too much. All the time she needs me, I don't care if she doesn't love me - he thought - I just want to be her support, that's all. I'll always be here for her. We have an unbreakable bond. She's the most important person in my life - more than, dare I say… my… wife, my children, my siblings, and all my friends. I can't live without her - it's unbearable. He began to feel like unhappy Philip Carey in Somerset Maughan's

"Of Human Bondage" - whose addicted obsession with Mildred leads him onto a path of self-destruction - Mildred calling all the shots and Philip chained to her spell - unable to detach himself - to his drug of choice (it was a platonic relationship). And here was Martin, addicted to Isabelle - finding himself spellbound - unable to say No to her requests - being used as her puppy on a lead - wagging its tail while waiting for small crumbs from its mistress. Isabelle felt empowered and adored all the attention she was getting - it made up for her bully husband.

Martin and Beatrice were like ships in the night and avoided each other - Bea was dreading his full-time retirement and decided she would not be retiring but would be out of his way. They annoyed each other and argued about most things. That love voice message should have been a red flag for Bea - and not long after that - another red flag reared itself - on her iPad, of all places.

One day, Bea was editing her photos on her iPad - to fill the time during the lockdown - she wanted to clear space, which meant trawling through years of photos. As she was going through them - she noticed a screenshot - one she did not recognise. She clicked on it and saw that it was a screenshot that had made its way onto her iPad from Martin's mobile phone. She knew it must have happened when photos were automatically shared between their Apple devices.

The screenshot was of a WhatsApp conversation between Isabelle and Martin - Isabelle's was of bouncy emojis and pink hearts, and Martin's was a complaint about Bea. Bea's heart tightened instantly as she thought, what the blooming heck was this conversation about? She was angry and deleted it instantly. It lodged in her memory, though, along with the love voice message.

Chapter 24 - Boxes of Fabrics and Chocolates

The lockdowns in England went on for much longer than people thought - it was cruelty which the government imposed unnecessarily on its citizens - with its scare tactics and daily death counts - the health secretary Matt Hancock-Up on the TV news - using his powers to gleefully wag his finger at the public, with that winey voice of his - the man who was caught fondling his mistress on camera and breaking all the rules he imposed on the public. He would soon be wagging his finger and coercing everyone to take an experimental injection, which he hailed as a miracle in the fight against COVID-19.

At the end of January 2021, Martin received his summons to take the experimental injection. He had no problems with it - he was a firm believer that the government always acted in its citizens' best interests. Bea was much more skeptical and had lost trust in the government for years. It was another source of arguments between them.

As he stepped inside the warm kitchen from his early morning walk, Bea was sitting at the kitchen table reading the paper on her iPad.

'I've been invited to take the vaccine - as I'm in the 'at risk' category. And you can have it too, Bea - they said so.'

Bea's brown eyes flashed incredulity at him - she was momentarily speechless. He gave her a questioning look.

'Sorry, but I'm not having it - jabs need years of testing, Martin - sorry, but I've been listening to good scientists about it, and they say not to take it as it's still in trials. And there's another problem with it

- morally, I won't take it as it has the line of an aborted baby in the list of ingredients[28].

'Oh well - that's your choice, Bea - I don't happen to agree with you' - giving her a disdainful look - 'I'll have mine anyway. Erm....you do realise you won't be allowed to travel anywhere without it, Bea - I may have to go on holiday without you', with a smug smile.

'Well, as you know, I'm not a great holiday person anyway. Actually, there are some destinations that don't require jabs for entry.'

'Yes - places I don't want to go to,' he said firmly.

'How do you know - have you looked at the destinations? And by the way, I'm going on an anti-lockdown march - with Liesel and some friends. In London - in March.'

'That's rather stupid, Bea - I suppose they're all whacky ethnicky types - rich hippies?'

'All types Martin - all types - I never go on protest marches Martin, but I feel so strongly that the government is wrong that I want to show solidarity with others who feel like me.'

'Well, don't blame me if you get covid.' 'Do I blame you for things, Martin?' Flashing him a defiant look.

Martin was so cross with Beatrice and her refusal to take the jab and now wanted to go on a protest march - he needed to tell Isabelle this news and ask her what she thought of it. To his great surprise, Isabelle explained to him that Bea was perfectly within her rights not to take the jab - and that her adult children had all refused the jab too.

---

[28] Leaflet for the AstraZeneca states amongst other ingredients that it contains "human embryonic kidney (HEK) 293 cells."

‘Are you taking the jab, Isabelle?’ He WhatsApped, ‘For sure, yes - Étienne also will ave vaccination.’

One night in February, Martin couldn’t sleep. It was a common problem since his heart operation - he was still mulling over Bea and her stubbornness over not having the jab and also thinking of Isabelle. He read some of his Kindle while Bea slept - it helped him sleep. He still couldn’t sleep, so he checked his phone for any messages and emails and found an old email from Isabelle’s friend Anne-Marie. It was past 1 am in the morning. The subject matter was Isabelle and her unkind husband - and how they were all coping with being locked down. He emailed,

‘Dear Anne-M… I do worry about Isabelle. She drives herself so hard and does not get the support that she needs from her husband, who I think is actually rather cruel. She wants so much to be loved by him and his family, but I fear that she will always be disappointed. You are the only person who really knows how I feel for Isabelle and have since the day we met. If I could have my life again….. But that cannot be and helps no one, so instead, I will always be here for her. We are each other’s support, and we have a deep bond. Love M.’

Isabelle did indeed have a large favour to ask Martin. During the lockdown, she had time to finish the soft furnishings in one of the castle houses. She wanted to source English fabrics and trimmings from the Designers Guild, as Belgian ones were not as good. She also wanted to order some Farrow and Ball paints - which were more expensive in Belgium. She emailed him to ask for his help with sourcing fabrics and paints, which he was more than happy to do. If Martin had no interest in fabrics before now, he was very keen now! It would mean that Isabelle and Étienne would have to pay them a visit to collect the fabrics and paints - as soon as England was open to visitors - hopefully in the summer of 2021. Yippee he thought.

Between them, Martin and Isabelle found the right trimmings and had them delivered to Martin’s address. When the boxes arrived,

Martin carefully hid them in his 'study' at the top of the house. He didn't want Bea to find them.

One day while Bea was cleaning the house - it took her the best part of a day as there were now five people living in the house during the lockdown - she went to dust and Hoover Martin's study. After a while, the Hoover banged into a cardboard box under the bed. She switched the hoover off and wondered what was under the bed. As she pulled the first box out, she saw a few more and pulled them out. They were all sealed boxes. She put them on the bed and went to find Martin to ask him what they were. She found him by the lake, sitting on the bench, watching the ducks.

'Oh, Isabelle asked me to help with fabrics for one of the guest houses in the castle grounds, and apparently, they can't get decent fabric in Belgium. They love English ones', he said sheepishly, 'They'll collect them when England opens to visitors - this summer, I think.' Bea looked questioningly at him.

'Sorry… you say… they can't get trimmings in Belgium? Are you sure? Do all High Life de Belgique people get their fabrics from England?'

'They like the Designer's Guild - and they want to get some Farrow and Ball paints when they come, so I've found a supplier locally - that massive new ironmongers near Herstwad.'

Bea started laughing.

'Since when have you ever been interested in sourcing blooming fabrics, Martin - is it a new hobby?'

'No - I'm just helping our friends out, that's all.'

A few weeks later, a large parcel arrived addressed to Martin. It was full of Belgian chocolate bars - his favourites. Bea watched him open it with interest. His eyes lit up when he saw the contents.

'Oh… Just a little thank you for helping them with the fabrics,' he grinned. 'Golly,' said Bea, 'that's a huge amount.'

'It'll keep me going until they visit in the summer.'

As the lockdown eased in Belgium, Isabelle was suddenly overwhelmed with work - all the castle bookings and everything that goes with running a large venue had to be got ready for when the castle re-opened. Her time was precious, and she had many other commitments besides the castle. Martin found that she wasn't as free as before, and he was very annoyed - she's so busy, he thought - why does she have to be so busy - why can't she give some of the jobs to others? I want to be with her again - I miss her voice so much - need to speak to her - she is the love of my life. He was looking forward to their visit as soon as England opened to foreign visitors.

The long-awaited opening of the borders happened in the summer of 2021, and the Tra-Vail-Durs were going to be one of the first visitors to take advantage of this. Martin arranged the compulsory PCR tests for them.

Shortly before the Belgians' visit, Martin had organised to take his sons to the 3-day Grand Prix in Silverstone - they would stay in a pub. It was their Christmas present. Both sons had inherited their father's love of fast cars, and Rufus had started racing from a young age, and it was his absolute passion. Rufus was 14 and a half when they went, and it was something to look forward to after the harsh lockdown. They drove on Friday 16th July - an important day in Beatrice's religious calendar, for it was the feast day of Our Lady of Mount Carmel - of the brown scapular, and her beloved grandmother had been a lay Carmelite.

During their time at Silverstone, Rufus noticed something about his father. He noticed that he was preoccupied with his WhatsApp. He thought it odd that his father didn't want to drink in the atmosphere of the event - was he bored of watching racing? But Rufus observed something else - something that made him feel uneasy. He saw someone's profile photo pop up quite a lot on Martin's WhatsApp -

the photo of Isabelle and her name by the photo. He noticed that his father had a different expression when he was messaging Isabelle - as though he was in a trance of sorts - a sort of dream world. Over the three days, he thought his father was messaging Isabelle a lot - and wondered why. I wonder if Ma knows how much he messages Isabelle, he thought. It was a gut feeling that made him feel worried and uneasy. He remembered the catechism lesson on marriage, the dangers of forming extremely close friends with the opposite sex, and how it could lead to affairs. Another thing he observed was that his father used Google Translate a lot.

When they returned home, Rufus kept his thoughts private, but when he felt it was appropriate, he voiced his concerns to his older brother. It was a weight off his shoulders, and he was very close to his brother - even though there was a 20-year age gap. Freddie explained that their father and Isabelle were very old friends and that there was nothing to worry about… however, he said he would keep an eye on things at the next event.

The next event was a One-Day International cricket match. Freddie kept a cursory glance on Martin and eventually saw exactly what Rufus meant. Both boys didn't like it - what would their mother think - did she even know about the messaging? Freddie knew that Isabelle turned down being his godmother because she couldn't play an active role as she lived in another country - and yet she seemed to have a lot of time for his father. The two sons kept it to themselves - but would eventually confide in their sister - when an opportunity arose.

Isabelle and Étienne arrived soon after the Silverstone trip. Beatrice was genuinely pleased to see them - she still had no idea of the depths of feelings Martin had for Isabelle. Martin played down his emotions when they arrived - was a little subdued, Bea thought. But like a child in a sweetie shop, his face broke into delight when Isabelle presented him with a huge box of his favourite Belgian chocolate bars.

It was a flying visit, and the Farrow and Ball paints were bought and loaded into the back of Étienne's sensible estate car, along with the boxes of fabric trimmings. Before they left, Martin was asked if he wouldn't mind doing some translations from French into English regarding wedding enquiries and giving his advice regarding the castle website and the Instagram account. He was more than delighted to do these jobs. Of course, he was.

Chapter 25 - Martin's 60th Birthday Party

Martin was better looking the older he got. By the time of his big birthday in 2022, his hair was almost white, giving him a distinguished look. He tried to keep his weight within the normal range, and this was a challenge. He liked decent wines and common milk chocolate - especially Belgian.

Bea and Martin still had a troubled marriage, and while Bea still made an effort to look good for her husband, he didn't really take any notice. They didn't like each other and had fallen out of love with each other - they tolerated each other at best. He found her views whacky, and she found his views equally annoying. How on earth would they survive another 20 years ahead of them - she dreaded it. She had absolutely no idea about his besottedness with another woman - it would have never entered into her imagination - it was utterly inconceivable. But the chasm between them was very wide now. Something was so wrong.

Occasionally, Martin taunted Bea and told her that 'Isabelle's more catholic than you.'

'Really - why? What aspect makes her more catholic than me?'
'Oh, I don't know - it's just a hunch.'

Martin decided to have a small catered dinner party in the barn for his immediate family and closest friends. He didn't invite Bea's family as it was a very large one, and he was planning to have a summer party for them instead. It went without saying that Isabelle and Étienne would be the guests of honour, and of course, they would be staying for a few days. The dress code was "favourite outfit." Martin wanted to wear an old green smoking jacket, thick red corduroy Pakeman Catto & Carter trousers, and green velvet shoes. Bea's favourite outfit at that particular time was an orange satin shirt and a gold pleated skirt.

As the canapé and champagne course was being served in the main house - Isabelle, as usual, made her svelte dramatic entrance - she was wearing a silver metallic jumpsuit with high stiletto shoes - the sort that made a clicketty clack with each step. Étienne was wearing his favourite Loden jacket. Bea wondered if Martin liked the jumpsuit - most probably, she thought - but then he wouldn't care even if she was wearing a flipping black sack!

During the dinner - Étienne was fixated by Freddie. 'Beatrice - you need to undo the apron strings.' 'What do you mean Étienne?'

'Little Freddie - ee's still too attached to his mother.' 'Oh, I don't think so, Étienne.'

'You must let go, Beatrice.'

Bea thought Étienne was becoming like a record player - going on and on about the same subject - as though he had drunk too much wine. But he was teetotal.

The party ended with Martin's off-the-cuff speech - where he thanked everyone for coming - and especially thanked his oldest friend - Isabelle, who had known him for longer than anyone present except his brother and sister.

Freddie and Rufus quietly observed that their father was indeed spellbound by this Belgian lady - in her silver space suit. Did their mother notice how enchanted he was by Isabelle?

As the Belgians said their goodbyes - they mentioned their youngest son's wedding, which was taking place in the summer.

'I don't think I can go,' said Bea, 'I haven't had covid and I'm not jabbed.' 'Is fine, Beatrice - you may quarantine with us,' said Isabelle.

'We'll definitely be able to come,' said Martin, 'that is absolutely fixed - we're coming.'

The thorny issues of COVID-19 jabs reared its ugly head again when Rufus was offered a jab through his school. It would require parental consent. Both Martin and Bea had the same letter from the school. They were sitting at the kitchen table in the cold winter of 2022. Beatrice was feeling a bit unwell with a cold and drinking hot water.

'I think Rufus can make his own mind up on whether to have the jab or not,' said Martin.

'Well - no - actually, he needs our consent, and I don't give it.' 'Well, I am giving consent then,' said Martin.

'Actually darling - if you read the letter carefully, it says that if the parents aren't in agreement, then they are siding with the non-jab parent. Did you not read that?'

Martin sighed in annoyance. He had read it, and it annoyed him. He knew it wasn't worth arguing with Bea. Not on this issue, anyway.

A few days later, Bea woke up feeling very unwell. Martin promptly went to the kitchen - letting the cats out, and removed a covid test from one of the many boxes they had piled up in a cupboard. Bea did the test. It was positive. Martin couldn't hide his elation if he tried - it was the best news and made his day. It meant that they could go to the wedding in Belgium now, as Bea would be granted six months of natural immunity.

'I still have to book for a PCR test - they won't just take my word for it,' she said weakly.

'Ok, we'll drive to the testing centre today.'

The confirmation came a few days later, and they would definitely be going to the wedding now. Bea thought to herself that her husband was only worried about the wedding and not the fact she was feeling unwell. She thought his priorities were not with her, so where were his priorities then? With Isabelle no doubt.

Martin wanted a new waistcoat for the wedding. The theme was "bold colours" - and instead of asking for his wife's help like most husbands would have done, he asked Isabelle what waistcoat to buy, and he bought the one she liked. It was a bright red one. When Bea saw him open the package - she said,

'Gosh, it's not like you to buy something like that without asking if I like it.'

'You know I wear red, so why would I ask you what you think?'

Chapter 26 - Another Belgian Wedding

It was late June and time to go to another Belgian wedding, that of the youngest Tra-Vail-Dur son, but this time was different from the last time. This time, the Charmers were regarded as family and were therefore invited to come the day before as helpers at the wedding. They would now be staying in the main house on the estate - along with family members. Bea was feeling more confident about the French language as she had studied it for a few weeks.

Martin was very anxious to get to Belgium as early as possible on Friday so that they could do the jobs set for them. He took his Aston and drove them fast to the castle with just the delay of getting through the Eurotunnel. The weather was dry and hot.

Once they unpacked in the beautiful bedroom suite, they were given the job of making waffles and soft drinks. Isabelle was very stressed out about the seat pads in the conservatory not being the colour she ordered. Bea asked her if she was OK, and Isabelle, in breathless tones from running around sorting things out and carrying a large bag of linen, sighed, 'This is my life, Beatrice - LOOK at me - this laundry - my life - ooff.'

'Oh dear - well, you let us know what we can do to help', 'Is fine - you are elping.'

When Martin and Bea finished their jobs, Martin wanted to look at the garden, and Isabelle came to join them - she wanted a break. She showed them the formal castle garden, which bordered a wild meadow and woodlands.

Bea was wearing the wrong shoes and couldn't go further than the end of the garden, so she stopped while Martin and Isabelle continued in deep conversation towards the meadow and woods, oblivious to Bea. Bea thought to herself - they haven't noticed I'm not with them - I expect that's what they want - their time alone. A tightness came over her as she felt things were not right. Not right at all. Bea's sister

Lucy was a counsellor and used to say that if you felt something was wrong, it usually meant something *was* wrong.

That night, after a family barbecue, they went to bed very tired from the long drive and having helped with the wedding. Martin got up very early as he wanted to see if he could help with any more jobs.

The dress code was bold colours, and Bea wore a yellow and orange dress with a pink hat. Martin was wearing his morning coat with the new red waistcoat - approved of by Isabelle. When Bea saw Isabelle's outfit, she was surprised at the audacity of such an outfit, which she felt rather inappropriate for a Viscountess at her son's wedding. Bea thought it looked like a spray-on onesie in gaudy colours. It was of a sheer material with a very low-cut neckline. Along with her stiletto clicketty clack sandals, she looked not very ladylike.

The wedding party was going to be taken on decorated farm trucks to the church. Martin went with Isabelle in the front truck, having abandoned Bea, who went in the other truck behind. Bea felt annoyed by this and thought - he has no idea where I am and nor does he care - he's in a little world where only Isabelle counts - just like yesterday when they both ignored me in the garden to go on their private walkabouts together.

The marriage service was noisy, with lots of loud voices and no reverence. It was as though no one was aware they were in a church. After the ceremony and photos, it was back to the castle in the farm trucks. A drinks reception was waiting for them, and a smart team of waiting staff.

After the drinks, they were ushered into the conservatory, which was even more sumptuous than the last wedding, and this time, there was no seating plan, so Isabelle grabbed Martin and Beatrice and led them to sit on each side of her - although Étienne placed his best friend next to Bea - the same friend she had sat with five years before at the daughter's wedding. It was altogether more informal as the guests were invited to get their own food from different types of buffets around the room. It was a very posh self-service.

After the meal, long speeches, and a big screen of photos, it *was* time for the evening party when another cohort of guests arrived, and Martin and Beatrice went to join in with the dancing. Isabelle was still fretting about the wrong colour pads on the chairs and went to change into a long silk gown - a much more demeur choice of outfit than the wedding onesie.

At an appropriate time, the Charmers made their move and quietly walked away from the castle and towards their accommodation. As they went - someone was following them. Isabelle had caught sight of them sidling off, and she wanted an excuse to get away from the party.

As they arrived at the house, Isabelle came up behind them and asked them if they were OK.

'It was a lovely wedding,' said Bea, 'and I don't think anyone noticed what colour the seat pads were - I honestly wouldn't worry Isabelle.'

'Yes, it was a super day Isabelle - and did everything go how you wanted - apart from the wrong seat cushions?' Asked Martin in his softest voice.

Isabelle started talking at length, and Bea quietly said goodnight and went upstairs - saying to herself as she left Martin and Isabelle lingering in the stairwell, 'You're welcome to him.' She had no idea why she said it - it was said instinctively. Deep down, she suspected something was going on between her husband and Isabelle - it was a hunch - a 6th sense. It was the first time she had felt like that. That trembling voice message and screenshot came into her mind.

Bea was already in bed by the time Martin came upstairs - he assumed she was asleep, and he quickly and quietly undressed and got into his side of the bed.

Martin was up early again on the day they were leaving - and he left Bea in bed while he went to look for Isabelle. A huge array of breakfast choices was all laid out beautifully by the resident staff, and Martin had a quick breakfast and coffee before wandering outside.

Bea got up and went down to join the other family members staying in the house and having breakfast - Martin and Isabelle were nowhere to be seen. Étienne was busy clearing up the castle grounds and filling the boot of his car with bags of rubbish and laundry.

Eventually, Martin returned after dropping Isabelle off somewhere on the castle grounds.

Bea looked coolly at him come into the breakfast room, and they both started helping put the plates away. Martin explained,

'Oh - I went to get petrol - and I didn't know where the petrol stations were, so Isabelle offered to show me where they were - if you were wondering where I was.'

'Oh - doesn't Waze help with that?' Said Bea, thinking to herself that her husband's explanation seemed a bit too rehearsed somehow. He had clearly thought about it; she felt - as though he was hiding a guilty secret. She also felt it a bit odd that he had dropped Isabelle off somewhere - it almost looked to Bea as though they had both decided it didn't look right if they both arrived together after the petrol trip.

'Apparently, they've had problems with some petrol stations, and some haven't had fuel,' he said.

Before the wedding, Martin had arranged to come to the 3-day Spa Grand Prix in Belgium in late August with his two sons. Isabelle and Étienne were going to put them up in their house in Brussels. Bea decided not to join them, as she would only have returned from seeing her mother in Cornwall a few days before.

As they said their Goodbyes, Étienne tried to persuade Bea to come and stay and that she could go shopping and sightseeing instead of watching the Grand Prix. Bea politely but firmly said that it was too soon after her trip to Cornwall. Étienne seemed genuinely sad.

As Martin drove the car out of the castle grounds, he turned and smiled at Bea, 'Bea, I think you have a fan - you've pulled.'

'What do you mean, Martin?' She looked sharply at him. 'I think Étienne is rather keen on you.'

'How very convenient for you,' she whispered. Martin didn't hear her. She thought to herself - how very convenient for you, Martin, if Étienne likes me - it would make life so much easier for you and Isabelle.

Out of the blue, Bea asked, 'If Étienne and I were dead, would you marry Isabelle?' 'Yes.'

'Oh, I'd better watch out then, hadn't I - if anything happens to me…' 'Of course it's not going to happen,' he teased.

'It's your other party soon - for my family. Can you think about what you want to serve? Asked Bea.

'Let's see what the weather's like nearer the time.'

Soon after their Belgian trip, Martin started receiving many photos of the wedding - the majority of them had Isabelle in them - naturally. One of the photos was of Isabelle with her two small granddaughters. Martin commented that while they were lovely girls, they were not quite as beautiful as their grandmother. Isabelle adored such comments - they fed her narcissism and vanity and encouraged her to send more. After all, she knew Martin loved her - he had told her - with those three universally understood words. Deep down, she knew she was the most important person in Martin's life. She knew about his troubled marriage - he told her everything - she would always be his confidante. Poor, poor Beatrice - being his second choice - I was always his first choice, but I could not marry a non-Catholic. Isabelle loved her husband, but he was unkind to her, so she needed Martin to fill in the emotional gap that she lacked from Étienne - Étienne, the workaholic who never stopped working.

Part 6. Hell Hath No Fury…

Chapter 27 - Martin's Party for Bea's Family

When Martin celebrated his big 0 birthdays - he didn't include Beatrice's family because 1) it was a very large family and 2) there was much infighting amongst the members, and therefore best to keep them apart - he felt. Bea understood this, so when it came to his 60th - he decided to have a separate party for all of Bea's immediate family. It was to take place in the middle of July at lunchtime - so that Bea's nieces and nephews could swim and play in the garden.

As there was a large number to cater for, Martin decided to use his new Paella kit, which he had been given as a birthday present at his winter birthday party - it was easier than a barbecue as everything was in one huge pan. And as it was the Queen's Platinum Jubilee year, Bea decided to make an easier version of the official winning pudding, which was a lemon and Amaretti trifle. It was still fiddly, took ages, and Bea thought it was probably the last time she would make it.

The day arrived, and so did the heat and sun. The Paella kit was assembled over a large gas cylinder, and the recipe was obeyed exactly - as it was the first time using a proper Paella kit. Martin enjoyed being in charge of the Paella as it meant he didn't have to socialise too much - and he could WhatsApp Isabelle if a quiet moment arose.

Freddie and Cecily were due to come to the party as they wanted to see their relations from their mother's side of the family. Freddie was slightly agitated on the train and voiced his concerns to his sister, 'Rufus and I… we're a bit worried about Dad…er, well, you know, he messages Isabelle rather a lot.' Cecily was unzipping a bulging makeup bag.

'Why - has mum said something about it? Asked Cecily while meticulously putting makeup on.

'Gosh no - she's never even mentioned it - but I'm not sure she knows how much dad messages Isabelle - we notice it at the sporting events we go to - he gets into another world when he's doing it. It doesn't seem right, Cecily.' 'OK - will see what he's like at the party later - I wonder if there'll be any rows with mum's family - there usually are,' said Cecily, smiling.

At noon, Bea's family started arriving, including Bea's mother, Therese - who came with her youngest daughter, Tessa, and family. Bea's other sister, Lucy, arrived with her new rescue Border Terrier, as did Bea's brother and his two little girls. All gravitated towards the pool area, which was where the Paella was being cooked. Small children started jumping in the pool, and little squeals of excitement were heard amidst the splashing.

Apart from a bit of tension between some of Bea's family, the day went remarkably smoothly, and the Paella was a huge success. Martin was very pleased with this new toy and was glad to relax with a very good red wine when all the cooking was done.

'The Jubilee pudding's heavenly, Bea,' said Lucy, lighting up a cigarette. 'Yes - it's very citrusy - but jolly fiddly making it,' said Bea.

'It's all fantastic,' said Therese, enjoying the superior red wine.

As the party was nearing its end with the cheese course - the guests started to leave - it was early evening and still hot. Bea's sister Lucy was staying the night as it was a long drive home for her, and she enjoyed the company of her nephews and nieces.

Cecily was lying on one of the loungers by the pool, and Bea and Lucy went to join her. Lucy was catching up on news of mutual friends and then asked Bea, 'Oh, and how's your Belgian friend - Isabelle?'

'Oh, don't ask that,' groaned Cecily, sitting up on her lounger and looking at Bea, who was raising her eyebrows.

'I must say I'm rather fed up with her name being mentioned - I mean it's as though she's an invisible member of this household -

Isabelle says this or Isabelle recommends that - I mean Lucy - we have a new sofa in the winter room - and guess what - it's an IKEA sofa - Martin assembled it, I kid you not!'

'Fancy you getting an IKEA sofa?' laughed Lucy.

'Well, guess who recommended it? St Isabelle of course. It's a very good sofa, I must say - but you know… it's getting a bit grating hearing her name so much.'

'Sorry I mentioned her,' said Lucy, stroking her small dog, 'It was a good lunch, Bea - and no family rows - phew.'

As the evening wore on, Bea was getting tired - she wanted to get ready for bed, so she went to get changed into her night clothes. Lucy went to join the Charmer children, who were chatting on the terrace, and she was looking around for her brother-in-law.

'Where's your father - did he enjoy his party? As she walked on the terrace with a cigarette - Cecily went to join her and got down to stroke the dog.

'I think he's gone by the pool - I can just see him at the pool table,' said Freddie, who noticed his father looking at his phone - with a serene expression.

'Why isn't he with us? Probably texting, you know who,' said Freddie quickly.

Lucy noticed that Freddie was a little agitated and a bit unsettled - he was tapping his right foot in a rhythmic manner. He had been drinking wine during lunch, and it made him more talkative and animated. While walking around with her dog, she was listening to their conversation - about Isabelle and their father. Rufus was a quiet teenager of a few words, but what he asked next triggered something in his older brother.

'Why's dad on Google Translate a lot?' He asked them. 'Is he?' Asked Cecily.

‘Yes,’ said Freddie, getting up and taking in a deep breath, the first of many - and walking around the terrace, ‘I need to speak to Dad.’

‘Oh…about Isabelle? What will you say?’ Asked Cecily nervously. ‘What I’ve been meaning to ask for a while but haven’t had the courage until now.’

‘No, I would wait,’ said Lucy to her eldest nephew - ‘Wait til tomorrow - when you’ve sobered up.’

Freddie felt his heart pumping, and he felt confident - this was something he needed to do - it had been on his mind for months. He walked down to the pool. Bea emerged from the kitchen French doors in her dressing gown and sat at the table with Lucy, Cecily, and Rufus. She offered to make some tea for Lucy.

‘Yes, please - Earl Grey.’

As Bea put the tea on the table, she saw Freddie and Martin under the old oak tree where the swing hung - next to the ancient apple tree groaning with apples. Martin was moving around and looking at the grass, and the scene struck her as a little confrontational. It wasn’t a calm scene - Martin looked uncomfortable, Bea thought.

‘Oh - I do hope they’re not having a row, are they - look over by the oak tree.’

‘I don’t know - Freddie just got up and went to find Dad, that’s all,’ said Cecily.

‘I think it’s what happens when the drink is involved,’ said Lucy seated with her dog on her lap and fag in her hand.

When Freddie went to ask his father if he could have a private word with him under the oak tree. Martin looked up at him and was perturbed by his son’s serious expression - he wondered what on earth it was about. He felt annoyed that his peace was disturbed after a long day. He only wanted to relax alone with a nice glass of wine. Theirs was a tricky father-son relationship, and Martin felt Freddie was more of an Eclectic than a Charmer. The Eclectic family were a vocal lot and said what they thought. He got up silently and followed Freddie to the oak tree, thinking, 'Oh no, here we go.'

'Dad - I've been meaning to ask you - it's just a simple question but - is…is… Is there something going on with you and Isabelle? - It's just something Rufus and I have noticed, that's all. You do message her a lot - even Rufus notices. I mean, you're always talking about her and the castle - you're clearly very in awe of her and her talents - I mean, why wouldn't you be?' He looked intently at his father.

'No - I am not having an affair with Isabelle - she's a very dear friend of mine - I've known her since she was 17.'

'OK, thanks for clearing that up.'

Fendi and Furla had joined them and were having a playful spat under the apple tree - Furla trying to leap out at Fendi, who daintily put her right paw out, ready to bop Furla on her black fluffy head.

The two men walked up to the terrace with the cats racing up behind them and sat down with the others - it was a dark and sultry night. Bea was fading fast and desperate to go to bed.

'OK, I'm hitting the hay - don't talk too loudly' as she moved into the kitchen and upstairs to the bedroom. The windows were open, and she heard soft voices below.

As Bea tried to sleep - Martin joined her and lay on the bed. 'Bea - I need to warn you about something.'

'Oh?' said Bea, rolling over to face him.

'Well, you know what Freddie's like - when he gets a bit…you know… argumentative.'

'Yes I do know - go on.'

‘Well, I’m worried he’s going to say something when we go on holiday next week.’

‘What’s he going to say - what are you on about?’

‘OK - I think he’s going to say that he thinks Isabelle and I are having an affair’ and quickening his voice, he added, ‘Well, now, of course, you know that’s not true, don’t you?’

‘Of course, that’s ridiculous - she’s just your very close friend - I mean, you’re always messaging her, aren’t you? Her name is mentioned a lot.’

‘Exactly so - Bea, she’s just a very old friend of mine - and she’s very devoted to Étienne - she would never leave him. I’m coming to bed now - the others are still outside.’

While Martin was in the bathroom - Bea suddenly felt angry - an anger that had been simmering in her gut for some weeks. She privately suspected something might be going on with her husband and Isabelle - but she convinced herself nothing could possibly be going on. Or could it? She sat up in bed and waited for Martin to leave the bathroom.

As he got into his pyjamas - Bea was no longer tired. She looked straight at him. He recognised anger in her sharp eyes. Her voice was swift and deep -

‘You know Martin - you know… *if* I find out that something *is* going on with Isabelle - you do know that we’re over - do you hear me? It’s curtains for us - finished - finito. Oh…and I mean in your head - is she on your mind - do you desire her mentally? - That’s just as bad, Martin - it’s coveting someone else’s wife or adultery of the heart - I’m not having it - goodnight!’

‘Nothing’s going on - really.’

They slept very much on their sides of the large six-foot-wide bed - and had done for some time. This was a deeply unhappy marriage,

Bea thought, and she found it hard to sleep - she wondered what on earth made her eldest son suspect his father of having an affair - what did he see exactly? Why on earth would he say something like that to his father? It was one thing for her to have a mild suspicion, especially after the recent wedding, where little things were starting to add up and make her suspicious - but why would her son think something was going on? I'll see what happens on holiday, and I'll be prepared if Freddie says something.

On their summer holiday in too windy Crete - Bea was watching out for Freddie to say something - which he did - quite casually, late, on the last night of the holiday - it was said jokingly, and Bea kept cool.

'Dad - what's going on with you and Isabelle?'

Martin quickly changed the subject, and nothing more was said. The holiday was just about over, and they would be packing soon.

Bea was just relieved that her two sons were going with their father to Spa in a few weeks' time and would hopefully keep an eye on what he was getting up to. The gulf between them was huge, and the marriage was going through the most trying time. She tried to avoid him, and they spoke only about mundane things like what the cats were up to - or whether the ducks had been fed that day, or whether Rufus was doing his homework, etc. No controversial subjects - just boring everyday stuff. Their relationship was polite and dreary. They really didn't like each other at all.

When they returned home, Bea kept herself busy with the parish council meetings and her eBay shop - where she sold all sorts of items picked up from charity shops. It kept her mind off Martin. But she kept dwelling on the day Freddie had challenged his father about Isabelle. She wrote the date of the party, and while she wrote it down, she realised it was an important day. It was the Feast of Our Lady of

Mount Carmel[29] - of which she wore the brown Carmelite scapular, and of course, her grandmother was buried in the brown Carmelite habit, having been a lay Carmelite. The date had completely escaped her, but she now pondered its significance. She had been extremely close to her grandmother, who taught her so much of the Catholic Faith. She thought - was it possible that granny had something to do with Freddie challenging Martin? Quite possibly, especially as Freddie was her first great-grandchild - who she knew for the first six years of his life before dying of bone cancer. Bea remembered that Granny loved seeing Freddie and Cecily and, while she was still able, would draw their portraits.

---

[29] 16th July

Chapter 28 - Spa Grand Prix, Belgium 2022

By the time Martin, Freddie, and Rufus went to Spa over the August bank holiday, Beatrice was delighted that she would have some time alone in the house - she couldn't wait for Martin to leave, and she was supremely happy when they kissed goodbye. She was going to have four nights alone, just with the cats. Her youngest sister, Tessa, had invited her to a pool party on Saturday, but apart from that, she was free to do as she pleased. She couldn't remember the last time she was alone in the house - it must have been before the COVID nightmare.

Martin had given Bea and their sons brief details of the trip. They were going to drive to Knokke resort and meet Isabelle and her close friend Anne-Marie, and then they would drive to the Tra-Vail-Dur's home in Brussels in time for the evening. The Grand Prix was starting on Friday for three days, and then they would be returning home on the Monday of the Bank Holiday weekend. Martin had insured Freddie to drive his Aston Martin so that the driving could be shared. All fine and good thought, Bea. Martin won't be spending much time with Isabelle - and he'll be with the boys anyway.

When they arrived at sunny Knokke - Isabelle was with Anne-Marie, now a stout woman but with the same smiley sense of fun. Isabelle introduced her to Freddie and Rufus. After a few pleasantries, Anne-Marie apologised that she had to get back to Brussels to see her sick father, and so she waved goodbye. Isabelle offered to take the Charmers to a trendy eaterie she was sure the boys would like.

'That's a shame your friend had to leave so soon,' said Freddie, looking squarely at Isabelle.

'Her fader is quite ol and now very ill,' explained Isabelle, 'You will see her later at my ouse.'

Martin sent Bea a WhatsApp to say they had arrived safely and that it was glorious weather. He sent a group photo of Isabelle, Freddie, and Rufus at an eaterie on the beach. Bea wondered where

Anne-Marie was but didn't ask. She didn't want to know the answer. Her instinct told her that she wasn't there. Her instinct was right.

After their meal - Martin, the boys, and Isabelle meandered along the promenade of typical resort shops, and eventually, they came across an electric- bike hire shop. Isabelle thought the two boys might like to hire bikes, and they could even go across the Dutch border. Martin thought this an excellent idea and sorted out the bike hire. Isabelle was keen to show Martin the large nature reserve, and the boys would be bored with that.

As Martin was organising the bike hire, Freddie felt he and his brother had been 'had' - he thought to himself - Isabelle's planned this all along - pack Anne-Marie off, pack us off on bikes- so we can get to the Dutch border - how flipping exciting! 'So where will we find you when we finish?' He asked his father and Isabelle.

'We meet you ere at the bike shop - yes - is OK?' said Isabelle in her most dulcet voice.

'OK, we'll probably cycle in the nature reserve as well - I'm sure it's very beautiful, Isabelle - we may see you there,' said Freddie, looking straight at Isabelle. He was worried for his younger brother and what he might think of the situation. The bike hire was for the rest of the afternoon - that was a few hours to cycle around. A few hours for his father and Isabelle to be alone - her plans undoubtedly - and his. He could see that his father was very happy indeed.

Martin was totally in his element - he felt this was heaven - spending hours alone with the love of his life - his angel, his goddess, his Isabelle. He'd been looking forward to this for months. They walked slowly, close together, towards the nature reserve. Isabelle was wearing trainer shoes with wedges, tight white jeans, and a bright orange top - her ponytail swung from side to side, and she gave him sly, coquettish grins as he impressed her with his news.

'You'll be pleased to know that I have resumed my helicopter lessons, Isabelle.'

'You have - oh thas good Marrteen.' 'And how is Étienne?'

'OOff - ee work - always working.'

The pair were so engrossed with each other that they forgot the time. It was only when Martin's Apple Watch bleeped - that they turned around and walked towards the exit.

When it was time to return the bikes, the boys waited for some time before they saw Isabelle and Martin meandering towards them as though they had all the time in the world.

'You can drive us, Freddie,' said Martin, 'You need to get used to driving on the other side of the road.'

Isabelle travelled in the back of the car with Martin. Freddie wanted to drive fast, but the dulcet voice in the back told him to stop speeding.

'But my father always drives fast, Isabelle.'

'No, I don't,' said Martin sheepishly - Rufus started laughing. 'Liar'

'Is true, Marrteen- you drive fast?'

'No, not really, Isabelle - I'm a safe driver,' he joked.

Freddie parked at the chic designer home in Brussels, which the Tra-Vail-Durs had built from scratch - it was light, large, and modern and had a large lift to the basement. They were still living in the house while their new abode was being built at the castle. Étienne greeted them cordially, and Isabelle showed them to their rooms, where they unpacked before supper.

Supper was informal in the large, airy kitchen, and they discussed the arrangements for the early start to Spa the next morning.

'You can drive tomorrow, Freddie - I've decided not to come tomorrow - the first day's boring - not much goes on,' said Martin, trying hard to justify his absence while his eldest son gave him a knowing look.

'Oh,' said Freddie, a little taken aback.

'It's more fun for you and Rufus to go,' said Martin, 'I'm going to see what's been happening at the castle - how the renovations are going - you know - and see some of the family.'

'I see,' said Freddie, looking at Rufus. Rufus was very quiet - his French was not great, and he was naturally shy, so he didn't speak much.

Freddie was perturbed - this was meant to be a few days away with their father, and all he really wanted to do was spend it with Isabelle - he must have planned it this way. Something's not quite right, Freddie thought. Not right at all. What will my younger brother make of this? - It's not good - he's already worried something's going on between those two, and this type of behaviour fuels those thoughts. He's not setting a good example - it's all too covert and planned - as though the pair of them know exactly what they're doing.

Meanwhile, Bea had a long, relaxing bath and decided to have an early night without watching television - She decided to have a break from the television and read instead - It was going to be a quiet time of not doing very much - with nice soothing music to listen to. It was also a break from cooking - she had planned to have easy meals like baked potatoes and cheese or canned tuna. She was also looking forward to a 4-day detox from wine. The Charmers were not alcoholics, but they were big wine drinkers.

When she went to bed, she couldn't sleep - it got later and later and into the small hours, and no sleep came. The nightmare of nightmares was about to begin.

She felt an inexplicable force grip her inside of indescribable agony, a living nightmare of hideousness - a searing pain in her heart - like daggers stabbing all night long - a horrible dark night of the soul - the sixth sense feeling that something monstrous was going on - something grotesque - horrendous shattering devastating crushing. Tears began to flow as she realised the shattered state of her marriage.

Bea was still wide awake when the birds tweeted outside - and she hadn't slept at all - she felt a desolation never felt before - a tortuous unhappiness that had been simmering below the surface for the last few years - she knew her marriage was in desperate trouble. The next few days alone terrified her - freaked her out. She had her sister's lunch party to look forward to - *anything* to keep her mind off her situation. She began to pray for guidance.

'God, what is wrong with this marriage - please help me in my dark hour - what must I do?'

On Friday morning, Freddie sent photos of Spa to the family via WhatsApp - he had driven Rufus early so that they could get the full atmosphere of the Grand Prix. Martin also sent photos to the family group - of Isabelle and Étienne and various friends - looking like a group outing in a park. Bea concluded that Martin was not with his sons at Spa. Of course, he wasn't - any excuse to be with blooming flipping Isabelle. Vomit vomit, she thought.

'Oh, so is it just you two at Spa?' asked Bea on the family WhatsApp group, 'Martin must have found more interesting things to do then.' No response to my sarcasm, she thought. Later on, Martin sent a photo of a statue of Our Lady in the castle chapel. 'You'll approve of this, Bea.'

Bea felt a seething anger thinking - Martin never ever went into Catholic chapels - let alone take pictures of statues - he should be at Spa with the boys - what's he blinking up to - undoubtedly worshipping that silky voice and taking pictures of religious statues!? - I feel sick, sick, sick.

‘Dear God - what’s happening to me - why do I feel so dreadful? - what’s going on? Please help me.’

A thought came into Bea’s head - maybe we should go to marriage counselling - maybe we’ve hit rock bottom, and this is what we have to do. I’ll do some research online.

While researching marriage counselling - she stumbled on “Relate” - the largest relationship counselling organisation in the UK. But something struck her on its home page. There was an article titled - “Should I be Worried if My Partner Has a Very Close Friendship with Someone of the Opposite Sex?” Her insides tightened as she forced herself to read it.

What Bea discovered shocked her as she realised that what the article said was everything she was experiencing in her marriage. It was like a light bulb moment for her. This article was about Martin and Isabelle - totally. It would appear that they were having what was termed an “emotional affair” - an affair of the heart or mental affair. Bea had never heard of this before - although Martin had mentioned to her a long time ago that colleagues in his office spoke of mental affairs - at the time, Bea thought how very strange. She strained back to try and remember what Martin had asked her decades ago, ‘Have you heard of mental affairs, Bea?’ ‘How absurd, Martin - no, I haven’t - why?’

‘Just some colleagues at the office were discussing it.’ ‘Well, I think it sounds ridiculous - completely mad.’ Bea felt rather ill as she remembered all the little incidents over the last few years - that trembling love voicemail sent by mistake - that screenshot of Martin complaining about her to Isabelle. These should have been red flags - she felt naive, stupid and deeply hurt - why hadn’t she properly addressed the relationship between her husband and Isabelle. Yes he messaged her a lot and her name popped up often in their family conversations. That seating plan at the daughter’s wedding - putting him next to her - mother of the bride for goodness sake. Bea was not at all happy with this friendship - it felt wrong and she felt violated and betrayed. How dare they? How dare Isabelle come crying to Martin just because Étienne wasn't being kind to her, and she knowing full well that Martin was like putty in her hands - and always was. That dulcet voice - Martin so enraptured by everything she did and said. Even the children noticed. Bea now regarded Isabelle as an appalling friend and more like a wolf in sheep's clothing or a crafty vixen. It explained why she and Martin were having such a torrid marriage these last few years. And of course - it was so easy for them, with smartphones and WhatsApp.

Bea spent another sleepless night of racing thoughts - of welling anger. She thanked God she was out for lunch the next day. The robot mower was making soft rumbling noises as it made its way to the lawn below the bedroom window, its headlights casting shadows on the ceiling - white lines moving in the dead of night.

The next day was a glorious late August day and Bea was tired after another tormenting night - she tried to get some sleep late morning as she would need some energy to see her sister Tessa's family and others they had invited to their barbecue pool party.

Bea had a long bath to try and calm her shattered nerves. She slowly chose a summer dress to wear - in a cheerful colour. She didn't feel cheerful. She skipped breakfast having lost her appetite, fed the cats and ducks and then set off in the Golf for the party.

The party was noisy and a day of many moving parts - small children shouting and jumping in the pool, food being taken to the barbecue and all taking turns to turn the steaks and sausages over - more guests arriving with small children, large blonde dogs looking for scraps, children climbing the tree house, then onto the trampoline, the swing - then a football game - so much noise thought Bea - so much noise. Bea was content to sit and watch the children in the pool and wear dark glasses and hat - she liked having her mind on other things than her troubled marriage. A couple sat with their wriggling baby nearby trying to shield him from the strong sun.

Tessa told everyone to help themselves with food and drink. Bea, having lost her appetite, took a small amount, which Tessa noticed, 'Not on a diet, are you, Bea?'

'No no - just lost my appetite - haven't been sleeping well lately' in flat tones.

'Oh - why's that?'

'Let me just sit down with my plate.'

Tessa went to fetch some children on the trampoline and gee up some adults who were loitering in another part of the garden.

'Lunch is ready - do come.'

Bea sat with some of her nieces and nephews and asked them questions while they ate quickly - wanting to swim again soon. Tessa was up and down like a yo yo with requests for this that or the other - a child wanted a particular drink - could the baby have some water as it wasn't allowed sugary drinks - a dog had just picked up the football puncturing it - was there another ball?

Eventually, Tessa sat down and wanted to know what Bea was up to while Martin and Rufus were away. Amid the noise in the pool and garden, Bea seized the moment quickly - whispering quickly, 'Freddie thinks Martin might be having an emotional affair with Isabelle.' Tessa took off her sunglasses and whispered, 'What! Are you serious?'

'The boys both see him texting her a lot at events - and I've been a bit suspicious for a while now - I ignored several red flags a few years ago - so naive it's unbelievable - I can't quite believe how thick I've been - for soooo long. I've been unhappy since the lockdowns - I think that's when it all started - that's when things started going wrong for us.'

'Golly - I'm shocked - have you asked him?'

'No. I've read an article on Relate about emotional affairs - and his behaviour fits the description - I'm going to show him the article when he gets home - I can't sleep - I'm so distressed.'

'Oh Bea I'm so sorry - you must feel awful - he's with her now isn't he?' 'Yes they're staying with her plus her husband.'

'Have you told anyone else?'

'No. Just you. I need to ask him on Monday.' 'OK, I won't mention it to anyone.'

'Thanks - I needed to tell someone as it's been a weight on me since they left for Spa - I feel a bit better.'

Tessa's daughter was calling her from the kitchen. Bea got up with Tessa and walked to the garden and watched her nieces and nephews in the tree house.

'I'm going to have an ice cream Bea' squeaked a little voice from the tree house.

'What flavour do you like?' 'Strawberry.'

Another 2 nights to go thought Bea as teas and coffees were being served. I hope I can sleep better now that I've confided in a family member.

The party was winding down, guests gradually leaving - Bea left and promised Tessa she would keep her posted.

Chapter 29 - Hell Hath No Fury

The days leading up to Martin's return home felt very long. Bea realised that she had missed him dreadfully but she needed to be calm and collected. Father and son arrived quite late on the Monday evening - laden with Martin's favourite Belgian chocolate bars.

'Looks like you had a fun time,' she said quietly.

Martin took Bea in his arms, kissed and embraced her - while noticing her reddened eyes from crying.

'We did indeed have a great time - didn't we, Rufus?' 'Oh yes - brilliant.'

After a simple supper, Rufus went to his virtual racing game in the annexe, while Martin opened a bottle of wine and poured out two glasses while Bea went to the winter sitting room.

'I need to speak to you seriously, and I'm going to get to the point, Martin - we've been having big problems, haven't we - and I think I may know the root cause - you know I haven't slept properly since you left - something extraordinary happened to me the first night - it was like a supernatural sign telling me to wake up.'

'What Beatrice?'

'Surely you know we haven't been getting along for a few years now?' 'I do know that yes.'

'Well I looked up marriage counselling - I think we really need counselling - but I came across an article which describes you and Isabelle.'

'We don't need counselling Bea - what are you on about?'

'Please can you just read this article on the Relate website - it's on the big computer in the study.'

Martin sighed and slowly went to read the article. 'Well I'm afraid I don't agree with Relate.'

'It says you should be transparent and show all the messaging between you and Isabelle.'

'I'm sorry but I'm not doing that' said a defiant Martin.

'Well, I'm sorry, Martin, but we need counselling - I'm not going to stay unhappy for the rest of the marriage when I think I know the root cause of all this. You're having an emotional affair with Isabelle…according to that article.'

'No I'm not - she's just a dear friend of mine.'

'I disagree - it all seems to tie in with the lockdowns - we didn't get on, and you seemed to be messaging her a lot.' Bea could feel anger welling up inside as she tried to contain her anger and her voice rising. 'That love voice message - that screenshot - Freddie's suspicions - these were all red flags, and I ignored them all.'

'All right all right - if that's what Relate say - then yes I am - in their opinion - but I don't agree with them.'

Bea covered her face in her hands and took a deep breath - then she ran around in circles around the coffee table and started hyperventilating - before falling onto the sofa and curling up like a small child. Martin came and held her hand, looking concerned, while in a clenched voice, Bea said, 'When did it all start - truth, please?' After a long pause Martin said.

'Soon after my second heart op. It was a life-changing experience, and I re-evaluated my life and who were the most important people in my life.'

'What!!? But that's nearly six years ago - what, so you dropped most of your friends and family - I mean, you stopped talking to me properly years ago because she, Isabelle's your one true friend now?'

‘She is, yes - but we got very close when lockdown started, and we had a lot of time - I didn’t like you, and you didn’t like me.’

Bea was trying desperately not to be hysterical but failing, ‘Why Martin, why did it start - what have I done wrong? It’s all my fault - I wasn’t nice to you - I ignored you - oh dear - sorry, so sorry, my fault - it’s earth-shattering - it’s too awful. This is just horrendous. What did I do wrong?’

‘OK - you and I disagree about a lot of issues… like Brexit, COVID vaccines, politics - you know…so I got close to Isabelle - we supported each other while we were both having marital difficulties.’

‘What else?’ Bea stood up and walked around the room - trying not to hyperventilate.

‘Look, Bea, you told me God was first in your life - so Isabelle…well..erm..she became first in my life.’

Bea waved her arms around in frustration, ‘But that’s absurd, Martin - God is above everyone - HE made us. HE gave me the vocation to marry you! - How can you possibly compare Isabelle to God!- are you in your right mind - or did you just want an excuse to idolise her - that’s it, isn’t it? - any excuse to worship your goddess. What else? ‘You’ve been banging on about moving house.’

‘Don’t I have any say in moving house - this is my house too you know, I supervised all the renovations and the builders while you worked 12 hours a day - oh that’s pathetic Martin - what else?’

‘You have absolutely no interest in my garden…or my hobbies.’
‘When you married me, you knew I had no interest in gardening - I don’t like you flying helicopters as I think they’re dangerous, and I don’t like flying, you’re right. But hang on a minute - you don’t take any interest in my hobbies - and you’re dismissive over my religion - what else, Martin?’

‘Let’s face it, Bea - you’re not particularly affectionate towards me - you never say I love you.’

Bea was so angry now that she was beside herself with rage.

'But Martin- you've treated me like "wham bang thank you mam" ADMIT IT!'

'OK- I can see your point - let's change that now.'

Martin went to pour out 2 large glasses of wine, Bea was weeping silently. 'Does her husband know about this about her being disloyal towards him?'

'Yes he's fine- he's a workaholic so he's got other priorities.'

'As you won't show the messages we need counselling - I'm not happy with this situation and I won't put up with it - I'm dropping her as a friend and I don't want to see her again - in fact she's not welcome here.'

'She's done nothing wrong.'

'She's stolen your emotional energy, which was meant for ME - your wife- instead, she used you as she knows you'll do anything for her.' 'You don't own me, and I don't like this jealousy, Bea!'

'How dare you! Of course, I don't own you, but you are my husband, and our marriage vows state that we're faithful to each other while we live- to the exclusion of all others.'

'Really?- Oh, I didn't know that you couldn't have emotional relationships with other women- Look, nothing physical has happened, so I disagree with what Relate says. Look - admittedly…it is an unusual situation -OK, I can see that it is quite unusual - this friendship.'

'Martin -it's actually worse than a physical affair. But hang on - you say nothing physical happened - yet you spent a lot of time alone - I'm thinking back to all those occasions -oh yes when you carefully explained why Isabelle had to accompany you to get petrol -your woodland walks - are you sure you're telling me the truth? OK -even if it is platonic, the emotional attachment is stronger than the physical

- I've been researching it while you were in Spa. And as your wife, I have every right to be jealous of any extremely close woman friend of yours -in fact, I don't know anyone who has this situation in their marriage.'

Martin got up angrily from the sofa, and in a deep voice, he said clearly and loudly, 'I love her, I love her, I can't help it, it's in my heart!' And with that, he went outside for a few minutes and came back to find Bea slumped on an armchair, muttering to herself silently.

'Well -that's it then -there's no possible way I can stay with a man who's clearly desperately in love with another woman - no possible way - so when Rufus has finished his exams - I will be asking you for a formal separation -it's the only thing a Catholic is allowed to do in this situation. I can never ever remarry while you're still alive, and I will always be married to you. There's no way I'll put up with this - I'm not being second best. You know -I feel like Princess Diana when she said Camilla was the third person in the marriage. And I suppose you've told her you to love her?'

'Yes.'

'What?!!!! -You said those 3 words to a woman who is neither your wife, your sister, your mother or your daughter! How blinking dare you! And does she reciprocate?'

'Er..No'

'Not verbally perhaps, but Martin - her behaviour suggests to me that she does reciprocate - I mean actions speak louder than words, - OK so what would you have done if she had declared her love to you?'

'I honestly don't know - look, you asked for the truth, so I'm telling you the truth - look, of course, I'm not leaving you, and there's no way she would ever leave Étienne and give up her title - look, I had a mad moment of fantasy and the reality - look I'm not giving up Isabelle for....Sorry, I mean I'm not giving you up for Isabelle' sighing in frustration at the Freudian slip and raising his eyes upwards. Bea's eyes glittered as she said, 'Freudian slip, Martin - Freudian slip. But this is even worse than I thought - I mean, if she doesn't feel the same way - then she's been leading you on, and you just adore the thrill of the chase, don't you - I mean, how many times did she turn you down as teenagers - was it twice? It's just too exciting to see if you can get her in the end like the knight in shining armour rescuing Isabelle at the castle from her blooming awful husband - fricking heck Martin it's La La land - completely and utterly insane madness!'

'Look Bea - what I meant was that I love her as a dear friend - not as a lover.'

'Sorry, Martin, but every woman in the world knows what those three words mean - including Isabelle.'

'No... she knew what I meant.'

'Look, you just told me you loved her - so are you now changing your mind to say you love her as a friend only? - And by the way, I don't believe you...in that case, you should tell her what you meant - otherwise, you're leading her on - like a duplicitous cad.'

'OK, I will tell her...in my own time, Bea.'

They heard the front door open and Rufus came in, and stopped their arguments. They drank some more wine before going to bed. Bea was emotionally charged - emotionally shattered - stressed out beyond belief - this was her whole world caving in - she never thought this could happen to her, she thought maybe I'm being arrogant to think he wouldn't fall for another woman - but I'm married to him - I've obeyed the marriage vows and I expected him to. He never got over that Isabelle - I should never have married a man who was still hung up over someone else. My mistake. I'm paying for it now.

In bed, Martin embraced Bea tenderly, who lay sobbing.

'I think we should sleep in separate bedrooms,' said Bea. 'No - I've missed you too much - let's keep talking - we've never talked so much in years.'

'We really need counselling, Martin.' 'OK… I'll consider it.'

'The next 10 months are crucial for Rufus - he's got his GCSEs next year - we need to appear totally normal with him while we go to counselling - I don't want him worried about us.'

'OK'

Bea woke up at 5 a.m. in a searing rage - Martin was sound asleep. Bea, getting out of bed, in a loud whisper, 'Hell hath no fury - hell hath no fury, Martin! Where was Isabelle when you came out of the hospital, Martin - who helped you in the loo - who looked after your needs for months after your operation - and that cunning Isabelle with her emotional outbursts and bouncing heart emojis on the hospital WhatsApp group?'

Martin was shocked at this outburst and lay silent, looking out of the window while Bea went to make her morning tea and let the cats in.

Bea got back into bed with her mug of tea. Furla jumped onto the end of the bed.

'How did this, you know, this thing with Isabelle manifest itself?' 'Oh…well, we had a morning call to talk about our plans for the day, and then we spoke in the evenings about how our days went.'

'Crikey - you sound like a married couple - so presumably you rang each other, and you must have done the calls secretly as you were never in the house when you or she rang - funny that - did you both plan the timings so I wouldn't be within earshot? That's so sneaky, isn't it - well, people having affairs tend to hide their activities, and you 2 were the same - if it was all so innocent, then why didn't you ring each other in the house? I'll tell you why…you both knew you were out of order discussing your marital problems with each other - and that is how 99% of all affairs begin.'

Martin didn't say a word. He stared blankly outside. Fendi jumped on the bed and got under the duvet.

Over the next days and weeks - Bea and Martin had an intense love hate relationship - they re-connected and talked a lot - they experienced a honeymoon type period. Then Bea would suddenly flare up when she got anxious about their situation - she found herself taking herbal anti-anxiety pills, and she started writing profusely - about the past, as it was cathartic. She wrote in her study. Martin stood at her study door one day looking quizzically at her.

'I'm writing about you and Isabelle - it's helping me cope - I'm starting from the beginning and I remember everything you told me about her - right from the day I met you as a totally naive girl of 18 at that tea party in our first week at Exeter.'

'I see - is it a character assassination? - thanks a lot.'

'No - it's not a character assassination - and you can read it if you like - I may write a novel based on it, a most extraordinary love story spanning over 40 years,' looking up and noticing his discomfort.

'I don't think I'll like it.'

'Oh don't worry - I'll change the names and appearances of the main characters - I was thinking of calling you Matthias - a good solid name and I think may call Isabelle - Pascha - and so forth', as she gazed into his still beautiful eyes and slightly pursed rosebud lips.

Bea began a new daily habit - that of praying for a quarter of an hour in the morning to ask God what to do. A big decision she made was to stop being a supply teaching assistant - which she regarded as a glorified babysitter role - much of the time dealing with challenging children. She kept her role as a parish counsellor as that was interesting.

Chapter 30 - Counselling

Bea booked some counselling sessions with Relate, but as they were very busy, it was a few weeks of waiting for the next available slot. While they waited, Bea ordered a book written by the famous marriage counsellor Zelda West-Meads, who used to write for YOU magazine in the Mail on Sunday. It was published in 2016, and in it, the author demonstrates why infidelity is on the increase. The book had a chapter called "The Internet and Affairs."[30] This was the chapter Bea wanted to read.

Zelda West Meads, in her experience as a marriage counsellor, saw that the internet was fuelling adultery and that if you wouldn't be happy for your partner to see your messages or texts from a very close friend, then you were having an emotional affair. She says - "Even if it isn't yet physically consummated, there's an emotional intensity many marriages no longer have. The constant to-ing and fro-ing of messages is seductive. Even more electric is the experience of re-connecting with your first love online". Bea thought this was Martin and Isabelle to a T.

It was clear as daylight to Bea, that with the advent of smartphones[31] (mini computers), and WhatsApp - the most popular messaging platform worldwide, the emotional affair with Isabelle was very easy to have, and was probably addictive[32]. WhatsApp offers free text, voice and video services, and Isabelle was sending 100s of photos (mostly of herself) at the click of a button. Studies have found that men are more affected by visual images than women.

30 "To Love, Honour and Betray - Why Affairs Happen and How to Survive them"

31 The first Apple smart phone, aka the iPhone, started in 2007.

32 WhatsApp became the most popular messaging application in 2015, with 2 billion users by 2020.

The day for the counselling session arrived - via Zoom, and Martin was twitchy - he was dreading it. When the counselling session started - the counsellor wanted to hear each person speak in turn, so it was Bea who spoke first.

Bea explained that up until a few years ago, their marriage was pretty good but went wrong 2-3 years ago when they didn't get on - that Martin had a very intense friendship with a woman he fell in love with 42 years ago - who turned him down twice as a teenager and again recently. This deep friendship intensified after his life-changing heart operation when they started a WhatsApp relationship - and Martin didn't want to show Bea the messages or photos. Bea said that if it hadn't been for her two sons being worried about the WhatsApps, she would not have kicked up a fuss. However, she did feel uncomfortable in Isabelle and Martin's presence, knowing that something didn't feel quite right - like a 6th sense. Bea also mentioned the mistaken love voice message sent to her in error. Bea told the counsellor that she refused to see Isabelle again as she felt she and Étienne were unwittingly enabling their little 'frissons.'

It was now Martin's turn to speak.

'Well, I can't really argue - what Beatrice says is true.'

The counsellor asked Martin if he was prepared to show the messages.

'No, I don't see why I should.' The counsellor was silent for a few seconds and then said in a low voice, 'Well, in that case - you're having an emotional affair.'

'Well, you see, I disagree with Relate - but OK, I see what you're saying.'

Bea looked at Martin to see his reaction at hearing the experienced counsellor confirm what she had been saying for weeks - he had a slightly reddened palour - although it might have been the Zoom camera, which made people look unnatural - Bea felt.

The counsellor mentioned that it was possible to be addicted to another person and this could be a possibility in Martin's case. And like alcoholics the addicted person had to want to be 'cured' of their addiction.

After some individual counselling sessions a few weeks later - Martin reluctantly agreed to show the messages as the counsellor told him that if he didn't, then he was continuing the affair. He was just relieved that his true feelings weren't on WhatsApp; they were either vocal (or not recorded), or written down in a secure place. Bea realised that the secret phone calls between Isabelle and Martin would forever remain a mystery as these were always taken elsewhere at pre-arranged times.

The Charmers decided mutually that no more counselling was needed. Bea was satisfied with the outcome - she realised she loved Martin and the thought of separating for an indeterminate period of time, whilst possibly necessary, was a horrible outcome - she hated the thought of living alone. But she knew she had to be prepared to separate if things got worse.

Throughout her crisis, Bea thanked God for all her immediate family and her close friends. They were all supportive and thought she was doing the right thing regarding the counselling, but some were concerned that she was happy for Martin and Isabelle to carry on communicating- was he going to visit her alone - would he be inviting her over? Tessa - her feisty younger sister, said when they next met, 'surely they should stop all contact Bea - how can you be happy knowing that the counsellor said it was a mental affair - and yet they're still…you know….continuing…HE…LLO!?' Janine in America felt the same way and continually checked in via WhatsApp to see how things were going.

'I've seen some of the messages - quite bland really - she's sent him over a 1000 photos though - I mean she's his top person on his WhatsApp data thing - I haven't looked at the photos - just glanced at some - mostly of her really, the odd risqué one, I mean I didn't know she was quite so vain - don't narcissists send photos of themselves?'

'Well, I don't think I'd be happy if that were me - that's all, Bea.' 'Look - they know I won't see her again, so I think it'll be difficult for them to meet up - if he goes alone, he'll be a gooseberry as she's always with her husband. I can't imagine that the husband will want him to go there alone - although he may not care - I have no idea really what Étienne thinks.' 'Bea - do you actually love Martin?'

'Yes I do….but I did fall out of love with him doing the lockdown - we both did. It would be much easier if I didn't.'

'Well, we'll have a nice break in the Isle of Wight soon.'

Bea went on a walking holiday to the Isle of Wight with her sisters soon after the counselling was over - and Martin used the time alone to find out if it was possible to go to Brussells for the day. He looked at return flights to Brussels and the Eurostar and concluded that it wasn't feasible. He thought it probably wouldn't look right if he stayed the night on his own and he had to be home for Rufus anyway. He was just happy to carry on with the special friendship with Isabelle - who was still the most important person in his life - or possibly equal to Bea - but he wasn't quite sure who. He loved them both.

Bea found out about his potential trips to Brussells as she looked up the search history bar on the family computer, which showed him searching for return flights and the Eurostar. When she asked him if he was going there he said it wasn't feasible to do a day trip.

One day while he was in the field taking his cats for their daily walk - he thought he had better tell Isabelle what was going on - she knew that Bea had unfriended her on Facebook and she wasn't going to try and contact her.

'We've had the counselling Isabelle - all is OK but I need to explain something to you.'

'Wat is it Marrteen?' Said the dulcet voice he loved so much.

'Well do you remember when I told you that er… em….I loved you - remember that it was during ghastly lockdown, and things were bad here?

'Of course, I remember - yes, for sure.' 'Well, I meant it as a friend, Isabelle.'

Isabelle laughed. She had a strong suspicion that Beatrice had made him do this. Of course she didn't believe him! She still had a hold over him and she knew it.

'Oh…Is OK Marrteen - is OK - I know, I know.'

'And are all the family well Isabelle?' Asked Martin.

'Is OK - some problems yes - but now I sink all good.'

'I got your email from the American client. I'll do that translation for you later.'

'Oh, sooo kind Marrteen so chouette.' 'It's all my pleasure Isabelle.'

When Bea returned after the Isle of Wight trip - all seemed fine between them - they got on very well and they were happy - they arranged to go away for the odd weekend and do more activities together - they were still in a honeymoon phase and Martin had agreed that maybe it was time to sell the house and buy a smaller home. He also re-connected with some old friends, ones he had 'dropped' temporarily after his heart operation.

Chapter 31 - The Notebooks

It was December and Beatrice and Martin were getting on very well - he still messaged Isabelle and was being transparent about showing the messages - Bea found it mildly irritating but she had agreed it was OK, and most of the time she really didn't want to see the messages. Bea believed him when he told her he had explained to Isabelle what he meant when he said he loved her. He knew Isabelle was never going to be Bea's friend - which he was extremely sad about. He was still trying to work out a way they could see their Belgian friends, but it was a bit tricky with Bea's intense dislike of Isabelle.

Martin's advisory role at a German bank came to a shuddering halt one day when the top dog announced he was shutting part of the business down and all his colleagues were told to pack up and leave the premises - in true City style. Martin decided he would no longer work for a bank which behaved in this way, and he packed his stuff away too. It was the end of an era.

'How awful to sack all those new recruits too' said Bea when she heard the news.

'Appalling I agree - I won't be going back in any capacity now.'
'Won't you miss the City though?'

'Yes I think I will - I may look for some non-exec roles after Christmas.'

As Martin emptied his work belongings he held up an ancient looking address book - which he had had since his very first job at Lazards in 1984. The spine was weak and pages were falling out.

'All these contact details I had - all in this blue book - before Blackberrys came along.'

'Are you keeping all that stuff' said Bea.

'Yes - it's a bit of history' as he neatly put some unused looking notebooks in a pile on the family computer desk.

'I'm going up to meet the team for lunch soon - to find out how they're all coping with being kicked out of the bank - see what their plans are.'

Bea was getting on with her faction[33] novel and wanted to get it finished before the school summer holidays - she set herself a word target of 10,000 words a month - she tried to write when Martin was busy with other activities - she knew it annoyed him.

One day when Martin was having a helicopter lesson she went to do some research on the family iMac in the study and her eyes rested on 2 lovely blue notebooks in a pile - Beatrice had a love for stationary - any stationary, especially notebooks. She had a notebook for the weekly menu planning, a notebook for jotting ideas down in her bag, a notebook by the sofa and a Christmas notebook. She looked at the notebooks on the pile and thought they looked rather unused. She thought - I wonder if I can use those notebooks for my writing - I'll just check them to make sure there isn't anything important in them before I use them.

She picked up one notebook and opened it - it had a fairly random list of business notes, numbers, and Zoom meeting info - only a few pages were written in an otherwise blank notebook. As she read through the notes, she saw a random sentence, and she read it twice - before her chest tightened and she felt her heart start to pump quickly. She covered her mouth in disbelief at what she read. It said,

She is probably the most wonderful human being that has ever been alive.

---

[33] A combination of facts and fiction.

“Instinctively, she knew this was referring to Isabelle. She carried on reading, and on the next page of notes - there was another random sentence - and by now, Bea was shivering with horror at what she was reading.

Miss her voice so much. Need to speak to her. She is my love of my life.

Bea thought this was appalling - when did he write all this? She noticed on one page that he had written that Belgium was fully vaccinated - so Bea looked up this information and found out that herd immunity had been achieved by August 2021. She deduced that these notes must have been written around then - which would have been after the Belgians’ visit that summer.

Bea carried on reading the notes and saw yet more random hidden sentences, one of which said,

I wonder why she is so busy - not helpful - want to be with her again. She is just so lovely.

By now Bea was beside herself with rage and rocking backwards and forwards in the chair grasping her shoulders. She tore the pages out and carefully put them somewhere safe. Then she took the other notebook and only 2 pages had been written on. She read it and there was information about Isabelle’s family but a sentence in smaller writing said.

Do you know how much I love you? Too too much.

What struck Bea as she was shaking and hyperventilating, bitter tears streaming down, while tearing out the page - was the intensity of feelings her husband had for Isabelle. It was now clear to Bea - the grotesque reality that her husband was in love with another woman - his first love - the love he never got over - it was just too monstrous - and was probably in love with her for many many years. The little hidden sentences were so terribly profound that she almost compared their intensity to the last sayings of Jesus on the cross. You could not make this up! She thought. Here was laid bare her husband's real thoughts about Isabelle - Bea felt her world was breaking apart - like shattered glass everywhere.

It was so bad, she tried to imagine worse situations that could happen to her - she picked up her notebook and jotted things that would be worse than her husband being in love with another woman. She thought this would make her feel not so bad.

1) Dying in a state of unrepentant mortal sin and going to Hell forever
2) Losing a child
3) Being eaten alive by a shark
4) Being attacked by an axe murderer
5) Being thrown into a container of boiling oil
6) Being thrown off a cliff
7) Being burnt alive

It didn't make her feel better.

As she carefully photocopied the pages - then put the originals in a safe place she felt she no longer knew her husband - these secret thoughts so deep and profound - she wondered if he ever felt like that about her - it was earth shattering - how long had he had these feelings she wondered - was it since the heart operation or years before, or was it just during the Covid lockdowns - did he still feel this way - would he tell Bea if she asked - would he tell the truth or would he wriggle out of it in clever lawyer style - his law degree gave him an edge with words - she knew - often when arguing with him he picked her up on some point - just like a lawyer. These hidden sentences were that of a tortured soul - had he told her Viscountness any of this or was it because she had turned him down - a third time - all these questions Bea had.

She was so upset she barely managed to WhatsApp Martin about the love sentences in 2 notebooks - and a few minutes later he rang her up in panic mode. He did not deny the sentences were about

Isabelle - even though Isabelle's name was not specifically mentioned.

'Bea - they're just doodles - ages ago - tear them up, please.' Bea shouted, 'THEY AREN'T DOODLES, MARTIN - THEY ARE SOME OF THE MOST PROFOUND FEELINGS I'VE EVER READ - I CAN'T GO ON LIKE THIS - IF YOU LOVE ANOTHER WOMAN, I'M OFF.'

'Please, Bea, I'm sorry - I love you - please wait til I get home.' 'CAN'T FACE YOU GO AWAY.'

Martin returned home later and Bea was silent - in a heap. He looked worried and was walking in short steps. She handed him the photocopies and asked him to read them out loud.

'Read each one please - so I can hear.'

'But you're the love of my life,' he pleaded unconvincingly, 'I love you.' 'You're just saying that - I don't believe you anymore - the way you hid those in your work notes - all like a cryptic puzzle.'

Martin read the sentences out quickly and promptly tore the pages up into little pieces.

'Look that was all in the past.'

Bea grabbed a Paul Smith scarf and started whipping the sofa with it to vent her anger. The fact they were 'in the past' was not the point - whether they were in the past or in the present - it was the horrible fact they were ever written at all - and in such a devious way - hiding them in other notes so as not to be discovered.

'You haven't been honest with me about your true feelings towards her, have you - how can I trust you to tell the truth?' And Bea hammered the scarf on the sofa, which made her breathless. 'Look, it was during the lockdown - you know we had a bad patch.'

Bea gave him her hardest, angriest, glitteriest look she could muster and thrashed the scarf on the sofa, 'The fact you wrote these about another woman is crushing me - the fact it's in the past, so you say, is totally irrelevant - how do I know you no longer think of her in this way?'

'You shouldn't have looked in the books.'

'They were on the family desk - I wanted to see if they could be used for my writing and I thought I'd better check there was nothing important in them before I used them.'

Martin was sitting silently on the opposite sofa - he was shocked at the ferocity with which the scarf was being thrashed against a sofa. Breathlessly, she asked, 'Martin - Martin…can I just ask you to have some time out from Isabelle for a month - do you think you can manage that? Just a month - you should be concentrating on us - not being addicted to her all the time - you know - you're addicted to me physically and addicted to her Viscountness emotionally - that's so not right, Martin.'

'OK… I'll do what you ask. I'm sorry.'

Bea thought to herself - what happens when the month is up - will he be able stick by the agreement - is his addiction that strong? Can I bear this friendship to still carry on?

'Just promise me Bea - you won't ever show those things to Isabelle will you? - it makes me look so pathetic.'

Bea thought to herself - why on earth would I show a narcissistic vain woman those sentences? - It would only make her more conceited!

'I won't show them to her.'

After a period of reflection and Bea had managed to calm down, she looked sadly at Martin, who also had a sad expression, 'You know - none of this had to happen, did it? I mean if you hadn't had this private relationship with her - we could have still been friends with them as a couple - you both ruined it - now I won't see her again. You should have included Étienne and me on your WhatsApps. Remember Martin your behaviour nearly ruined our friendship with our other friends - you overstepped the mark then. I mean there's no comparison with what's been going on with her over the Channel, but…I hope you get the picture. It's a shame as I like Étienne - but then again - if he'd paid more attention to his wife, she wouldn't have come crying to you, would she, causing you to fall hopelessly in love with her? So I'm afraid I'm not terribly keen on him anymore - actually, I don't want to see them again.'

Chapter 32 - The Burst Pipe

Martin having agreed not to contact Isabelle for a month - was finding it excruciatingly hard. He was addicted to her emotionally and he was suffering. Badly. Bea noticed. It was the time between Christmas and New Year. Bea saw his sad face one evening in the winter sitting room and made an observation. Their daughter was with them and Bea had kept her updated on things.

'You look as unhappy as I feel' said Bea getting up to give Rufus his weekly catechism lesson in the study. They had stopped going to Mass regularly as Bea didn't think Francis was a true pope and therefore she joined the growing sedevacantist movement in the UK - of which there was a quarterly mass in Surrey, with a very elderly but sprightly priest.

Cecily went to sit by the wood burner so that she could chat quietly with her father. In low tones, she said, 'Dad - I honestly think you should end this friendship with Isabelle - you clearly have feelings for her, and it's just making things worse for Mum.'

'I can't - she means too much to me.'

'Dad - if you can't live without her - well you know what mum might do don't you - do you really want that?'

'Of course I don't Cecily - but it simply, it simply isn't black and white', while he got up and poured another glass of very decent red wine - one of his special Christmas wines.

Bea finished the lesson and came in to the middle of the conversation while Cecily went to get ready for bed.

'Martin - I know you're unhappy about the 'no contact' with her - I have to be compassionate if you're addicted to her.'

'There's nothing going on with her - she's just a friend.'

'But we keep going over and over this again, Martin - you have proved time and time again that you have a habit of falling in love with her - how does that make me feel? Blinking awful and second best.'

'I know' he said with extraordinary anguish, and Bea thought he was holding back tears.

'OK - I can't stop you - go ahead - I'll just have to trust you, won't I.' 'Thaaaank Youuuuu- I think... I think you may have saved the...marriage...I love you.'

Bea thought that her husband was addicted to Isabelle - it was as though they had an unbreakable bond - of human bondage, made possible in the digital age of smartphones and WhatsApp.

One cold January morning Martin set of for a 2-day shoot in Devon. He was leaving at 8.30 sharp. As he was getting ready to go, one of the gardeners came running up from the pool area and told Matin that water was gushing into the shower area - and that it looked like a burst pipe. Martin ran up to ask Bea to contact a plumber to come and sort it, as it was an emergency, and he had to leave on time. He was extremely agitated about leaving on time.

As he was about to drive away - Bea wanted to know the contact details of the pool man - as he may know where the stopcock was. She ran out in her dressing gown and as she opened the car door - Martin's mobile was ringing.

'What's the number of the pool man?' 'Oh that's Isabelle ringing.'

Bea lost the plot - she looked in horror at him - daggers shooting out of her eyeballs and ran to the house. Martin stopped the car and ran after her.

'Flipping heck - that's why you had to leave - you had a planned phone call with her! Never mind the burst pipe - her call is more important.'

‘I wanted an update on the castle - they had a small fire there.’

‘These phone calls with her - they’re all planned aren’t they - for when I’m not around - I have no idea what sweet nothings you’re saying to her do I?’

It’s one thing to show me the text messages, but these secret phone calls - not sure I can carry on much longer like this, Martin - I’m so fed up with it all.’

‘Sorry - look, I need to go - you did say I could still contact her.’

‘I know, I know - but the phone call brought it all home to me - the reality of it all - go go - I’ll deal with the burst pipe.’

‘I won’t contact her Bea.’ ‘You said that last time.’

‘OK - see you in a few days - let me know about the burst pipe.’

Bea could barely say goodbye. She was so upset.

‘Martin - look I’m sorry I flew into a rage - I couldn’t help it, the phone call - it seemed so planned so cosy so intimate, I’m so sorry - you need to go.’

Luckily for Bea the pool man lived locally and he came immediately and showed Bea where the stopcock was. Bea felt embarrassed that she was still in her night clothes and all flustered and dishevelled.

Bea composed herself - she was due to meet her sister for a dog walk later.

Before getting dressed a little voice told her to look at Martin’s emails.

The family computer had the same password for every person in the family. Bea had never looked at Martin’s emails but when the emotional affair was discovered, the advice from Relate was that emails etc. had be accessed by the wounded party - it was all part of the healing process. Otherwise the trust would never return.

Bea looked up Isabelle's name and she came up in a separate folder. The emails dated from 2013 with her begging him to go to her 50th party, after not having seen each other for 9 years. Then Bea found the emails asking him to source designer fabrics and Farrow and Ball paints for the castle, but more recent ones were asking him to translate emails from English speaking customers to the castle. Some of the newest emails from Isabelle were of a slightly flirtatious nature - she referred to Martin as an 'amour'[34] in one.

Bea wondered if Étienne and Isabelle knew about Google Translate, so she emailed both Étienne and Isabelle a very polite email - explaining that Martin was on a shoot for a few days, and would not be available to translate for them, but had they heard about Google Translate? Then she said that Martin was going to be rather busy when he got home from the shoot. She was hoping that the email would be a polite but veiled message to Isabelle to step back.

Isabelle emailed back copying in Martin and said that she did indeed know about Google Translate - but sometimes the English nuances were too obscure, and that's why she liked Martin to do them - however, she said she wouldn't send anymore translations.

Bea told her sister on the dog walk about the hidden sentences in the notebooks, and Tessa just sighed at Bea, 'He's not going to get over her, is he? He doesn't want to, does he? - you're Diana, and she's Camilla - smell the coffee Beatrice smell the coffee - he wants his cake and eat it - you know - all the time you're happy for them to be in contact - well they'll find a way to meet up I bet they will, of course, they will. You need to accept the fact that your husband is in love with

---

[34] Oxford Languages translates "amour" as a love affair or lover especially one that is secret. Brittanica Dictionary translates it as a physical relationship: a love affair, especially a secret love affair. It can also mean "a Love". Merriam-Webster translates "amour" as a usually illicit love affair.

another woman - the one that he can't have. I can't imagine what you're feeling - you must be so stressed by it all?'

'Yes I am - not sure where it's all going in the long term - but I'm tied at the moment - Rufus has his exams in June and I need to stay sane and normal - it's hard yes very hard - but if this is my cross then so be it - I made my bed and I have to lie in it - more fool me for marrying a) a non-Catholic and b) a man who was clearly never going to get over his first love. How stupid was I?!'

A naive stupid girl. But I love him - and women love cads don't they - always have and always will. It's human nature. 'Do you know someone admired his Aston the other day and said he looked like Sean Connery - can you believe it?'

'No I can't - look Bea - can't you get an annulment?'

'For goodness sake we're validly married - so no that's not possible.' 'What even though you married in a Methodist chapel?'

'That still doesn't invalidate it - it's what they call valid but illicit. An annulment would only apply if - at the time of our wedding vows - Martin was having an affair at the same time. I asked him and he definitely wasn't having an affair when we said our vows. The only option if things get worse is to legally separate - for an indeterminate period of time. I can never re-marry while Martin's alive - and I couldn't date anyone else, so I could end up a bit of a hermit in a house somewhere. I don't want to separate but I know I may have to if he starts going over to see her on a regular basis.'

Tessa gave Bea a strange look.

'It's in the Bible, Tess - you can't undo what God has joined together in a valid marriage. The regret I have is that no one, not even the priest, warned me of the dangers of being in a mixed marriage. Would I have taken any notice? I was in love, so probably not.'

'I'm in a mixed marriage, Bea.'

‘I know - but your husband isn’t ~~anti Catholic~~anti-Catholic and he doesn’t have a problem with Catholicism - he goes to church with you doesn’t he?’

‘I guess so.’

Chapter 33 - Bea writes to Isabelle

One day while Martin was having a helicopter lesson Bea was going through old emails and she found a strange one from Martin to an old PA - no longer working for him. He had asked Wendy out for "din dins" as Bea and 5 year old Rufus were away in Cornwall. Wendy an attractive woman was also on her own as her husband was away. Bea was unaware of this at the time as Martin hadn't told her about the dinner date.

Bea quizzed him about it.

'What happened after din dins with Wendy?' 'Oh we went our separate ways.'

'Did anything go on between you - while you were working together? I mean you were always talking about her when you came home from work.'

'Nothing ever happened - she's a very good friend, that's all.' 'Ok.'

Another savage blow to Bea was finding Martin's email to Isabelle's best friend Anne-Marie during the 2021 winter lockdown. It was like a knife to her heart when she learnt that 1) Martin had always loved Isabelle since the day they met, and 2) If he could have his life again…

Bea thought that Martin confiding with Anne-Marie could only mean one thing - that he wanted what he said conveyed to Isabelle - he was using Anne-Marie as his go-between knowing that the women told each other everything. Bea was so distraught and her self-esteem nonexistent that this was like a final nail in the coffin as far as she was concerned, and that Martin would really have to make a choice between Bea and Isabelle - it was that simple - in her eyes.

When Martin returned home - she said she needed to speak to him seriously, and he wearily said OK, thinking - oh no what now? They went down to the lake. Bea was calm and collected - she meant business and Martin knew it.

'I saw what you wrote to Anne-Marie regarding your love for Isabelle since *the day you met*! And if you could have your life again… Martin, it's as clear as day now that I have always been your second choice and that you are still love sick for Isabelle. So, I'm telling you - either finish this inappropriate, damaging friendship - or you lose me - I will separate from you judicially. You see, you're that arrogant you don't think I'll do it, do you? Well, I've found out what to do, and it's all ready to go. I really am not putting up with this much longer - I can't act yet as we have Rufus to think of. Oh, and by the way - if he does badly in his GCSEs, we can't get cross as he's deeply concerned about our situation, and that may have a bearing on his results. He's been worried since he saw you texting her years ago.

Martin was pacing towards the wooden bridge leading to the woods, and he was silent for a few moments, then said, 'You've made your position clear - but I'm not finishing via WhatsApp - I'll go to Belgium and tell her in person.'

'Fine - and I expect you to be a man of your word' while he faced her in slight defiance and said, 'And her friendship is on a par with our marriage.' 'That's just so wrong - how does that make me feel?' 'I'm not talking about it anymore, Bea.'

Bea had been mulling over a letter she was mentally composing to Isabelle. She planned to show it to Martin before sending it. She was going to call her a femme fatale, a teaser and a cunning vixen. Martin asked her to remove the offending words, so her final version was,

March 2023

Isabelle

It's necessary for you to know why it's not possible for me to be your friend. It is very, very simple.

You know that Martin fell in love with you when he was 18. He told me this.

And during the Covid of 2020, you were very disloyal to Étienne because you discussed your problems with Martin. So Martin fell in love with you again. I know this because he told me so. It was a knife in my heart! And you know full well because you encouraged him. You know what you are doing! Women know what other women do. That's true isn't it?

Also I found some profound love sentences which Martin wrote about you. It was another knife in my heart!

I think you are a temptress with my husband. It is very obvious.

You do secret phone calls with my husband. It's like an emotional affair.

I don't trust you. It's difficult to trust you and Martin.

I can't stop your friendship, but I can't be your friend. Martin knows this.

I hope your husband is happy - does he know you discuss your marital problems with Martin? Does Étienne have a very intense lady friend? I don't have a close male friend. If I have problems I speak to my family. Never another man. It's not appropriate.

I pray every day for our marriages.

ADIEU

Beatrice Mary

Bea decided to use the term "Adieu" because it meant goodbye forever.

Martin read the letter but didn't think Bea would send it. Bea had every intention of posting the letter and a few weeks later she had a pathetic reply from Isabelle telling her that it wasn't her fault and that she was not the things Bea was accusing her of. She said Martin was like a brother and that was all. Bea regarded it as a short curt letter - and not that truthful. She thought - well does a woman really send all those photos of herself (some quite tantalising) to a brother?! Of course not!

Bea gave Martin the letter. He made no comment.

Chapter 34 - Trip to Belgium

Martin had organised for Rufus to go and stay with a Belgian family to improve his French speaking during the Easter holiday. He told Bea that he would accompany Rufus as he would be staying with Étienne and Isabelle - and do what he said he would do.

'You need two nights to…er…do what you said?'

'Well, yes - we don't get there til the evening, so two nights is fair - and it takes a while to get through passport control from this end to Brussels on the Eurostar.

'OK - that's fair enough.'

Bea was really hoping that Martin would be a man of his word but she wasn't entirely sure he would be. She knew how weak-kneed he was whenever he saw his ladylove. She never imagined this bond had gone so deep and his feelings for Isabelle so crushing for her. The weeks went by slowly and they had stopped discussing Isabelle. They were getting on well but always at the back of Bea's mind was, will he do it or not - I don't think he will the bond's too strong, and maybe I do have to prepare mentally for separation.

While Martin and Rufus were in Belgium, Bea went on a walking holiday with her sister Lucy - they were going to do 5 miles a day on the South Downs.

Lucy, an addictions counsellor, was skeptical of Martin's trip and she warned Bea to be prepared for nothing to actually happen.

'Look, Bea - you need to get your head around the fact that your husband is in love with another woman - have you got that yet?'

'Yes - and I won't stay with him if he's still going to hanker after her - look, I have to wait for him to come back and see what happens - I don't think he'll finish the 'friendship' either - he's too involved with her and her family now. I'm fully preparing for the fact that nothing will change.'

When Bea returned home from the walking holiday - Martin was already home and there were boxes of Belgian chocolates.

'Oh, these look very smart,' said Bea after they hugged hello. 'Yes - the boxes are for you.'

'Thank you' said Bea while taking her case upstairs - she thought Martin seemed quite happy.

'How did it go then? Were you a man of your word?'

Martin was shuffling his feet and holding the Aga bar, looking sheepish.

'No - look, when I got there, I had a change of heart - they were so so kind to me, taking me out for supper and then all these chocolates for us - for you. And also, I realised that I no longer fancy Isabelle.'

Bea thought this was an incredible excuse - and she didn't believe Martin about him not fancying Isabelle - it was a red herring she felt - to get her off the scent. How could a man with the depth of feeling for Isabelle and all those written love sentences, suddenly decide he didn't fancy her anymore. Bea thought it was just too planned - he had no intention of doing what he said and she wasn't surprised.

'I knew you wouldn't do it - so just because you now say you don't fancy her, erm - not sure I really believe that Martin - makes it all all right does it?'

'Look, I love them both - they're both my friends.'

'Étienne - who you describe as cruel is now a great husband is he?'

Bea welled up angrily, 'You're not a man of your word - you had no intention of finishing it, did you?'

'Yes - I went with that intention but changed my mind - we're allowed to change our minds aren't we?'

'OK - nothing has changed then - they're both your pals, and you will be going there regularly.'

'I don't see why I can't go every six months.' 'Well, I'm not having them here - no way.'

'I wish I could invite them here,' he said with a sad look.

'It's your house too - how can I stop you from inviting them - but I won't be here, so it'll be a cosy threesome, will it? Won't you be a gooseberry? Look - you've shown no remorse, Martin - you don't seem to care that I'm hurt and that you may lose me - it's incredible - you just want to think of your next 'fix' of her - you're already making plans to see her again - you really are addicted to her!'

'Oh my remorse, Bea - my remorse is your book - your novel, whatever it is - that's what I don't like.'

'I've repeated several times that I'll rip up the book if you end what I consider a dangerous and inappropriate friendship with another woman whom you happen to have a habit of falling for - and now, all of a sudden, you no longer fancy her? - You're just saying that to take me off the scent.'

'It's true,' he laughed, 'I don't fancy her anymore.' 'Would you still marry her if you were free to?' 'Yes'

'So you would marry someone you no longer fancy?'

'It would just be for companionship, that's all - platonic.' Bea was laughing with incredulity.

'The marriage would be invalid in that case.' Bea was sighing at Martin's absurdity of saying he no longer fancied a woman but would still marry her! Bea thought he might be a little mad.

‘So I continue my novel, and you continue your friendship.’ ‘I suppose so,’ said Martin.

‘It’s a deeply unhappy compromise,’ said Bea, remembering that Martin considered Isabelle on a par with his marriage - the two Freudian slips when he said he wasn’t giving Isabelle up for her, and she remembered the time she asked Martin, who out of Isabelle and Bea would he throw out of a balloon if he had to - he didn’t know - he really didn’t know!’

Martin shrugged.

‘You can’t tell me who I can have as friends.’

‘I’ve never done that, Martin - it’s just one person who I find a threat, and any other woman would be exactly the same - don’t you dare tell me I’m controlling who your friends are.’

When Bea told Lucy what had happened, Lucy wasn’t surprised,

‘Look, Bea, Martin went to Brussels with the intention of doing something, and then he didn’t. Not only that, but when he got home, all he wanted to do was sort a way of inviting her over, I mean to get his next ‘fix.’ As an addictions counsellor, this is typical behaviour of someone addicted to another person.’

‘Yes - you’re right. I think he has an addiction, too. I really don’t know what’s going to happen - just take each day as it comes, really.’

The Charmers muddled along and kept calm for their son’s critical time of exams - Bea went on long walks with Martin - in different parts of Sussex to see if they would like to consider other places to move to. Martin also encouraged Bea to come around the garden and the woodland walk he had created now that the days were long.

Chapter 35 - King Charles III's Coronation

The date for King Charles III to be crowned was Saturday, 6th May 2023, and the Charmer family was invited to spend part of the day with friends they had known since moving out of London. Thc build-up to the ceremony was going to be televised well before the crowning - in true British style with a lot of horses and chariots in royal blue, gold, and red, and magnificent uniforms to match.

It was also a significant day for Bea - it was the eve of the 30th anniversary of her Grandmother Ursula's death.

On the way home from the gathering, where much food and wine were consumed, Freddie and Martin were having an unpleasant disagreement about something someone had said - it was nothing unusual - when too much wine was drunk, arguments often followed - sometimes heated ones. Wine loosens the tongue and removes inhibitions. It did on this day.

But what Freddie came out with jolted Beatrice, and she felt a clenching inside her chest and palpitations.

'How can I look up to you while you're still dating Isabelle?' said Freddie, pointing his finger at Martin.

'Well, I don't really know what's going on either,' said Bea. 'Stop it!' Shouted Cecily, who was driving.

There was silence from that moment on, and when they arrived back to the farmhouse, Martin sat down momentarily - poured a glass of wine but left it on the table before going upstairs to bed, leaving Bea with their children, who wanted answers.

'Mum - what's going on - you know - with you and dad?' asked Freddie with his big questioning brown eyes, 'Is that why he's gone to bed - because I mentioned Isabelle?'

'Well - your father went to Belgium with Rufus, who was doing an exchange…' Freddie looked shocked and interrupted Bea,

'Sorry, but who arranged the exchange - wasn't it the school?' 'No - your Da arranged it.'

Freddie frowned and sighed.

'Ma, I had no idea. I thought his school organised this - so dad arranged the exchange so he could see Isabelle?'

'I'm sure that was partly it, but what you don't know is that he made an agreement with me to go and tell her that he wasn't going to visit her anymore. Well, that didn't happen - and frankly, I didn't think it would happen.'

'Dad thinks he can just be friends with her… but I'm a man, and I know that those situations never work - there's always one who wants more - it just doesn't work these close friendships with the opposite sex - I've been there!'

'Well, he said he didn't have the heart to do what he'd agreed to do - as they took him out for a meal and were so hospitable - and also that he no longer… er fancies her…which I don't really believe.'

'Hmm - that doesn't sound right. Dad's not showing you any respect, Ma.' 'So - the current position is this - dad is still in contact with her, he's still their friend, and he plans to see them… maybe every six months. Am I happy about it? No, I'm not! - I certainly won't be seeing them.'

Cecily shot a look at her mother and shook her head, 'Mum - that's not on - you need to put your foot down.'

'How can I stop him? - Look, I need to stay calm for your little bro while he does his GCSEs. After those have finished, we will have another conversation about our situation.'

Bea left the conversation and went up to see if Martin was OK. He was asleep.

Freddie and Cecily were discussing the situation and told Bea that they wanted to contact Isabelle and tell her to leave the family alone.

'I'll email her,' said Freddie.

'No, Freddie - I think it's better coming from me,' said Cecily.

'And I can tell you both that your father says if you contact her, he will leave us all!'

'I think if Isabelle was as innocent as she claims, then she would have done everything to tell you that right from the start. OK, so you broke contact with her, but she has the landline - she could have rung you - the fact she didn't makes her look pretty guilty', said Cecily.

'I totally agree,' said Bea, 'and on that note, I'm going to bed.'

When she was in bed, Bea couldn't sleep thinking about what the children had said earlier, and she suddenly realised it was 30 years since her grandmother's death - oh granny did you have a hand in all this - I mean, when Freddie asked Martin if he and Isabelle were having an affair, it was the Carmelite feast day - and now it's 30 years since you died - did you prod Freddie again granny?

The next day, Martin saw that Bea was crying - he sighed - here we go again - what is it this time, he thought.

'I'm crying because of what the children said - they don't like our situation, Martin - they think you're not showing me any respect.'

Bea's immediate family felt the same way as her children.

Over the days and weeks that followed, Bea grew more and more upset about the situation. Ultimately, nothing had changed - he was still in contact with Isabelle, and not only that, he planned to see her regularly. He was showing no concern for his wife's feelings.

Bea had printed out the separation form and filled it in - together with the marriage certificate and a cheque for £365. She was finally accepting that Martin's priority was Isabelle, and that was all that mattered to him. She lost the will to fight anymore and was resigned to a future living alone. It was gut-wrenching, but she felt she had no option. How could she stay with a man who regarded her as 2nd best?

A few weeks later, Bea told Martin what her plans were. He shocked her with his threatening response.

'If you stop my friendship, then I won't like you anymore - I'll regard you in a different light.'

'Ah, I see - Martin - your love for me is conditional upon you having Isabelle as your close lady friend. That's not right, Martin, or fair or true love. I love you unconditionally, and you only love me conditionally.'

'Let me think about it.'

Bea thought bitterly - he needs time to think about who his priority is - that's disgraceful. I'm posting the separation papers.

Bea found the situation of waiting for her husband to make up his mind intolerable - and she told him flatly.

'Martin - it's now totally clear to me that you can't live without Isabelle - and you can't choose between her or me. You know…this whole thing should have ended retrospectively when you declared yourself to her. So I've filled out the separation form and the cheque - I'm not going to be a doormat for much longer.'

Martin got up abruptly, took Bea's arm, and led them outside to the table by the oak tree, where the grass was wild. They sat down on the old, rickety wooden garden chairs that they had purchased when they bought the house 24 years previously. Martin cocked his head sideways and looked seriously at Bea.

'Look, Beatrice - I'm not going to see Isabelle or invite her over - it's…it's not practical - look, I realise I don't have your blessing, so I'm going to respect that.'

Bea studied his serious expression for a few seconds and said quickly, 'I didn't know that Martin - well…you didn't tell me that before,' she said wearily, feeling a sense of 'Déjà vu - and not entirely convinced he would stick by this decision. She knew by his next expression that there was a big 'but' coming.

'But she *is* the 2nd most important person in my life - and she will always be my friend - I'll still be in touch.'

'Oh…is she more important than your children?' 'Sometimes… yes.'

'Above your siblings?'

'Yes…Well, we don't really talk our family, unlike yours.'

As they made their way back to the house, they both noticed that the apples were just budding from the tree leaves.

Bea wondered if this next phase was going to be more swings and roundabouts and decided only time would tell. She also felt it was a bit cunning of Martin, as he probably wouldn't tell Isabelle he wasn't going to see her again. She sensed he would always want to keep the door ajar - keep his options open… just in case.

Bea felt that nothing would ever be the same again and that she would have to learn to live with the fact that her husband had fallen in love with his first love, which he called the love of his life. It was something she could never forget – like a static dark cloud. Would she be spending the rest of her life metaphorically glancing over her shoulder?

She now saw clearly why her religion was against mixed marriages. The Catholic Church is very clear about what constitutes infidelity - thoughts, words, and actions all count. At the beginning of every Mass, the people say the "Confiteor," which is a general confession of sins and includes the words - 'I have sinned exceedingly in thought, word, and deed, through my fault, through my fault, through my most grievous fault.' The Church of England does not have this in its services, and therefore, for a non-Catholic, thoughts and words don't count - or if they do, it isn't explicit. What constitutes infidelity for one partner may not constitute infidelity for the other - which can have catastrophic consequences. Bea thought that "Relate" - which had no religious affiliations whatsoever, was actually very Catholic in its approach to infidelity, as it regarded affairs as being emotional or physical or both.

Three Sundays later, on a hot June day after lunch outside and after a few glasses of red wine, Martin startled Bea three times and told her that she, Beatrice, was the love of his life.

Bea was so taken aback she could not quite believe it but so wanted to believe it. She hoped he meant it. She gazed up at the beautiful eyes and rosebud mouth and said, '*You're* the love of my life. And do you realise- it's 40 years to the month since we got engaged!'

And Bea swiftly got up from the table and walked down to the ancient apple tree, where she turned on her newly formed playlist on her iPhone, and started dancing to old disco hits. For now, she was content. But how long would it last she wondered. She had got used to being on an emotional rollercoaster for the best part of a year - her husband was and always would be a very restless man. She had a nagging feeling that this dark period in her life may not be quite the end of the story. As she danced towards the lake - the afternoon sunrays were dancing in the tree leaves. For now, she was content. But vigilant.

To Be Continued…Or not…it all depends…

Appendix

Chapter 1, footnote 2;

A 'mixed marriage' (i.e., a marriage between a Catholic and one who, though baptised, does not profess the Catholic Faith) is strictly forbidden, nor will the Church even tolerate it unless, in a special case, there be a grave reason and the following conditions be fulfilled:-

1) That all the children who may be born of the marriage shall be baptised and brought up in the Catholic Faith. 2) That the Catholic party shall have full liberty for the practice of the Catholic religion. The Catholic party is bound to pray and do everything he or she reasonably can for the conversion of the other to the Catholic Faith. It is strictly forbidden that any religious marriage ceremony should take place except the Catholic ceremony. See Pg 80, A Simple Prayer Book, CTS, 1957.

Page 67 - Clean Love in Courtship by Fr Lovasik says;

Thus, the Catholic Church implicitly forbids courtship between Catholics and non-Catholics. Experience has proven the following facts about mixed marriages:

1) One of the great barriers to unity of mind and heart is difference in religion.

2) Mixed marriages have been and continue to be the cause of an alarming and ever-increasing number of fallen-away Catholics.

3) The majority of the children of mixed marriages are either not reared in the faith or lose their faith.

4) The modern non-Catholic attitude towards marriage is so different from the Catholic's attitude that mixed marriage almost invariably leads to serious disagreement between the man and the

woman, particularly about birth control, Catholic education, and religious practices.

5) A non-Catholic can always end a marriage in divorce, which is in complete opposition to Christ's law. But marriage for the Catholic is a lifelong contract. Christ so ordained it, and the Catholic so regards it.

6) If the Catholic in a mixed marriage is faithful to his religion, he is extremely lonely; he feels isolated from his partner, and he finds it almost impossible to explain the situation to the children.

7) Marriage itself presents enough problems without adding the problems that are created by religious differences.

8) If you insist on marrying a non-Catholic, you should take the person to the priest at least six weeks before the marriage, that there be ample time for the necessary instructions. The non-Catholic should at least know what his/ her future spouse believes, what promises must be made, the nature of marriage, its duties, responsibilities, and privileges.

9) Conversions before marriage are often more or less pretended and are seldom the fruit of sincere conviction. 9 out of every 10 Catholics who contract a mixed marriage do it to their own and their children's serious detriment. It is preferable to be single rather than be in a mixed marriage.

Chapter 9, footnote 7;

Regarding the Catholic Church's teaching on birth control;

In Genesis 1:27-28, "Male and female he created them. Then God blessed them, saying 'increase and multiply; fill the earth and subdue it'" - also repeated after the Flood (Genesis 9:1).

The first Biblical condemnation of birth control is in Genesis 38: 8-10, often referred to as the "sin of Onan," where Onan practices the withdrawal method, and God kills him on the spot.

The Catholic Church teaches that one cannot separate the unitive from the procreative, which artificial birth control does.

A person who a) knows that artificial birth control is a serious sin, and who b) freely commits this sin, and c) with the full will - commits a mortal sin. If a, b, or c is missing, it is a venial sin. Mortal sins can only be forgiven in the confessional unless there are no valid priests available, in which case a perfect act of contrition suffices - however, if a valid priest does become available, it is still imperative to go to confession.

Bibliography

The Complete Knox Holy Bible - 2nd edition 1956 - London Burns & Oates

Douay Rheims Holy Bible - 1899

Dressing with Dignity - Colleen Hammond - 2005 - TAN Books & Publishers Inc.

Clean Love in Courtship - Father Lovasik - 1974 - TAN Books

The Official Sloane Ranger handbook - Ann Barr & Peter York - 1982

Brideshead Revisited - Evelyn Waugh - 1945

Of Human Bondage - Somerset Maugham - 1915

To Love Honour and Betray - Zelda West-Meads - 2016

Contraception - a history - John Noonan - 1965

A Simple Prayer Book - Catholic Truth Society - 1957

Wonders of the Catholic Faith - Fr Radecki - 2015 - St Joseph's Media

The Catechism of Christian Doctrine - CTS - 1958

Printed in Great Britain
by Amazon

62607972R00137